PRAISE FOR PAIGE HARBISON

"For fans of *Gossip Girl*."
—*Teen Vogue*

"*Here Lies Bridget* is an ideal read for victims of this
⸍ smal behaviour [bullying], offering keen and witty
insight into the emotional motivations of privileged
narcissists… What's so engaging about *Here Lies Bridget*
is its honest insight into Bridget's self-perception…
[A] solid and intriguing read."
—*Los Angeles Times*

e novel unfolds with a certain sweetness and a lack of
cism, which I found refreshing. This may be because
nor Paige is only twenty years old, so her connection
with a young audience is natural and easy."
—*New York Times* bestselling author Jen Lancaster on
Here Lies Bridget

ls Harbison wrote a fantastic book. It was filled with
great life lessons as well as great entertainment."
—Books with Bite blog, 5 Bites

I totally loved this book! From the moment I opened
it up and read the first page I was hooked. I seriously
couldn't put it down… Overall a fantastic, captivating
page-turner every high-school–aged girl should
pick up and read."
—My Precious: The Ramblings of a
Kindle Addict blog

'*Here Lies Bridget* is a fun, sweet, cruel and wonderfully
delightful story that is part *Mean Girls* and part
A Christmas Carol."
—Fiktshun blog

Books by **Paige Harbison**

HERE LIES BRIDGET
NEW GIRL

PAIGE HARBISON

NEW GIRL

mira ink is a registered trademark of Harlequin Enterprises Limited, used under licence.

Published in Great Britain 2012
MIRA Books, an imprint of Harlequin (UK) Limited,
Eton House, 18-24 Paradise Road,
Richmond, Surrey, TW9 1SR

© Paige Harbison 2012

ISBN 978 1 848 45063 9

47-0512

To Angela Petrunick,
who lost her computer privileges at work because of this
book—and who helped me make it what it is today.

"Oh, for the time
when I shall sleep
Without identity."

— Emily Brontë

chapter 1 me

THE PANORAMIC VIEW OUTSIDE THE WINDOWS of the bus showed a world that wasn't mine. It was chilly in early September and the trees were pine, not palm.

I grew up in St. Augustine, Florida. My life so far had been made up of conversations over noisy fans, shrieking at the sight of pony-size bugs in the shower, and coming home from the beach to find an alarmingly sunburned reflection waiting for me in the mirror. When I took my Labrador, Jasper, for a walk, it meant running in the surf and tossing a tennis ball into the waves. I hardly ever got in the car without my thighs sticking to the hot seats, and most of my neighbors were renters or vacationers. It wasn't Hawaii, but it wasn't New Hampshire, either. And that, unfortunately for this warm-weather girl, was where I found myself now.

Towering trees of dark, thick green loomed over the highway we rode down. It was fifty-five degrees out, the sun had already set at six, and it was only September second. St. Augustine isn't bliss all year round, and I'm the first to admit it, but it's never this cold *yet*. Not this early in the year. My friends back home were still going for swims after school every day and requesting outdoor seating at restaurants. Restaurants that I was already craving to order from again.

Behind me I was leaving all of the warmth of home, my best friends, and a really comfortable queen-size bed that lay next to a big window that overlooked the beach and filled my room with the smell of salty sand. I was leaving all of that for a boarding school. Up north. Where I knew no one.

I'd never been the new girl before, and I barely knew what to think. But every time I remembered that that would be my new identity, a surge of nervous anticipation spread from my chest right down to the pit of my stomach. I was about to step into the spotlight in front of eight hundred other students. Would they wait for me to dance and entertain them, or would they expect me to walk right across the stage and back out of sight?

And which would I do?

My parents had called this a "surprise." Poor, deluded, lovely things that they are. It turned out that they had been submitting an application for me every year since I'd begged to go to boarding school in eighth grade. I'd found this place on Google somewhere, and excitedly called them to the computer where I'd gone on and on about how much fun it would be.

This was right after I'd finished all of the *Harry Potter* books, unsurprisingly, and would have given anything to be swept away and told that my life was more than it seemed. When my first application was submitted and rejected, I'd burst into adolescent tears. When I had stepped into my new huge, public high school for the first time, I'd felt sick with regret that I couldn't be somewhere else. It felt so plain, so black-and-white.

But by the time my parents presented me with the fruits of

their secret labors, I'd grown to really love my "plain" life—largely thanks to them, admittedly. Not even in that "never know what you've got until it's gone" kind of way. I was happy all the time. Sheltered and comfortable, true. Dreading college and being away from everything, also true. But I was happy.

I had a best friend, Leah, who was regularly in and out of the same relationship with one guy, a crew of other fun friends that I wasn't as close to but had plenty of fun with, and a seriously fantastic little family that I loved to come home to. If anything went badly in the rest of my life, there was always my mother to reassure me that the thing I really needed was a pedicure, and off we'd skip. My father could always come back from the grocery store with a York Peppermint Pattie and a tube of Pringles, knowing that my way to my happiness is often found through junk food. My four-year-old sister, Lily, could always cheer me up with a crayon drawing, or even the overheard sounds of her tiny voice in another room playing out some story with her toys. Not to mention again the warm breeze that whistled through my window every night, while I drifted off to sleep with Jasper curled up on my feet.

Oh, that feeling…I missed it already.

Last night seemed like forever ago.

But one lazy afternoon, my parents had called me in from the backyard, where I was tanning and listening to a book on my little white earphones, and into the kitchen. Lily was flinging macaroni and cheese, and my parents were beaming.

"What's going on?" I could tell something was up. My mother, the open book, looked like she was about to burst.

"We have a bit of a surprise for you." My dad grinned.

"We got you into Manderley!" my mother spilled.

She loved good news, gossip, excitement, parties and wine. She'd grown up in the heart of Paris with equally marvelous sisters, and so every word that came out of her mouth sounded like champagne bubbles. So I smiled, not registering what she'd said meant, or even—as was often the problem with my dear mother's accent—what she'd said.

"Sorry?"

"Manderley Academy." My dad held up a brochure. "We know how badly you've always wanted to go. You got in, honey!"

He came over to give me a hug. My mother, who had been bouncing from foot to foot, her hands clasped together, followed him.

And, like that, there was nothing I could say. They were too excited. I tried to drop hints over the coming weeks, suggesting that maybe my going there wasn't worth the money, considering that it was only for one year. But they told me the money was already spent and that it would probably help get me a scholarship at one of the schools I'd already been accepted to.

"See, it's actually *saving* money," my father had decided.

My mom cooed from the next room that it was, "perfect, just pozee-tiffly *perfect!*"

Leah, ever the devoted best friend, patiently spent the rest of the summer helping me soak up as much of home as I could before leaving. We were having fun, when I wasn't catching her looking at me mournfully. At those points I'd say, "Lee-*ah*, I'll be back for college soon, and you'll be absolutely sick of me."

She'd nod, but then doubt would fill her eyes as she looked at me and she'd say something like, "But what if you *don't* come back?"

I'd laugh and assure her that there was no way that would happen. It had always been our plan to go to college together and be roommates. I ignored the voice in my head that asked if I was sure that's what I really wanted.

Of course it was. It's what I'd always wanted.

I ordered coconut shrimp from my favorite restaurant every other day, in an effort to get sick of them. Instead, I think what I did was grow more desperate not to leave them behind. Leah and I went to the beach every single day, without fail. As she put it, I was going to need my tan to last through the year. The whole, long, cold year up north. Sometimes it was like she was trying to convince me to stay, but since I had no control over it, all it did was make me dread my impending departure more.

When it rained, we just moped and looked out the windows for a while before watching something obsess-worthy for the rest of the day.

The days were shorter than ever in those three months. My legs felt leaner and tanner, and my shorts shorter and more frayed. My friends were funnier and more exuberant than ever before. The boys were cuter, the neighbors more neighborly, and my home was cozier. No one argued, no one was snappish; everything was perfect.

But then the summer wound to a close, like all good things eventually do. Though you'd never know it from looking outside, where it was still sunny and warm.

My mother took me shopping for things with long sleeves—and I learned that these make my wrists feel strangled—boots, which make my feet hot, and a good coat, which made me feel panicky and claustrophobic. I said goodbye to all of my friends, knowing it wouldn't be the same next time I saw them. I gave Jasper the biggest hug, soothed my distressed sister with a bag of Pirate's Booty popcorn (her favorite for some reason) and the promise that I'd be home soon, thanked my parents again for the surprise, and trudged onto a plane for New Hampshire. Now here I was hours later, passing by neighborhoods with big old Victorian-style homes, trying to forget about palm trees and mango salsa. I pushed thoughts of football on the beach at night and the ability to actually *leave* school at the end of the day from my mind.

I knew I would be okay. I always was. I wasn't going to feel nostalgic forever. I wasn't going to hate everything just because it was unfamiliar. It'd be tough to jump into a new life, but that was okay. It was my last year of high school anyway. What did I have to lose?

I could be anyone I wanted to be now. I could adopt an accent—I'd always been ace at mocking my mother. I could become a slut maybe. I could be carefree and exciting....

A small, irritating voice in my head told me that I wouldn't be any of those things. I'd lose confidence as soon as I stepped off this bus, and that was just a fact.

The neighborhoods that passed by the windows died away, and we turned onto a long, narrow, gravel road. A road like a hallway, packed with cabs, cars and other buses, with walls of tall green trees on either side of us and reaching up to the clouds. We inched our way up for fifteen minutes, and then I finally saw the actual boarding school for the first time in real life.

Manderley.

It truly took my breath away the second it unveiled itself to me. The building was old, *enormous,* and I could just barely see in the waning daylight that it was covered in thick ivy. Lively golden glows poured from its shuttered windows. Surrounding all this were jade lawns and a wrought-iron fence. Lamps illuminated bustling, shadowy figures in the roundabout, all unloading luggage and heading down the long path of brick that led to the building.

The campus had always been striking in the pictures I saw,

but to see it in person made me feel like I was in the presence of some omniscient queen.

We filed off of the bus, and cold air hit my thighs. I had been freezing for the entire ride from the airport until I figured out how to direct the stream of air they call a fan away from me. Everyone around me was wearing long jeans, scarves, Lacoste polos, and sweaters. My Jax Beach Lifeguard sweatshirt (a real one, not a touristy one), frayed jean shorts and Rainbow flip-flops looked so out of place. I'd been sure it couldn't be *that* cold here.

I'd spent my life in Southern states. I'd never even seen snow in real life.

"Oh, you'll see a lot of that," Dad had said.

"Hush, Daddy. Tell me there'll be unseasonably warm weather this year," I'd replied.

I also had brought the most stuff out of anybody I'd ridden in with. I'd gotten a lot of looks throughout the ride, and I assumed that was why, although that annoying part of me felt kind of sure I had a big embarrassing something somewhere on me. According to the snotty girl sitting in front of me— who seemed intent on informing me without speaking *directly* to me—everyone always leaves their things in their rooms over the summer. Still, weren't there freshmen and transfers? Why was it so weird I should have a year's worth of things before living somewhere for a year?

"Miss?"

I turned and saw a guy with a flashlight and a notepad.

"Yes?"

"Do you need to check in some luggage?"

"Check in?"

"There's only a service elevator, so we just take it up for you."

His practiced tone told me that he'd had to explain this many times.

"Oh." I smiled. "Okay, great. I was wondering how I was going to bring it all in." I gave a small laugh, and he smiled politely back at me.

"Write down your student ID number and room number here, please." He handed me a clipboard. I filled out the indicated lines, referencing the letter I'd gotten over the summer for both, and handed it back. "Thanks, it should be up there soon."

He slapped stickers on my things, and another guy put them into a cart. I followed everyone else up the walkway toward the school, taking a deep breath and letting it out slowly. I would not be intimidated by this place. I refused. I ignored that little voice in my head again.

As I walked down the path, I remembered when I was thirteen and looking at pictures of Manderley. I'd imagined myself prancing down this very path full of optimism, maybe already with a brand-new friend acquired on the ride in, ready to have an adventure.

I felt a little silly thinking about it, but something in me still had a flicker of that same excitement.

Once in the hall, I saw that there was a woman directing each wave of students to a line for the cell phone drop. Yes. Oh-ho yes.

The cell phone drop. In an effort to be more "traditional," the school mandated that we could use cell phones only between seven and nine at night or on weekends, and we had to check them out, leaving our room keys behind as collateral. Leah and I'd read *all* about it in the letters. We'd sat on her back porch in the gray-blue of a mosquitoey twilight waiting for her dad to finish grilling the burgers and hot dogs, and read all about the new restrictions I'd be living with.

I'd be living in a dorm with a girl I'd never yet spoken to, sleeping in a twin-size bed. There would be no interdorm visitation between guys and girls, no social-networking sites except on a special computer in the library. We'd be wearing uniforms, and, perhaps most disappointingly as a new student with no friends here, the no cell phones thing.

It was like prison. Without visitors.

After reluctantly dropping off my beloved, brand-new iPhone and getting my key, I realized I didn't know where to go.

I got up the nerve and approached two girls standing by the stairs. "Hi, um, I'm sorry, but do any of you know which way I go to get to room fifteen?"

The girls exchanged a meaningful look I didn't understand. I resisted the urge to shrink away.

The brunette with big pearl earrings and a very thin nose tossed her hair and looked at me. "So you're the new girl?"

"Yes, I'm—"

"Great. My name is Julia, and this is Madison. We live right across from you."

"Oh, good." I smiled.

She did not.

"You can follow us, we're going up."

"Okay."

Follow seemed like a weird word to choose. *Walk with.* Or, *come with.* Instead, I got *trail pitifully behind like a stray cat.*

They started off, and I tried to keep up.

"So did you two know whoever used to live in my room?"

Another exchanged look.

The one called Julia looked straight ahead and responded, "Yep."

"Ah." I nodded. Trying to fill the silence I said, "That cell phone drop blows, doesn't it? How do you guys survive?"

Madison looked back at me. "You get used to it."

It was clear that I shouldn't ask any more. I stayed silent for the next two flights.

The hallway was all open doors and girls gabbing and shrieking. The noise quieted as we walked up. Everyone was looking at us. Or at me. I didn't know whether to wave or what, so I just walked on.

"There it is," Julia said, and pointed at the only shut door on the hall.

Everyone was silent now, and no one tried to conceal their stares.

I went for the knob, hesitated, and then knocked. No answer. Pushing the door open, I was surprised to find that the lights were on and my roommate was there, reading a book.

"Hi, are you Dana?" I asked, and then realized that both sides of the room were fully decorated. "Am I in the wrong room?"

Was that why everyone had stared? They were just trying to embarrass me for some reason?

"No."

"No you're not...Dana, or—"

"You're in the right *place,*" she said impatiently, not looking up at me. A curtain of shiny black hair hid her face.

I stood there, feeling like an idiot. She wasn't being helpful at all, but still *I* felt like I was harping on the subject. "Sorry, but...then why is there someone else's stuff over there?"

"Those are Becca's things."

Another few seconds of silence passed as she slowly, deliberately, turned a page in her book.

"Um. Okay." I cleared my throat again and shifted my weight to my left foot, still aware of the quiet outside as everyone listened to this conversation. It seemed that Dana would be perfectly content with me standing here for the rest of my life trying to figure out if, in fact, I should take another step in or not.

Finally she revealed to me her face. She looked like a skeleton. The skin that stretched over her high, sharp-looking cheekbones was as white as Julia's pearls. Her lashes were black and long, and trimmed narrow eyes. Thick black liner encircled them, and she looked distinctly exotic. I didn't think I'd ever seen someone who looked quite like her.

I immediately felt the twinge of intimidation.

"Is…she coming to get her stuff?" I asked, when she said nothing.

"I don't know."

"What am I supposed to do with it, then?"

I blushed as my confidence promptly ebbed.

Her cat eyes moved to look at the other side of the room. "I already put some of it away for her."

I followed her gaze and spotted a Louis Vuitton suitcase underneath the bed.

"I see," I said.

A thoughtful moment passed before she said, "You shouldn't sleep in the sheets."

"No."

I took a few steps toward the bed. The floorboards groaned.

"Stop." She said it quietly, but exhaustedly. As if she'd told me a hundred times to stay away from that comforter.

I backed away, watching as she very slowly and carefully removed each layer. When she got to the pillow, she stopped for a minute and gave it a very slight squeeze before removing its case. Odd. But I said nothing.

When she finished, Dana walked silently back to her side of the room, and removed her own sheets, replacing them with Becca's. I got a chill, and then realized the noise had resumed outside.

Once she'd finished, she lay down in the sheets and closed her eyes. I averted mine quickly, feeling as though I was spying on someone unaware of my presence.

My suitcases hadn't arrived yet, so I just sat down on the nylon-encased mattress that was begrudgingly left for me. With a furtive glance in my roommate's direction, I leaned forward and looked at the Polaroid pictures on the wall across from me.

Most of them starred a pretty girl with long, platinum-blond hair. She was pretty in that sort of affected way that you can tell she practiced. Maybe I was wrong, maybe that's how she always looked, but to me she seemed a little pinched. I noticed in one picture that she was one of those girls who looked good in a hat. I always look stupid in them.

I scanned the snapshots of her with different friends, almost always posed and never candid, and usually including someone who was probably her boyfriend. There was more than one picture of them kissing. He was really good-looking. Not just hot or sexy, but handsome in that kind of old-fashioned way. His hair was dark and his eyes were light. He wasn't smiling in any of the pictures, and something about him made it hard to look away.

All the girls stood with their stomachs sucked in and their hands on their hips, either squinting "sexily" at the camera or making some other very-on-purpose facial expression. Madison and Julia, the girls I'd just met, were in several of them. I could already tell that they weren't the kind of people that I was used to being around.

Suddenly my bright pink toenail polish looked tacky, and my clothes ratty.

I was startled a moment later by a knock at the door. I glanced at Dana, who didn't move.

"Come in?" I said, standing. It was Madison and Julia, who, clearly, never left each other's sides.

"So, are you down to come to the party later?" Julia asked.

"Is it like a school thing?"

Madison furrowed her brows, still smiling. "No?"

I hesitated, weighing the options between risking getting in trouble but being social and taking the safe route of staying in my room. What was the worst that could happen, I'd have to transfer back home?

"Yeah, sure."

They both smiled, said, "Cool," and then they walked off, leaving Dana and me alone again, as if the brief exchange had never happened.

"Are you going?"

Her eyes opened, and she stared at the ceiling. "Maybe. Probably not."

"Okay." I sat back down.

She grabbed her book and went back to "reading."

After a few more minutes, my things finally arrived, and I told the guy to just go ahead and set them on the floor. I stood above the pile, considering it for a long moment.

"Dana?" I said quietly. She looked up, and I withered. "Sorry. Um. Do you think... Should I take down these pictures and the frames and everything?"

She said nothing. This was unnecessarily uncomfortable.

"I mean...I could pack them up...." I trailed off lamely, not looking forward to the prospect.

She still said nothing. All I wanted to do was text Leah and share with her how completely, totally weird this all was. I wanted to tell her how I couldn't wait until next year; we'd both been accepted to Florida State University and fully intended to be roommates.

Instead, my phone sat in some lockbox downstairs, and I

tried to arrange my things neatly and accessibly in my boxes and suitcases. After that quick task, I lay down in my new bed and tried to ignore the bright blue eyes staring down at me from almost every picture. I picked up the first *Harry Potter* book in an effort to get excited about boarding school again, and waited quietly in my bed for Madison and Julia to fetch me for the party that would begin it all.

chapter 2 becca

One year ago

"I MEAN, CAN YOU BELIEVE THEY SENT ME HERE?" Becca sat, legs and arms crossed, in the backseat, complaining to the taxi driver she wasn't even sure spoke English. He nodded every now and again, but that was about it. She didn't even care, she was venting. "And you know why?"

The driver made eye contact with her in the rearview mirror.

Becca leaned forward. "Because I can't 'keep my grades up.' They think that'll be easier *here?* All of these kids probably study *nonstop*. They're probably all supersmart." She sat back again, with a disgruntled noise. "I mean that's not the only reason they made me come. I just…I hate both of my parents. My mom used to be okay, but now she just does whatever my dad says."

Nod from the driver.

"Yeah, it *sucks*. They don't know how to handle me so therefore they—what—ship me off? That is *fantastic* parenting." She was silent for a moment before another thought struck her. "This is *their* fault anyway. Isn't it all *about* the parenting? Isn't the 'troubled teenager' thing just the lashing out of an ignored or neglected child?"

Nod.

"Ex*actly*. See, even *you* understand it." She sighed as they pulled up to Manderley. "But I don't know. Maybe this will be better."

The taxi stopped by all the others along the very long entryway road, and the driver got out to remove her suitcases and boxes.

"Lot of stuff," he remarked with a smile when Becca clicked over in her high-heeled boots to join him at the back of the van.

"Yes, because this is my last two freaking years of high school, and they don't even want me at home. So I just brought all of it with me."

Nod. *"Pay."* He held out a hand.

"Ah." She dug into her purse. "You do accept cards, right? *Cards?*" She held one up when he clearly didn't know what she was saying.

Nod.

She looked down at her things, and then at the sidewalk, which was another six or seven feet. Becca smiled and looked at the driver. "Could you be a sweetheart and move them up there for me? Please?"

He cleared his throat and then did as she asked. When he came back, she handed him her credit card and waited. He brought back a receipt. She signed it, putting twenty dollars on the tip line. The next minute, he was back in the car and driving off.

For the briefest of moments, she felt weird watching him go. She was alone. This was her first year at a brand-new school, and she knew no one. Even that driver, whatever his unpronounceable, all consonant name was, had felt like company on the ride from the airport.

"Miss?"

Some guy with a cart startled her. "Jesus, what?"

"I can take your things and deliver them to your room."

"Okay, it's all right there." She pointed.

"Student ID number and room number?"

She screwed up her face. "I have *no* clue."

"It should have come in the mail with your roommate's name and your rule book."

She shrugged.

He looked down at his pad of paper. "Okay, just give me your name, then."

"Rebecca Normandy."

"You don't know any of your information?"

"No."

He clicked the side of his walkie-talkie, and it bleeped. "Hey, Bill?"

A few seconds passed before "Bill" answered. "Yeah."

"Can you look up a student's information for me?"

Another couple of seconds. "Go ahead."

"Rebecca...Normandy." He spelled her last name, and then wrote down what Bill's muffled voice reported.

She was getting impatient, and then had a terrible moment where she realized she wasn't eager to get anywhere.

"And how many items?"

Becca looked at him for a moment. He was looking *right* at them, did she really need to tell him? She glanced meaningfully down at them and then back to him.

He took a deep breath and counted, then handed her a

ticket he'd recorded it on. "Okay, hang on to this. On the back I wrote down your room number and student ID number. You'll need those to get your key up there at the cell phone drop."

She froze. "*So* sorry, the *what?*"

He gave her a look. "Didn't read any of the info, huh?"

"Uh-uh. Did you say *cell phone drop?*"

"They'll tell you the hours you can check it back out."

Becca sighed and followed the rest of the students up to the line that ended at a window. It was way too long to wait in. She went up to the next person in line. Luckily, it was a guy.

"Hi, I'm new here, and I'm so sorry to ask this, but do you mind if I just drop off my cell real fast? I wouldn't ask, but I'm just feeling so sick from the ride up here."

He nodded. "Yeah, sure."

"Thank you *so* much," she cooed. She looked apologetically at everyone else in the line. "Sorry!"

They all looked forgiving. She stepped into the line and then up to the window.

"Rebecca Normandy."

The boy behind the window was skinny and unattractive. He was the type that needed to learn that big shirts only make you look smaller.

"Freshman?"

She looked askance at him. Did she *look* like a freshman? "Um, no? Junior."

"Fill out the card." She did, using the information from the janitor guy, and then slid it back to him.

"Here's your key and information packet," the boy said.

"Okay, and where are the girls' dorms?"

He pointed. She smiled at him and then again at the boy who'd let her cut in front of him.

As she turned to walk away, she saw that almost everyone in the hall was looking at her. She couldn't help but love it.

But what a lot of average-looking people, she thought.

She had nothing to lose now that she was at Manderley. She might as well choose to be a hit while she was still here. She could be remembered when she did finally leave. But for a better reason than last time she left a school. There wasn't exactly a plaque hanging up at Waterford High School.

The following eyes continued the entire way up to her room. When she finally got there, the door was open. There was a dark-haired girl sitting on one of the beds, and the other side of the room was empty.

"I'm Rebecca. Call me Becca if you want," she said, making brief eye contact before looking around and taking in the *entirely* dreary room. The floor was a flat and ugly all-colors carpet, the walls were dingy white, and the bed looked like one you'd see in a dollhouse, i.e., not one for *sleeping*.

"I'm Dana Veers." Even she sounded bored with herself.

"This room is horrible," Becca said, and walked moodily to the empty side.

"It's ridiculous. I hate it. I've been here two years, and I feel like the walls are slowly moving in every day."

Becca looked at her new roommate for the first time. She was thin and pale, but was very pretty.

"Rocking the vampire look, I see." Becca started to unbutton her coat.

"That means a lot coming from you, Barbie."

Becca froze, and then started to laugh. She could see that her reaction surprised Dana.

"What are you laughing at?" Dana's tone sharpened.

"You! That was funny. Barbie. I *never* get that." She rolled her eyes.

"Because *vampire* was so creative?"

"Touché," Becca said with an arched eyebrow raised. "So what happened to your old roommate?"

"She graduated. Most of the girls end up with a roommate in the same class year, but sometimes they have to combine ages." She shrugged. "She was quiet, we didn't really talk very much."

Becca nodded, and then looked at her suitcases and boxes. "Wow, do I not feel like unpacking. What time is it?"

Dana hesitated before answering. It was clear that she didn't quite know how to handle her new roommate. "Eight-thirty."

"Mmm-kay. Is anything going on tonight?" It had been a while since she'd been social. She needed it.

"Anything...like what?"

Becca sighed. "Like, a party or something?"

"No one really parties here."

Becca laughed. "Now that is just not possible. It's a *boarding* school. That is the only thing that makes these places tolerable."

And then Becca was out the door. She stuck her head in the doorway of the next room over. Two girls were chatting and unpacking.

"Hey, I'm Becca." She smiled winningly at them in an *omg-we-r-about-2-b-bffs!* kind of way.

"I'm Julia." The taller of the two girls ran a hand through her caramel highlights.

"I'm Madison."

"Great. So, what's going on tonight?"

"What?" Madison asked.

"Any kind of party or anything?"

Madison looked confused. "No..."

Becca looked to Julia, who shook her head.

"Well, we should have one. Is there anywhere we can go?"

Madison shook her head, but Julia raised an eyebrow in consideration.

"I've always said we should do something down at the boathouse, but we never have. They have cameras. Not on the actual beach, but in the hall on the way there and stuff."

"Hmm…who watches the security tapes at night? Is it a student or, like, a security person?"

"He's a security guy, but he's kind of…" She looked uncomfortable. "He's just kind of off…."

"What, like, retarded?"

"Mentally challenged. Yes." Madison nodded.

"Let's go talk to him. What time's he go on to his shift, anyone know?"

"I always see him in there at night. He might be down there now."

Becca smirked. "Lead the way."

Madison looked nervous.

"Come on," said Becca, "don't be spineless."

Julia straightened up almost imperceptibly and walked out of the room. Madison followed. Then Becca. They led her to a wing off the great hall.

"That guy?" Becca pointed to the lanky, red-haired boy in the small, all-windowed office.

"That's him…." said Madison meekly.

Becca adjusted her hair, pulled down her shirt a little and knocked on the door. When he turned to look at her, she smiled and waved. "Hi!"

"Come in?"

"Hi, I'm Becca." She leaned down and held out a hand, which he took. "What's your name?"

"Danny."

"Danny? I like that name." She smiled again when he did. "So, Danny, I was wondering if you could help me."

"Help you with what?"

"Some people want to have a little get-together tonight, but we don't want to get in trouble." She stuck out her lips a little. "We just don't want to get told on. And we were just sure that you would be the right person to talk to about that."

He groaned. "I don't know...."

Becca smiled. "Oh, come on...it'll be our little secret! And maybe one of these times when we do it you can come down? Maybe?"

Danny laughed. "That would be nice."

"Good. So when you see everyone walking down the stairs to this boathouse, you won't say anything?"

He bared his teeth in worry, but shook his head. "I won't say anything."

"Good. *Good*. That's very, very sweet of you." She took his hand. "Thank you so much, Danny. If you ever get in trouble, I'll take full responsibility. But let's not let that happen, okay?"

He nodded eagerly.

"I'm going to go now, but I'll stop by soon to say hello, okay, Danny?" He nodded again.

She walked out and looked at the girls. "Okay, we're all set."

"Oh, my God, how did you do it?" Julia asked.

Becca shrugged. "Okay, now we need people. Guys."

"That's going to be difficult," said Madison.

"Why?"

"We're not allowed in the boys' dorms."

"Ugh, are you *serious?*"

Both of the girls nodded, looking somber.

"Okay, well then I'll do it. I'm new. *I didn't know.*" She gave a wide-eyed dumb-girl look and then smiled.

Madison laughed. "You're so...ballsy."

"Take me to the boys."

Their next stop was a door directly across from the one that led to their own dorms. While Julia and Madison stayed put, Becca walked through it, nonchalantly as could be, and into a long hallway, where she knocked on a door at random.

A chubby but okay-looking guy opened it. He looked surprised to see her.

"Hi, I'm Becca." She smiled.

"Cam. What's...what's up?"

"Hi, Cam," she said, looking up at him. "We're having a party at the boathouse. Get as many people as you can to come. I have a bunch of tequila and stuff."

"Really?"

She nodded. "Tell everyone."

"Sure. Are you new?"

"Yes, I am. Okay, so tell people. I'll see you tonight."

"I will. Nice to meet you." As soon as he shut the door, she walked to another room a few doors down. She had to tell someone who at least looked like they had friends to tell. It took a few doors until she finally decided she'd told enough people of the right kind.

When she emerged from the boys' dorms, it was to find Madison and Julia looking impressed.

"Okay, now let's just get the things we need." Becca smiled, and set off with her new posse to find cups for beer pong. She didn't have much beer, but they could just play with water when they ran out.

They returned to their hall with their collection, stolen from the dining hall.

"Hold these." Becca handed Madison the sleeve of cups she'd been holding.

She set off down the hallway, pounding on every door she passed. "Ladies! Everyone out of your rooms! Come on! Whoooo!"

By the time she reached the end of the hall and her own door, the hallway was filling up. She turned and smiled at them all.

"Good evening, girls. My name is Rebecca Normandy. Call me Becca. Tonight we are sneaking out of our dorms."

The girls exchanged glances, all looking eager and ready to be told what to do.

"We're going down to the boathouse. I've got a few bottles of tequila, and I've already started recruiting the boys."

"But we'll get in trouble," said a small, strawberry-blonde with tight curls, "won't we?"

"What's your name?"

"Susan."

"No, Susan. I've already handled that." She looked back to everyone else. "So are we all in?"

Most of the girls nodded.

"Good. See you out here at eleven."

She turned and went into her room.

"So, Dana, are you coming to the party tonight?"

"Um. I don't know."

"Just do it. I couldn't possibly go without my roomie." She smiled, and Dana smiled back.

chapter 3 me

WE SNUCK DOWN SOME CREAKY, SANDY STAIRS
to get to a beach that was so, *so* different from the ones back
home.

My bare legs were swathed in chilly air and I wished I could
go stick my feet in the water and have it be warm. But, alas,
this was not Florida.

There was a boathouse at the foot of the stairs. It was
pounding quietly with music, and a slivery border of gold
indicated the door to us. When the door was opened, sound
and light poured out and smacked us in the face.

I followed the other two and their booted feet with my
sandaled ones, and took a deep breath. I was ready.

No you're not, said that nag in my brain.

"I brought the new girl!" Julia said once we were in view
of the rest of the party.

"Hey," I said with a wave. My insides melted and I felt my
face grow hot.

She introduced me to everyone. I smiled and gave them
my name, promising them we'd have to remeet later. After

that, Madison and Julia went off to different guys, and left me alone.

I surveyed the scene and immediately felt out of my element. I had no guide. There were a few people on a shabby couch taking deep, strained breaths out of a bong. Another few were playing beer pong, a game I was familiar with but entirely awful at. And some people just hung around like me.

Some guy rose from a chair nearby and sidled up to me. "Hey, sweetie."

"Hey." I almost felt like I would rather be ignored.

"I'm Ricky. And you're the new girl."

I nodded and laughed, unable to think of anything to say.

He gave me what I was sure he thought was a winning smile, and asked if I wanted a shot.

"Oh, no, thank you."

"Oh, come on, you're fun, aren't you?" another guy asked, wandering over to us.

He said it in the distinct tone that usually goes with, *"Come on, little girl, you want some candy?"* Either that or like he was starring as a villain in some 1950s after-school special.

My cheeks, I was sure, were growing even redder. "I'm not a prude, I just…I'm not thirsty."

That was a stupid response. They looked like they knew it, and walked off.

I sighed and took a step backward. There was a yelp behind me, and I leaped as I realized I'd stepped on some girl's foot.

"Oh, jeez, I'm sorry."

"No problem. I'm Blake."

"Hi, I'm apparently 'the new girl.'"

She laughed. "This is my boyfriend, Cam."

"Hi, Cam." I glanced back at the two guys who had just walked away from me.

"I'd stay away from them." Cam took a sip from a red cup.

"Really?"

"Yeah, they're harmless, but I mean, they're pushy."

I looked around at everyone else. It was strange, because there was music and drinking and there were games, but everyone was kind of quiet. It was like a detention pizza party. "Everyone's sort of…subdued."

"Yeah." She looked around, too. "It's not usually like this."

I nodded, as if in understanding, and looked back out. Then the two of them started talking, and I felt like I should drift away. So I did. I sat down against a wall, suddenly eager to leave.

"You want to play?"

Another guy I hadn't met yet walked over to me. I really hoped they weren't all skeevy. This guy didn't look like he would be, though. He had shortish blond hair and an overall pleasant look about him. He probably didn't have to resort to being creepy.

"Play?" I asked.

He gestured to the table behind him. "Beer pong? Well… water pong. We don't have any beer." He smiled.

I envisioned the scene. Me playing, being terrible and being entirely lame and disappointing. "No, thanks, I'm really bad."

"That's okay," he said. "With no beer it's just for fun."

"No, really. Thank you, though."

Now I was being antisocial.

"Well, then." He held out a hand. "I'm Johnny."

"I—"

"Oh, new girl, right? Can I get you a drink?"

I sighed. "Right." Then, abruptly feeling like it might not be a bad idea, I said, "Maybe one small drink."

Johnny laughed and made me one. He added one shot. I thanked him, and took a sip.

"So what brings you to Manderley in your senior year?"

"My parents. I used to want to come here when I was younger. My parents got me in because a spot opened up, thinking I still really wanted to come."

His features hardened a little.

"Not that there's anything wrong with it here so far, I just...I liked my old school, too."

"Are you... Is Dana your roommate, then?"

"Yes, she is. I haven't really talked to her yet." I thought of her stony silence. "She didn't want to come down tonight."

"That's too bad. Not surprised, though." He looked behind him. "Well, if you change your mind about playing let me know. I have to go find someone since you don't want to." He gave me a smile, and found a new partner.

I stayed for another half an hour without being approached by anyone. I drank my drink and then headed out after saying goodbye to the few people I'd talked to. Ricky tried to convince me to have more shots before I left. I declined, and then hurried away from him as politely as possible.

Outside, I turned the corner on the dark, dusty stairs and nearly screamed as I ran into a figure.

"Whoa," he said.

"I'm sorry." It was dark, and we were illuminated only by the running lights at our feet. I could just barely make out his face, which seemed almost familiar. I looked away and started up the steps. I stumbled, dumbly, and he caught my wrist.

"Are you a freshman?" he asked.

"N-no." I shook my head. His hand was warm, and still held on to me.

"Then you're the new girl."

It wasn't a question. "Yes."

I saw his pale eyes squint briefly, and then he dropped my hand. A small chill ran through me, and I wanted him to say more. *I* wanted to say more, but I didn't know what.

"Sorry for running into you." I turned and walked up the steps, not understanding at all what had just happened.

As I snuck quietly through my door, I realized I didn't know where the light switch was. More than that, I couldn't turn on the overhead light since Dana was apparently sleeping. I flicked on my flashlight and stepped carefully to my bed, but not without stubbing my toe painfully on the suitcase under the bed. I bit my lip to keep from swearing, and then searched in the darkness for any of my things.

In the end, all I could find was my comforter and my pillow. I took off my jeans and slid noisily into bed. It was hard at first to fall asleep. I was cold and uncomfortable. I missed my big, cushy bed and the rest of my pillows, and even Jasper's annoyingly frequent snoring that would only cease after a nudge in the ribs from me.

At home when I couldn't sleep, I would make myself a little crudités plate like my dad always did, with Ritz crackers, cheeses, Wickles Pickles (the only kind worth buying), different kinds of meats, grapes....

Or maybe just a cup of tea and some of those jam-and-shortbread cookies my mom made and almost always had around. Suddenly nothing would be better than to tiptoe into my quiet living room, always lit by the fancy dim light in the corner, and cozy up on the couch to watch old *Frasier* reruns until unconsciousness swept me away.

I couldn't even think about it without getting a pain in my stomach.

I finally fell asleep, into weird dreams filled with distorted elements of Manderley I must have subconsciously taken in, but which I still didn't recognize.

Suddenly I was on the beach by the boathouse. It was pitch-black and freezing cold, even colder than before. I stepped into the water, which was so sharp and frigid that it felt like broken glass. Despite the pain, I kept walking. Before I knew it, I was swimming in the middle of the black sea. I couldn't see where I was, or how far away the shore was.

Panic wrapped around my heart as I realized I couldn't find my way to safety. There was a thunderous roar behind me, before a wave curled around me. It was strong, like a million forceful hands pushing me under. Every time I felt air, it would suck me under again and thrash me around like a Raggedy Ann doll.

A memory of those pale eyes I had barely been able to see floated into my suddenly aching head. He was mad, he was shouting. I couldn't stand to see him like this.

I couldn't catch my breath. I tried, and got a mouthful of salty water instead. I thought I reached the dry surface and took a breath. Instead I breathed in a rush of water that made my throat ache. My salty tears were mixing with the water around them and my body was contracting oddly as if I couldn't control it.

"Anyone who has not already, please proceed to the Kenneth L. Montague auditorium for the First Day Assembly."

I was shaken from my dream very abruptly when a voice I didn't expect came over a PA system I didn't know existed.

Why hadn't my alarm gone off? I inspected it, to find that I'd set it for 6:00 p.m., not a.m.

Without thinking, I threw on some jeans and grabbed my bright yellow staff T-shirt from my last year at the Jax Beach Surf Competition. I flip-flopped out the door thirty seconds later with only my key in hand.

It took me fifteen minutes of running around like a rat in a maze before I found the auditorium. I pulled on each of the doors, but they were all locked. I looked around for anyone, but I was completely alone. Left with no other option, I knocked.

The door opened suddenly, and a youngish man let me in. "Freshman?"

"Oh, no, I'm a senior. But I'm new."

"Try to be on time from now on." He was stern but not unkind. He glanced at my clothes. "And at the end of the assembly, please put on your uniform."

A shock of humiliation ran through me. I looked at the sea of navy-blue, white and khaki uniformed students in the seats. "Sorry, I'm coming from public school, I've never had—"

He nodded politely, though a touch dismissively, as I drifted into my annoying habit of overexplaining. I stopped, and he told me there was a seat down in front. To get to it, I'd have to walk—duck—past everyone.

I got there as quietly as possible and ignored the stares I could feel on me. Once seated, I stared straight up at the stage where I was only just noticing that there was a woman speaking.

She was reminding the students of the rules. Mostly everyone had no doubt heard the spiel as many times as I'd read it over the summer. I cringed when she got to the part about wearing uniforms every day to every function but Saturday and Sunday and social events. Weekends were mostly our own. We were allowed out from 9:00 a.m. until 10:00 p.m. on Saturdays, and from noon till 7:00 p.m. on Sundays. There were shuttles that would go back and forth from town to Manderley.

"...and absolutely no sexual relations of any kind anywhere on school property," the speaker said, a tad optimistically, and adjusted her papers. There was a snicker in the audience that she must have heard but ignored. "And now I'm inviting Professor Andrews up to the stage. Thank you for your continued attention." She took a seat at the back of the stage with several other teacher-looking people.

I clapped once, but the rest of the auditorium stayed silent. I shrank in my seat.

Professor Andrews turned out to be the man who'd let me in. He walked to the podium looking a little frazzled.

"Okay, well, I think Eloise, er, Headmaster Jenkins, pardon me, did a pretty good job of welcoming everyone, and reviewing the rules with you, so I won't be getting into any of that." He took his glasses from the neck of his shirt and put them on. "I'm sure most of you, at least many of you for whom this is not your first year, have already heard about Rebecca Normandy."

There was a slight rustling in the audience, but an immediate halt in the whispering.

"In the interest of providing correct information to all of you at once, and keeping the school from crippling rumors, I'll tell you what we know. Since May fourteenth, Rebecca Normandy has been missing. It's not clear what happened, only that she was here one moment and gone the next. If anyone hears anything from her, sees her, or is in any kind of contact with Miss Normandy, you *must tell someone.*"

I listened carefully, and then felt my stomach plummet through my seat.

Rebecca Normandy was Becca, the old roommate. Hers was the "slot that opened up" at Manderley.

"This is a very small school, and I'm sure that everyone here has been affected by the event. Because of that, I hope you all know that Dr. Morgan—" he gestured behind him to one of the seated women who was small and older and looked quite nice "—will have her door open at any time and will be offering counseling. I advise everyone who wants to or needs to, to make an appointment with Dr. Morgan. It can't hurt. And now, Dana Veers would like to say a few words on behalf of Miss Normandy's parents."

He stepped aside, and was quickly replaced by Dana. She peered out at the audience through her narrow eyes.

"So, we all know Becca is missing, but way too many people are just assuming she's dead. Anyone who can should write to her on Facebook and beg her to come back. Because I am *sure* she is out there, and probably checking it. If there is any way that she might come home, we have to make her want to. Her parents and the police have pretty much given up hope." She looked sick. "But I haven't, and I *hope* the rest of *you* haven't." She glanced down to the front row.

Then, abruptly, she thanked us for our attention and went back to her seat.

I was horrified at how I'd acted the day before. Dana's old roommate was missing. They had probably been friends.

Professor Andrews replaced her behind the stand. "Now Dr. Morgan has a few words she'd like to say, and then we'll release you to go to your first classes. Dr. Morgan?"

The tiny woman shuffled up to take his place, pulling the microphone down to match her height.

"Hello, everyone." She had a nasally English accent, and reminded me a little of the fairy godmother in *Cinderella*. "I know this is a very difficult time for each and every one of you, no matter how well you know Miss Normandy, or in what capacity. What you *must* remember is that you are *all* in this together. You are *all* going through something as one, unified group." She grasped the air and made a fist, as though collecting all of our leashes. "If you need someone to talk to, you could simply look left or right, and find someone who knows what you're going through." She smiled tenderly. "Why don't you do that now? Just look to the person sitting next to you, and tell them you're here for them. Go ahead."

There was a small murmur of reluctant participation, and some giggling. I looked to my left and saw the back of a girl's head, and to my right to see a boy slouching in his seat and leaning his face on his fingers.

I faced forward.

"Good." Dr. Morgan clasped her hands together. "Now take the hand of the person sitting next to you. Everyone, please?" She looked down at the front row, and with a surge I realized she was looking at me. Or...the boy next to me. "Mr. Holloway? You of all people..." She said the last part away from the microphone, but trailed off when the boy held out his hand for me to take. I put my hand in his.

As soon as we touched, it felt like an electrical current ran through me. I remembered the touch of the boy on the stairs the night before and wondered if this was him. I glanced sideways, not wanting to make it obvious that I was looking at him.

Dr. Morgan went on. "Now shut your eyes. And put your-self in the place that makes you the happiest." She was silent a few seconds, and shushed the people who laughed. "Wonder-ful. Now take a deep breath, and think to yourself, *I will get through this. I will get through this. I will get through this.* Deep breath in...and now out."

I was afraid my hand was clammy. Was I holding too hard? Did I seem eager?

"Good," said Dr. Morgan.

At her word, the boy let go of my hand as though it had burned him.

"Remember that everyone around you *understands,* and that you are abso*lutely* more than welcome to come visit with me. Over the next two weeks, I will be meeting with each one of you. We will discuss your plans for college, and anything else you might need to get off your chest. Thank you all for listening so carefully. Welcome back to Manderley, and if you're just starting, then welcome to your new home."

She smiled kindly, and went back to her seat as I and every-one else filled the room with the spattering of polite applause.

I was locked in my own head. There had been one spot at Manderley, and I'd gotten it. I was Rebecca's old roommate's *new* roommate, and the whole school was hoping she would come back at any second.

The boy next to me gave me a nod and then stood to leave.

Everything came together with a horrible lurch in my stomach. He *was* the one I'd run into on the stairs last night. Not only that, but the reason he was familiar was because he was the one pictured with Becca.

That startlingly handsome boy had been her boyfriend.

chapter 4 becca

ELEVEN O'CLOCK CAME. BECCA HAD ON A SHORT
black pencil skirt and a low white tank top.

"I'm so glad you decided to come," Becca said to Dana, as
she sprayed her Givenchy perfume where it mattered: neck,
wrists and boobs.

"Me, too."

"Here, before everyone else drinks it all." Becca took a swig
of tequila and handed the bottle to Dana.

"Oh, no—"

"Oh, come on, please!"

Dana took a deep breath and then took a sip. Becca tipped
the bottle a little higher and Dana gave a shriek as it filled her
mouth and spilled onto her cheeks.

Becca laughed and handed her roommate some tissues.

They emerged from their room to find that every girl on
the hall had put on their best outfit and stood waiting to be
led. Madison and Julia were standing with big purses filled
with cups and balls slung over their shoulders. Becca had her

new girl

own bag, filled with all the liquor she had brought with her to Manderley.

"You really think we won't get caught?" one of the girls asked.

"Oh, God no, we're not getting caught." She waved away the very idea. "Come on, stop worrying. You only live once, so live like it's your last night. Okay? Let's go." She smiled at all of them. "Lead the way," she said to Julia.

They walked down some side stairs and through an emergency exit that apparently didn't set off any alarms anywhere.

"Where are we going?" Becca heard someone ask from behind her.

"The boathouse," Julia answered, wielding a blue LED flashlight. "No one's ever down there at night, and it's out of view of all the teachers' rooms. It's the perfect place. I can't believe we never did this before."

They got down to the bottom of the stairs and to a small beach. There was some sand, but mostly a lot of rocks. In all, it looked like what you'd find at the bottom of a cartoon cliff.

Walking up to the boathouse, Julia pushed open a screen door, then a storm door. The light was already on and exposed a small house filled with dust and boating equipment. She wondered if she'd ever have to learn to use any of this stuff. Hopefully not.

"This place is disgusting," Becca noted, not helping matters.

Some people were already there, sitting around on the floor. One of them, Ricky, she thought his name was, was leaning on the speakers she'd told him to bring. She'd seen them in his room and "pretty-pleased" him into bringing them.

"Here." She handed him her iPod. "Put this on. It's the first playlist on there."

People trickled in for the next fifteen minutes. Becca got

the guys to help her put together a makeshift beer pong table. She took the Ziploc bag full of Ping-Pong balls and set them next to the case of beer and bottles she'd managed to stuff into her suitcases. The stolen cups were piled, and her plastic shot glasses set out next to the water bottles she'd had Dana fill with soda for chasers.

Soon the room was filled with laughing, talking, singing and squealing. As everyone got drunker and the room grew warmer, Becca felt more and more like herself. This was who she liked to be. She loved a chaotic atmosphere she could lose herself in. When everyone was drunk, no one was watching her too closely or looking for mistakes. If she said something she shouldn't, she could blame it on the drinks. Not like in real life, when the world was quiet and everyone could see and hear perfectly.

"Yeah, I'm rooming with some girl named Dana." Becca was shouting over the music to Ricky.

"Where is she?"

"Right over there," she pointed. "Don't you know her?"

"No, I've seen her around, but…"

"Dana!" Becca shouted her name across the room. Dana looked up, and then crossed the room to her. Becca took her hand. "This is my roommate!"

"Damn," said Ricky, looking between them, "you girls are so fucking hot."

Two other guys walked up. One of them swallowed his drink quickly. "Are you two gonna make out?"

Dana looked shocked.

"What, are you *scared?*" Becca asked with a laugh.

"What? No, I just—"

Becca looked to the group of guys suddenly surrounding them. "You dare me?"

All of them said yes, nodding.

"But—" Dana started, but was cut off by Becca, who had just planted a kiss on her.

Becca pulled away, laughing. The guys were all laughing and clapping at them.

"Oh, shit, she really did it!" One of the guys threw an arm around Becca. He let go of her and held a hand out to Dana. "I'm Barry."

Becca slapped his hand. "This is her *third* year here, the fact that you don't know her yet means you don't *get* to introduce yourself."

She looked at him playfully, and led Dana away.

"That guy was so annoying, wasn't he?" she said to Dana. "Barry? He totally tried to hit on me earlier. I'd ignore him."

It was a lie. But that didn't matter. It wasn't Dana's time to get looked at. *Becca* was the new girl. Not her.

"Let's have another drink," said Becca. She took Dana's hand and led her to the alcohol table.

When they got there, a tall boy was already pouring two shots.

"Make it four." Becca sidled up to him and saw that he was not just tall, but attractive, too. Blond, light brown eyes—and a good smile. He looked like he'd play baseball and was always nice to his mom.

"You the new girl?" he asked, and then turned to Dana. "Hey, what's up, Dana?"

"*Yes,*" Becca answered quickly, before Dana could say anything. "I am the new girl. I'm glad you know Dana, no one else seems to. What's your name?"

"Johnny." He smiled and looked down at the shots he was now pouring for them. "Of course I know Dana. She's that girl that sat next to me in Algebra last year." He mouthed *hot* at Becca, and then smiled at Dana.

Becca was about to say something about how little anyone

else seemed interested in Dana when another boy walked up. He was about the same height as Johnny, but an utter contrast. His skin was tan, like he'd spent the summer working outside and maybe had some Italian or something in him. His hair was black and a little messy, and his eyes were light blue. There was something in them that intrigued her. He looked... she tried to think of the word to describe him, and landed on *sly*.

"Hey." He nodded curtly at her, then turned his last words to Johnny. "Pour me one."

Immediately intrigued by this person who ignored her, she said, "I'm Becca."

"Here, Max." Johnny handed him a shot. They all clinked their glasses together, swallowed the burning liquid and then pounded back chasers.

"Becca," Max said, finally acknowledging her. "Hey."

"So, where'd you move here from?" asked Johnny, leaning back on the table.

"Chicago." Becca cast a side-glance at Max, who was now in conversation with Dana about how awful some teacher had been.

"Chicago? That's pretty cool. I've never been there. Why'd you transfer here?"

Chatty, wasn't he? "My parents can't stand me and hope someone else can." That was the simple answer.

He laughed. "I bet that's what a lot of people here feel like."

"Come on," Becca said suddenly to Dana. Her conversation with Max was going too well. And Becca was the one that wanted attention from him. She smiled. "Let's go pick some other music to put on, huh?"

Half an hour later, Becca had been flirted with by another group of guys and had her self-esteem restored. Now she was talking to that guy Cam and looking for a way out of the conversation. She spotted a girl staring at them. As soon as Becca caught her, the girl looked away.

"That girl," she said to Cam, and pointed. "Is that your girlfriend?"

A small smile and a tinge of pink appeared on his face. "No, that's Blake."

"But you like her."

He laughed it off. "What? That's crazy, I didn't... She's not... She wouldn't like me. She's gorgeous." His eyes were on Blake, but she had turned to talk to someone next to her.

"She likes you, I can tell."

"No..." he said, but something in his tone asked for an elaboration.

"She was just looking over here at you, and looking totally jealous that I was talking to you." It was obvious, and it's not like she wanted Cam's attention for herself, so she might as well tell him.

"Really?" Cam looked doubtful.

Becca rolled her eyes. "Blake!"

"No, don't—"

The girl looked up, surprised to see who was calling her name.

"Come here!" Becca motioned.

Blake glanced at Cam, who looked like he wanted to run but was too paralyzed with fear to do so. She walked over to them.

"I'm Becca. You know Cam?"

She nodded and smiled at him sheepishly. "Yes. Hi, Cam."

"Hi."

Ugh. "Yes okay, so you guys totally like each other. So," she said, and shrugged, "talk or whatever," and then she wandered off.

A little while later, Johnny sat down next to Becca and

asked if she was having fun. This close, and with a little more light on him than before, she could see that he was cute. Or maybe that was just that last shot sinking in.

"Yeah, it's pretty good." She felt Dana's eyes on her. She was jealous that Johnny was all about talking to Becca. And Becca couldn't help but rub it in. She tossed her hair and looked charmingly at him. "So tell me about *you*, Johnny."

"Well, what do you want to know?"

"Becca!"

She turned from Johnny to see Madison beckoning her over with a flapping hand.

"What?"

"Come outside with us!"

"Sorry," she said to Johnny. She saw that her roommate was now talking to Max.

Careful, Dana dear, you don't want to mess with Becca and what she wants.

"Come on, you!" She pulled Dana away. "You *will* be social from now on. I accept nothing less. I can't believe you don't know anyone at your own school."

Dana smiled apologetically at Max.

As soon as they were outside, she untangled her arm from Dana's and sat down on the sand with Blake (who was positively beaming), Madison and Julia. Everyone was clearly less worried about being quiet than they had been at first, and were laughing and talking without filter.

"So, *Becca*," Blake started, "who do *you* think is hot?"

All the girls laughed. Becca simply smiled back. "I'm not telling."

Of course not. She needed to be told who everyone *else* wanted first.

"Oh, come *on*," Julia cooed. "Who? Is it Johnny?"

She started to shake her head when Madison cooed.

"Ooh, he's so sweet. He'd be, like, the *best* boyfriend."

"Max is pretty attractive, too," Becca said.

"Well, obviously." Julia rolled her eyes. "Everyone knows that, but he's not even worth it."

"Why not?"

"Everyone has had a crush on him at some point," Madison elaborated. "But he's just…"

"Unattainable?" Becca filled in the blank. That's who she'd have to go for, then. Too bad he'd already exhibited little to no interest in her.

"Exactly." Blake nodded. "I do want to warn you though, Becca." Blake leaned in a little bit. "The girls at this school will be crazed with jealousy if you get together with Max."

So she couldn't act like that was her plan…. Becca shrugged. "Maybe he's gay and that's why he doesn't date."

Everyone laughed again, but then made it very clear that no one thought that was the case.

Madison, who was clearly seeing the world in double, leaned toward Becca. "No, but seriously. Seriously. Max is so hot. But you and Johnny would be so cute together!"

"I don't know, Max is okay," she said, playing it cool. He was much more than okay. And that's why she had to have him. But she couldn't seem too interested—not to anyone.

"What?" Everyone squealed in unison.

Madison's jaw dropped. "I'll be right back." She darted inside.

"What's she doing?" Becca asked.

"Probably puking," Julia said simply. "Okay, but so you're not into Johnny. I don't know, I mean—"

The boathouse screen door flew open and Madison stumbled out, dragging Max behind her.

"I got Max!"

Julia and Blake burst into laughter.

"Oh, my God! I can't believe you did that!" said Julia.

Becca stood cautiously and raked a hand through her hair. "Are you even drunk?"

"Not as drunk as you."

She raised an eyebrow.

Madison slung an arm over each of their shoulders. A struggle for her because she was probably about five feet, Becca was five-nine, and Max had to be about six-two.

"Guys, I have a secret." Madison was trying to whisper but barely succeeding. Julia and Blake were listening intently, ready to laugh at any second. "Max. Becca thinks you might be gay."

He raised his eyebrows and grinned, exposing straight white teeth. "That so?"

Becca smiled. "I was hypothesizing, since it was said that apparently you never date."

He nodded and looked away from her.

"Sh-sh-shh. Also," Madison said, reeling her audience back in. "She doesn't think you're that unattractive. Or...that you're not attractive. Or...wait..."

He looked back to her, appearing amused.

"I didn't mean you weren't *attractive*. I just meant—"

"It's okay. I don't think you're all that attractive, either."

He was obviously kidding, but Becca didn't think it was funny at all. She scoffed, trying to mask her embarrassment. Three other people had heard him say it. They might report that to other people, who would then think he wasn't kidding. She was going to have to make him want her.

Immediately.

"Well, aren't you sharp?" She looked him straight in the eyes.

"We should let you two get to know each other." Blake

stood and pulled up Julia. Madison nodded vigorously and led the way back into the boathouse.

They were alone. She smiled at him and walked toward the waves that were breaking quietly on the shore. She turned to crook a finger at him. "Come on."

He followed her. She stepped into the water.

"Cold?" he asked.

Becca didn't look back before answering. "How scared are you?"

He chuckled, and a moment later he'd rolled up his jeans and stood next to her. The water wrapped itself around their ankles, and he sucked air in through his teeth.

"Yup. It's cold."

"Wimp."

They were silent together for a moment, looking out at the black water and sky. It all ran together, with no horizon.

"This is seriously the worst beach."

"Are you always so unhappy with your surroundings?"

She glared at him. "No, I'm not unhappy with them. I'm just saying. It's hardly a beach. It's just sand and rocks that happen to be next to water."

Max stepped backward and sat down on the sand, away from where the water was breaking.

She followed him.

She leaned back like a pinup girl, and was quiet for a moment. "Why doesn't anyone here *drink?*"

"What're you talking about, there's a bunch of people in there drinking as we speak."

"Yeah, but at my old school, there were parties all the time."

"Public school?"

"Yep."

"Where can you have parties 'all the time,' doesn't everyone live with their parents?"

"Yeah, but there was this guy Vince that always had people over. He was like nineteen and lived by himself."

He nodded. "We drink in the dorms, we've just never come down here."

"That's because of the cameras, but I handled that."

"What'd you do, blow the guy?"

She turned sharply and was about to look angry when she saw that he was smiling.

She smiled, too. "No, I didn't *blow him*. I just talked to him."

"Okay." He said it like he didn't believe her.

So her conversation wasn't doing it for him. She'd try something else.

She put her hand on his hipbone and moved it up his stomach. He didn't flex, but it was still flat and solid.

She looked up at him and moved her hand across his stomach muscles. "Should I stop?" *Please don't say yes…*

He shook his head. She ran her fingernails up his chest. She put her face close to his. Her hand, now in his hair, tugged lightly. He kissed her. A moment later they were making out.

He was on top of her. He kissed her cheek, her neck, pulled up her tank top and kissed her more.

They took each other's shirts off. He put a hand on her thigh, and then up her skirt. She let him. She was getting nervous, but fought it off. He was strong and a little forceful—but not in a bad way. Then Becca made a decision.

If he wanted to, then she was going to. And it seemed like he did.

He was an amazing kisser. He was hot enough that everyone else was obsessed. He was evidently popular. And she was sixteen already. This needed to happen.

"Do it," she whispered in his ear when the time seemed right. The second he did, Becca realized she didn't even know his last name.

That was messed up—even Becca knew that. You should seriously know the full name of the guy you lose your virginity to.

chapter 5 becca

"HEY, BECCA."

Johnny stopped in front of Becca. He, Cam and Max all had lacrosse bags over their shoulders. Blake smiled at her, her hand in Cam's. Apparently the last two had taken her advice and had been talking, a lot.

Becca smiled, her eyes slightly narrowed. "Hey," she said to Cam and Blake. To Max she said, "Mike, was it?"

He had not said anything to her since they'd hooked up. That was weird. And she hadn't just made out with him. They'd actually *done it*. He was really going to act like it hadn't happened?

Max grinned. "Yep, that's it."

She looked back to Johnny, wondering if he knew what she and Max had done. "I was just on my way to the courtyard," she let out.

"Mind if I come with you?" he asked.

No, she didn't mind. Maybe Max would get jealous and then realize he should really *talk to her*.

"Sure." She glanced back to Cam, Blake and Max. "I'm sure I'll see you all soon."

Cam said nothing, but smiled and started off with Blake. Max held her gaze a few extra seconds, laughed, and followed them. Something in her plummeted as he did it.

She shook it off, and turned her focus to Johnny. Walking with him to the courtyard felt like walking the red carpet with Brad Pitt for all the stares they were getting. In the tabloids, she'd be a "mystery blonde."

Not for long.

He held the door open for her. "After you."

She walked through and sat down on a bench obscured mostly by bushes. "These socks are so ugly," she remarked, taking a cigarette from the top of one of hers.

"Everyone has to wear them, so it's not like you're going to stand out. You're not going to be the girl with those weird, ugly socks."

Becca raised her eyebrows. "Well, at least I found a use for them. They're so freaking bulky you can't even see my cigarettes—" she reached for her other sock "—or my lighter."

"You kind of can," he said, and watched her as she lit it. "I didn't know you smoked."

"What, do you not like it or something?"

He made a face. "Not my business."

True.

"I'd stop if I had to." She eyed him, and took a drag. "So, why did you want to come out here with me?"

He looked as if this was a subject he'd hoped she wouldn't broach. "I don't really know. I kind of…just wanted to talk to you."

"Oh, *really?*" She smiled playfully. She was used to this approach. This was much more comfortable for her than what Max was doing. Or wasn't doing.

People passing by the windows that overlooked the court-yard were noticing them. She blew some smoke out of her lungs and stood in front of him.

"Do you like me, Johnny?"

"I barely know you." He looked into her eyes. "But I'd like to get to know you."

"Good. I like you, too." She focused on the grass beneath her feet. "But I don't want to get a bad reputation."

She raised her head, hoping he'd say that Max had told him about what had happened. She envisioned a proud scene in which Max went for high fives and everyone was jealous.

But Johnny just furrowed his brows. "Bad reputation?"

Dammit. "Oh, you know. I don't want to jump into some-thing with someone too fast."

"That's okay, I'm not saying— I just feel like I want to know you. It's stupid...."

More looks from inside. She smiled winningly at him. "It's not stupid at all. Let's go eat lunch."

They walked down the hallway, Becca telling a story about her old school. He made a joke, and she laughed, laying a hand on his arm. "You are *so* funny."

Together they waltzed into the dining hall.

"Let's sit by ourselves, okay?"

"Sure," he said.

Becca set her purse down on a table and got a small bowl of soup. As they ate and he talked about whatever it was he was talking about, Becca surreptitiously scanned the hall for Max. Finally she caught him at a crowded table across the room. He wasn't looking at her. She couldn't help but glance up every now and then at him. Finally he did look in her direction, then quickly averted his gaze.

It was working, she could tell. He cared if she talked to

Johnny. So she didn't look up again, but directed her attention
to Johnny only.

"So how long have you and Max been friends?"

He ignored the change in subject and took a bite of his
sandwich. "Since we were kids. We both grew up in D.C."

"Cool. How come he doesn't date?"

He looked at her with a small smile. "You like Max, don't
you? See, here I thought you *weren't* like every other girl
here."

She laughed, trying to look as though this were prepos-
terous. "I do *not!* I'm just curious. He's not even that good-
looking, I don't get the appeal. So many girls like him, and
he never dates." She took a sip of her water. "It's just weird."

"Girls are always throwing themselves at him. He doesn't
need to date." Johnny shrugged. "I guess he's never gone for
the desperate type."

"Well, who does?"

"True."

"So," she said, "tell me something about you."

Whatever he said, she didn't listen. She was just trying to
look like she thought every word he said was fascinating.

A couple days later, as Becca left her last class of the day, she
saw Max going into the gym. She hurried upstairs to put on
her "workout clothes" and then walked in, too. She stepped
onto a treadmill a few down from his, her headphones on,
and acted like she didn't see Max.

She had to run for fifteen minutes before he came up next
to her.

He was in a gray T-shirt, soaked with hard-earned sweat
in all of the right places. She lowered the speed and took out
her pink headphones.

"Hey," she said, with a small smile.

He smiled back. "So, you're hanging out with Johnny now?"

"What do you mean 'hanging out with'?"

He shrugged. "You tell me."

"I'm getting to know him, but I'm not *hanging out with* anyone."

"Right."

Not being able to take it anymore, she turned off the treadmill.

"I'm going to get in the sauna. You want to come?"

He considered her for a moment, and then said, "I thought you weren't hanging out with anyone?"

"I'm not," she said, and led the way. Then she added, without looking back at him, "And besides, we've already done our hanging out. What interest are you to me now?"

"Ha!" he said.

The sauna was already warm. She took off her shirt and her shoes, leaving her in her neon pink sports bra and black nylon shorts. He followed her lead and stripped down, too.

It was the first time she'd really seen his body. It was perfect. The type of body artists would want to sculpt and poets could gab endlessly about. He was lean but strong.

They sat next to each other for a minute in silence, him leaning against the wall with his eyes shut, and her looking around the small brown room. The door had a lock. She leaned forward and turned it.

He turned to her, a small smirk on his face. "Yeah?"

Determination filled her. He *had* to want her. She couldn't be just another girl throwing herself at him, but she needed him to do something.

"What? I'm generally quite modest," she said, "and I just want to make sure no one comes in while I don't have my shirt on." She indicated her sports bra.

He nodded, visibly not believing her. "Come here," he said.

Yes. Now she had the power. "Why?"

"You know why."

She smiled and stepped up to where he was and lowered herself onto his lap. She wrapped her arms around his neck and let him kiss her. Soft at first but then with urgency.

The surge she felt in her chest was not romantic. It was victorious. She knew that as soon as he started to show interest in her, that she'd have no trouble walking away. But right now...

He laid her on the surface of the wooden bench and they did it again. By the time they emerged from the room, their faces were pink, and their bodies were slick with sweat from the heat.

chapter 6 me

ONE OF THE THINGS THAT HAD BEEN INTIMIDAT-
ing about heading to Manderley was its boast that almost
every student had a 4.0 GPA. My 3.2 was pretty good, but
who knew how that would translate from a public high school
in a beach town to a private New England boarding school.

I suspected "not so well" when I sat down on my first day
in my first class.

"Good morning, everyone." The teacher was a small
woman with black, beady eyes and hair that looked like it
would feel like straw. Her voice was a bit low and booming.
"I am Professor Van Hooper. Welcome to English. I'll tell you
now that this class will not be easy. Expect a C to be a good
grade."

I got a chill as I imagined what we'd have to do to stay
afloat. As if she'd read my thoughts, Professor Van Hooper
went on.

"Every two weeks, we will begin another book. At the end
of those two weeks, you will owe me a paper written on your
own choice of topic. The only restriction is that you must

find something worth investigating in the book and write about it."

A girl in front raised her hand. "Like a book report?"

"No. Not like a book report." The way she responded made me sure I'd be keeping my hand down as much as possible. "For example, this week, we are reading *To Kill a Mockingbird*. You may, for instance, choose to theorize on how the main character, Scout, grew through her experiences in the book. Or you might get a little bit more creative, and talk about her relationship with her father or brother. It's up to you to write something I want to read. It's up to *you* to find something about the book that isn't on the back cover. Now. Let's talk about basic formatting. Times New Roman, one-inch margins…"

There was a sudden shuffle as people dug through their backpacks for pens and notebooks. At my school back home we'd pretty much started using laptops, but the brochures had made it perfectly clear that they were not allowed in class. Stupid rule. I have terrible handwriting.

She switched on the overhead, and it hummed into life.

She sped through what she expected technically from us, and skipped straight into finding the deeper meaning in the classics. I loved to read, so I wasn't dreading it.

"I assume you've all read *To Kill a Mockingbird,* yes?"

There was an uncomfortable shuffle from the students who I guessed had skimmed through it and used SparkNotes.

"So as you read it this second time, I want you to start thinking more about the underlying themes. Yes, we know it's about prejudice and the struggle between right and wrong—but what *else* is there? What else did Harper Lee bury within her pages?"

World History demanded a lot more prior knowledge than I had. The teacher started off the class by asking us what we

knew about the religious beliefs of the Neanderthals. I sank
in my seat and hoped to God I wasn't called on.

Math, which was always my worst subject, started off with
a quiz. Really? Day One of Algebra II and we're taking a
quiz? *Just to see what we know,* but still. It's a quiz. Everyone
else around me seemed to know what was going on, making
my inability to follow along stick out like a sore thumb.

And then I walked into the huge concrete studio on the top
floor of the main building. The windows went from floor to
ceiling, and there were big black filing cabinets with wide,
skinny drawers lining the walls. There were about thirty easels
standing on the hard, cold floor, which was splattered with
the paint of a million masterpieces gone by.

The room echoed the music that came out of a silver Mac-
Book Air on one of the black cabinets. It wasn't until then that
I realized I'd gone almost three days without hearing music,
and thought how unusual that was for me.

There were a couple of people there already, sitting on
stools and talking to each other. I sat down on an empty one
and stared at the floor while people filtered in for the next
five minutes. I didn't talk to anyone and they didn't talk to
me. Maybe I was being paranoid, but as their whispers echoed
throughout the room, I heard a lot of "she," and I automatically and self-pityingly felt sure they were talking about me.

Professor Crawley walked in as the clock struck three,
marking the beginning of my last class of the day, and smiled
at us. He'd been the first teacher to crack a smile all day long.

"How's everyone doin'? Good first day?"

Silence.

"Yeah, me, too." He sat on a stool and looked down at the
papers on his clipboard. He ran through attendance, reading
our last names and waiting for the small murmur of acknowl-
edgment.

"...Francis? Gordon? Hanover? Holloway?" He looked up and around. I did, too. Had I not noticed him somehow? "Nope, no Holloway. All right, Langston? Marconi?"

My stomach dropped. I didn't know why, but I was disappointed he wasn't there. Maybe he was just late.

As Professor Crawley reached the end of attendance, everyone's heads turned toward the door. I followed the collective gaze to see—

"Mr. Holloway, there you are. Don't let your tardiness become a habit. You go by Max?"

He nodded his head and sat down on the stool next to mine. I looked straight ahead, suddenly unable to feel natural.

"So on to class, then. Welcome, all of you. Some of you I know, some of you I don't." Professor Crawley looked at me. "But I'm absolutely sure we'll get to know each other in no time. I'm Professor Crawley. You can just call me Crawley while we're in the classroom. Too many syllables otherwise. So how many of you have any experience in painting? Or art of any kind, really? Drawing, sculpting, maybe just doodles in your biology notes?"

A few people raised their hands. He smiled at them. "Right after piano lessons and right before tennis, huh?"

There was a small titter of appreciative laughter.

Crawley went on. "I'm just going to assume, for the sake of starting on the same foot, that we all have no experience, which is totally fine."

I breathed a sigh of relief, and felt Max's eyes shift to me. I glanced at him, and saw the smallest trace of a smile. I quickly looked away.

"So here's what we're going to do. I'm going to pair you guys up, and you're just going to start painting, see what comes out. This is your Gamsol." He held up a glass pot with a lid. "You rinse your brushes in here. It's like turpentine, except I'm not allergic to it."

Another titter from the girls.

"You've got your brushes, your oil paints, your palette, your palette knife and a rag. Make sure you rinse your brushes thoroughly or all of your colors will go muddy. Squeeze out only the smallest amount of paint. I assure you, this stuff goes far."

He paired us off. In this kind of situation I usually ended up partnerless and had to work with the teacher. But not this time.

"All right, so go ahead and grab a canvas and an easel and then stop off with me to get your box of supplies."

Once we were set up and sitting across from each other, I gave the boy in front of me an awkward and probably very unpretty smile.

"Max," he said, holding out a hand. "We met by the boat-house."

Oh, did we? I hadn't recalled…

"Yes, I remember, I nearly fell to my death on those stairs."

With a sickening lurch, I realized what poor taste that had been in. I wanted to say something to make up for it, but before I got the chance, he just nodded as he squeezed out some blue paint and said, "But here you are."

"Here I am."

I squeezed out a couple of colors and blended them until it resembled Max's tanned skin tone.

"So are you any good?" he asked.

"Good?"

He nodded at my canvas. "At painting."

"Oh." I laughed nervously. "I doubt it, I've never really done it before. I helped paint a mural back at my old school, but it was basically like painting in between the lines. Like a huge coloring book."

"Where'd you go to school?"

"St. Augustine. In Florida."

"Did you grow up there?"

"Yeah."

He gave a small smile. "You're in for a hell of a winter, then."

I took a deep breath and said, "Oh, I've heard."

"Ever seen snow?"

I shook my head.

"You're gonna see a lot of it here." He furrowed his brow at his canvas and looked at me.

"Are you any good?" I asked, indicating his canvas.

"Not at all. Don't be insulted by my portrait of you. I just took this class because I needed an elective and Crawley is awesome."

"He seems cool, yeah."

We settled into a silence I struggled not to fill with stupid rambling. I mixed up some more color to match his dark hair. I laid the brush on the canvas with the blackish color I'd mixed up. But it wasn't quite right. There was a small tinge of another color in there somewhere. I sifted through the paint tubes and found Alizarin Crimson. I added a tiny bit. Yes, that was a lot better.

"Look at me for a sec," he said.

I looked up. "What?"

He squinted and leaned toward me. "Green, okay. But…" He stood and came over to me. He put his hand under my chin and lifted up my face. My heart skipped.

"Trust me," he said with a smile. "I'm an artist."

"Paint me like one of your French girls."

Oh, the words spilled from my mouth before I could stop

them. I was too used to my group of friends. My cheeks turned hot.

He dropped his hand and looked at me. "Did you just make a *Titanic* reference?"

"Maybe."

He smiled and raised an eyebrow. "My older cousin Sarah watched that for the entirety of a family trip at the Outer Banks once. And if I remember correctly, in that scene, he wasn't just painting her face."

"Well, we probably won't be asked to do that in here."

"Probably not." He smiled. "Now look at me, I need to look at your eyes."

He tilted my head so that my eyes caught the light.

"They're not just green. They have some brown in them, too. Right in the middle." I looked at him as he studied my eyes.

"Really?" I said, even though I fully knew it.

"There's also..." He narrowed his own eyes. "Also some blue. They're like the color of...a pond or something."

I laughed, and it echoed in the otherwise silent room. Everyone looked at us. I bit my lip and looked around apologetically.

Max smiled. "What?"

"A pond? So, like, the brown is mud and the green is pond scum?"

He laughed, too, sitting back down. "I didn't mean it like that."

I laughed and focused back on my canvas.

The end of class came, and we were able to reveal our paintings to each other. I actually kind of liked mine. It didn't look like a photograph or anything, but it really looked like Max.

"You ready?" I asked him.

He furrowed his brow once again at his painting and said, "I guess."

We turned around our paintings. I don't think I'd laughed so hard in weeks. I was one big circle with pink tinge in my cheeks, little dots for freckles, and huge blue-green-brown eyes. I had no eyelids, and my lashes were like little black spiders.

"All right, all right, so I'm *not* an artist." He put his canvas back on the easel. "But at least I got your eyes right."

The rest of the week passed by in a frenzy of getting situated in classes and talking about the year full of work that lay before us. I could already tell that the huge studio was going to be my sanctuary, because as far as the other classes went, it was looking like the year wouldn't be an easy one. Manderley had block scheduling, so one day we'd have four classes, and then the next day we'd have four different ones. Fridays we had all of them, but they were cut in half. On A days, I had English, World History, Algebra II and Painting. On B days, I had Gym (a bummer because at my old school we didn't need to take it in senior year, and also because it's at *freaking* 8:00 a.m.), Biology, French II (a breeze, since my Paris-born mother had mostly taught me the language) and study hall (which I could hardly believe was a real thing).

A couple days into this schedule, I approached Blake in the dining hall as we slathered bagels with cream cheese, and she assured me things would settle down soon.

"It's always like this," she said. "It's superbusy and then teachers cool off. Trust me, two weeks from now it'll be ten times better. It's like they sprint and then get tired and drag their feet for the rest of the year."

I saw her and Cam every day in the hallways and a few times during meals. They were clearly a very happy couple, and I got along with both of them. I saw a few other people in the halls that I'd met, but no one said much more than a passing hello. I didn't see Max as much as I wanted to, but when I did, he was usually coming in from lacrosse practice with slightly flushed cheeks and a sheen of sweat on his sculpted cheekbones.

It was odd for me to be mostly solitary. Back home I was out all the time and did something at least *kind* of social every day even if it was just watching TV with Leah. I was missing home more each day. Every memory I had of home was suddenly set in a perfect sunny day, whereas Manderley was set to the backdrop of gray rain and cold drafts that seeped through ancient walls.

I was alone and cold, and since the food was nothing like my mother's or what I was used to, I was hungry. Even the salad, usually a safe go-to, tasted like nail polish remover.

It was really hard to stay positive. And that's normally a talent of mine.

Unable to simply quit school or even tell my thrilled parents about the mild disappointments of the past week, I sat by myself and read or did homework during meals, went to class alone, and then headed to my room where Dana would look disappointed to see me and then ignore me. Sometimes I wanted to just kick her in the shins and tell her to stop being such an unpleasant cloud of gloom, but then I'd remember Becca—it was hard not to, when my side of the room still displayed a wallpaper of her pictures—and feel guilty again.

So that put me in the dining hall at nine at night on my first Friday evening. I was filling my travel mug with hot chocolate. I'd decided I wasn't ready for bed and that I didn't want to spend time in the same room as Dana quite yet. I figured I'd read *To Kill a Mockingbird* and try to find the deeper motifs in the rotunda until I got tired.

It was meant to be a social place, but the chairs were clearly not built with comfort or extended sitting in mind. They were all stiff, and some of them were mysteriously itchy. The rotunda itself was pretty noisy, what with the entrance hall directly beneath us, but it was better than my room.

My hot chocolate looked thin and watery, but it was deceptively delicious. I turned to see Blake putting a piece of bread in the toaster.

I summoned the nerve and then said, "Hey, Blake."

She looked up, and took a second to register. "Oh, hey! I'm sorry, I didn't know you were there."

"That's okay, I just walked up."

She smiled kindly. "I'm just taking this up to my room or I'd sit with you."

"Oh, me, too," I said, not wanting her to think I was desperate. "I'm just getting some of this and then reading a little for English."

"I suggest reading on the second floor of the library. Have you been up there yet?"

"Not yet."

"There are some spiral stairs near the back of the library that lead up to a bunch of study rooms. Go into the room right across from the landing."

"What is it? Am I allowed?"

She giggled. "Yes, it's the senior study room. There's a gas fire in there, and a bunch of armchairs. It's *really* nice. It's empty a lot at night. Most of these kids do their homework right after classes."

"I'll go check it out, thanks." I brought my hot chocolate to my lips.

"Oh, and hey," she added quickly, "we're going down to the boathouse tonight, you want to come?"

"Um…" I scrunched up my face in consideration.

"I know you can. Harper Lee can wait until tomorrow."
She looked knowingly at me. "You just don't want to go.
Well, look, it'll be better this time. Last time you went, it was
just a little weird. The last party we had last year was the one
when…Becca went missing. Not only that, but she was the
one who kind of…started the parties down there."

"Oh…" Then the question I'd been waiting to ask all week
fell from my lips like an anvil. "What…what happened to
her?"

Blake's toast popped up in the toaster. She removed it and
concentrated on smothering it in butter and jelly. "She and
Max got into a fight about something to do with Johnny…
and it was right after Dana and she'd had a fight…and then
the next thing we knew she was just gone. So was the training
sailboat." Her hand slowed on the knife. "It was really strange.
There was a horrible storm brewing, so it doesn't make sense
for her to think she could go out in the boat…that would
be suicide. But maybe that's what it was…or maybe she was
pushed out onto the boat. Or maybe she just left, and the boat
thing was a coincidence. It's really not clear what happened."

Blake went silent, and it was clear to me that she'd spent a
lot of energy trying to figure this out.

"That's awful."

"It was also the last night though, so she might have just
called a cab and left for the summer. She had her purse on
her. And her family is incredibly rich. I don't know… It just
doesn't make *sense*. I'm sure you've heard all of the talk about
it. All the theories."

I shook my head. "No, not really. People talk about her a
lot, but…what do you mean by *theories?*"

She sighed and took a bite of her toast. "She's been missing
for so many months now that it's kind of…the longer she's
missing, the more likely it is she won't come back."

I didn't know what to say, so I said nothing.

"So I guess…" Blake went on, "I guess people are starting to wonder if she was killed."

"*Killed? Really?* By someone—by a student?"

She nodded somberly. "Yeah. It's hard to believe, but the whole thing is so surreal."

"Who do they think did it?"

"You know how it is—everyone became a suspect at one time or another, really. Rumors are like that. Since she and Max were a thing, *he* became the most consistent rumor…."

I felt like my blood had frozen. I pictured Johnny, asking me to play beer pong, and smiling at me with blond hair almost touching his bright eyes. I thought of Dana, so deep in mourning she couldn't seem to see straight.

And of Max. Max looking into my eyes. I'd looked into his, too. He wasn't capable of murder; surely I would have seen it. I knew that wasn't true—I didn't even know him. But still, I couldn't imagine it.

"But she's not even necessarily dead," she added quickly. "A lot of people think she's alive. That's just as likely." She looked at her toast for a quiet moment. "So you'll come?"

"Come?"

"To the party tonight."

No. No. Say no. "Sure."

"Great! Any time after eleven." She gave a small smile and then walked back out of the hall.

I set off for the library a moment later, and as I walked, my mind reeled as I thought about the missing girl. No one knew what had happened to her, and yet this time last year she'd been walking the same halls as me. It had been her first year, too. Had everyone been as chilly toward me? Probably not. She was probably *why* they were like that toward me. They all hated me for coming along.

I was like the new baby sibling that everyone resented.

The study room was empty when I arrived. The lights were off, and I had to feel around the walls until I found a switch. But rather than turning on a fluorescent overhead as I'd expected, it turned on a floor lamp in each corner of the room. They illuminated a smallish, cozy room paneled in dark wood, with comfy-looking armchairs and couches filling the place. Along one wall, there were desks with those old-fashioned green bankers' lights with the gold, beaded pull string. Right in the middle was a huge ornate mantel, with a modern electric fireplace. I flicked on a light switch and fire burst into life.

This, I supposed, was the charm of Northern states and cold places. It was a different type of charm and warmth than I was used to, but as I read for the next few hours with the fire warming my bare feet and I drank my hot chocolate, I could see that this wasn't bad, either.

I fell asleep and into another strange dream, as I had on my first night.

I was standing on the beach again. Someone was yelling at me. It was a male voice. I wanted to cry, but I couldn't let myself. I felt determined and strong, but sick and weak all at once. Everything was blurry, as if I was looking through the water of a chlorine pool.

My chest stung and my head pounded. I wanted to hit him, whoever he was. I wanted to scream back at him. But no...I didn't need to. He was wrong. He'd see. I wasn't like he thought I was. I could be better. I would be from now on....

chapter 7 me

I AWOKE WITH A START AND LOOKED AROUND, disoriented.

I had no way of knowing what time it was. In a world where cell phones were barely allowed, you'd think there would be a clock on every wall. But there wasn't. I put the fire out, turned off the lights and ran to my room. It was eleven forty-five. Just in time for bed, and I was fully awake.

I remembered Blake's invitation. I wasn't sure if I had the nerve to go down alone.

I got that butterfly flutter in my stomach as I wondered if Max was there. I ignored the thought. Of all ways to start off at Manderley, developing a crush on the most unavailable guy there was probably not the best.

The flutter turned to a shudder as I went down to the beach.

The breeze coming off the ocean felt good. Refreshing. A little bit like home, only way colder than usual. The air, in only these few days, had dropped a few degrees. But at least today it hadn't rained.

I clutched the fabric of my new peacoat closer to me and walked to the boathouse. I measured my breath carefully, loosened my grip on the book I still had in my hand and opened the door. I could tell immediately that the mood here was better than at the last party. Not so somber. I was met with a few astonished faces, and an immediate approach from my across-the-hall neighbors.

"You came! *Finally!*" Madison said, her smile big.

"I did." I smiled, too. "I'm sorry I'm here so late."

Julia hooked her arm with mine, as if we were best friends. "It's no problem."

I could smell that she'd already been drinking, and I could see by looking at and hearing everyone else that they had been, too. She dragged me across the musty room.

"Take a shot of this," she said, holding up a blue bottle. "It is whipped-cream-flavored vodka and it is *so* good."

I let her pour it into a shot glass and tried not to mentally relive the experience of the last time I'd had straight liquor. No one I hung out with back home really drank because we were always driving places, and didn't want to bother with the expense anyways. Sometimes at parties if someone else was driving I'd have a drink or two if Leah was, but not usually. One time, we were at my friend Lucy's aunt's house on Vilano Beach. I had about seven margaritas, made for me by someone else. That night I learned what it felt like to not care about how intimately close I was becoming with a toilet, and what it feels like to wake up with the imprint of a bathmat on my cheek. Bad. That's what it feels like. Freaking. Bad.

Especially when it doesn't go away for the next forty-eight hours. The sickness or the imprint.

"How do you get this stuff in here, anyway?" I asked, warily postponing the shot.

"Take it!" Madison said, and the two of them clinked their

glasses with mine, sloshing the slightly syrupy liquid onto my hand.

Three, two, one. And with the burning, numbing *yuck* came the memories and the churning stomach. They laughed at my facial expression, and I indicated that Madison should hand me a can of Sprite. My head spun instantly, and the deep bass of whatever heavy bass song was playing vibrated right through me.

"Whoo," I said, after a few sips of the soda. "It's been a while."

"Let's do it again!" Madison said, and poured another.

"No, really, I had a terrible hangover once—"

Julia put a hand on my shoulder. "Look. I drink all the time. I'm not gonna let you get a hangover. Cuz we're friends, right?"

I mean, that might be a slight exaggeration.... "I believe you," I said, "I just—"

Before I could object, they refilled my glass. I hesitated before taking it with them, and decided that one more shot couldn't hurt. And clearly this was the way to get in with these girls.

I downed some more Sprite and took a deep breath.

"So," said Julia, inching a little closer to me. "So. Who do you like?"

"Who do I what?"

"Like! I mean, so far do you think anyone is hot?"

I tried not to think of Max Holloway. "I don't really know anyone yet."

"You don't need to *know* them." Madison looked at me like this was obvious.

I felt under pressure, trying to think of someone, anyone besides Max to say. But I couldn't. "Really, I don't even know anyone's name."

"Just look around and point at someone!" Julia said, a little louder.

They were clearly not letting this go. I looked around for someone to point to, and landed my gaze on Johnny. He was smiling at some girl with strawberry-blond hair. I thought of what Blake had said earlier.

"Johnny?" Madison asked.

The girls exchanged a meaningful look.

"Oh, no, I didn't mean him, I was just looking at him. I didn't mean him—"

"Let's go back outside." Julia pointed toward the door.

Madison grabbed me and the next thing I knew, we were outside and walking away from the house. My flip-flops slapped cold pricks of sand into my calves.

"What?" I was sure my face was red, and was glad we were in such shrouding darkness.

Julia looked as if she was trying to say something tactfully. "That's Johnny Parker."

"Like I said, I didn't even know him or anything. I didn't say anything about thinking he was cute."

"Well, do you?"

This is the kind of question that girls ask each other, with the one intention of screwing the other over by her answer. So I just said, "I have no opinion on him, because I don't know him."

"There are only two guys here who are off-limits," said Julia. "One is Johnny Parker—"

She followed my gaze as it shifted over her shoulder. Max had just loped down the steps. Madison said, *"Shh…"*

"How many cats did you say your mom has? Ten? That's *like so many.*" Julia's voice was loud and fake. My face grew hot.

Max looked at us as he walked by, and then went through the boathouse door without a word.

"I don't have *any* cats, why did you say that?" I asked.

"Why do you care? Oh, no, you like *him,* don't you?"

"What? Like him—no!"

They clearly wanted to back me into the Bitch Corner. They exchanged another look.

I looked at each of them, my heart skipping a little at being so accurately pinned. "I don't *know either* of them."

"But do you think you might like Max?"

"Why are you asking me that?"

"Because." Julia looked helplessly at me, and then to Madison.

Madison gave me a pitying look. "Because you really shouldn't. He's not going to like you back." She rested a hand on my shoulder. "Not because there's anything wrong with you...just..."

"He's in love with Becca. Like *crazy* in love."

I shook my head, and smiled. "No, no I don't like him. Don't worry about it."

"Good." Madison looked relieved. "We just don't want you to get hurt. And when she comes back..."

"*If* she comes back." Julia looked morosely down at her feet.

"Right. *If*...if and when she comes back, you just wouldn't want to..."

"No, really," I said, my voice unnaturally high, "it's fine! Let's go back inside."

We did, the two others drifted off, and I found myself surprised to learn that Dana was *not* in our room back up at the school. She was here. And by the looks of it, she was wasted. When I passed her she didn't notice me.

Johnny was at the makeshift bar, pouring himself a shot of Captain Morgan.

I stood next to him. "Hit me."

He laughed, and wordlessly screwed the cap back on the Captain, and opened the blue bottle of vodka.

"How'd you know that's what I wanted?"

"It's girl stuff." He cast a side-glance at me and smiled.

"Hey, I don't need to pretend to be tough, *Captain Morgan.*" I smiled. "I hate straight liquor. At least this stuff is easier."

"Well, then," he said, handing me my shot, "cheers to not pretending."

We clinked, swallowed, and then I made that face again. He popped open a soda and handed it to me.

"Thanks." I swigged it. "I had a can, but I don't know where it is."

"Never leave a drink unattended and then drink from it again. That's how girls get roofied."

"Are there people here who would do that?"

He furrowed his brows. "I really don't think so. But Ricky is the pill guy." He shrugged. "You should just always be careful anyway."

"There it is!" Johnny said, as I made the winning cup in beer pong. "You finally made one, and right when it really mattered."

He smiled at me.

"Took long enough." I smiled back, all too aware that Max had just come into our part of the room.

"Who wants next?" Johnny asked loudly.

For a small moment I hoped Max would volunteer.

"We do!" Blake said, pulling Cam to the table.

Probably for the best—I didn't need to make a fool of myself when I knew he'd be watching.

"Your shot," Johnny said, nudging me with his elbow.

I aimed, shot and missed.

My head spun every time Cam or Blake made a shot and I had to take a sip of the vodka and pineapple that she'd made for me. Finally they made their last cup, and Johnny and I had lost. I tried very hard to concentrate on the game, but even though my eyes were on the red cups, my brain was in the crowd around us.

I turned to Johnny with an apologetic smile. "I'm sorry I'm so bad!"

I sipped my drink and wavered a little. Closing my eyes, I took a deep breath and tried to steady myself.

"You want some water?"

I nodded, my eyes still shut, thinking it was Johnny. But when I opened my eyes, it was to see Max.

I felt my stomach lurch, and I took the bottle he handed me. "Thanks." Then, to overexplain as usual, I said, "I'm kind of a lightweight."

"That's better than being a hardened alcoholic by seventeen." He sat back down, and I saw that next to him was Dana. She was finishing a red cup filled with something and wobbling into the wall behind her.

I fanned myself with my hand, suddenly feeling hot.

"You okay? You wanna step outside?"

"Um, sure." My skin grew even warmer as surrounding gazes shifted to us when we stood and walked toward the door. It was like they were all motion-sensor security cameras, and I was a clumsy thief.

We stepped out into the chilly air, and I breathed deeply.

"So, how do you like it here so far?" he asked.

In that moment I was very aware of how cute he was.

"Max, get in here. Dana's freaking out."

He looked puzzled, but went inside. I followed him

"—doesn't anyone even *care?* You're all just acting like it never happened! Like it didn't happen *here,* only a few months ago."

"Dana, come—" Johnny tried to pull her away from the center of attention, but she swatted his hand away.

"Shut up, *Johnny,* you're...you're one of the reasons she's gone and you know it. I will *never* look at you the same way."

She may as well have slapped him. His eyes turned to stone, and he stepped away from her again. I glanced at Blake.

"Nobody cares," shrilled Dana. "Nobody understands what it's like to care about someone. You're all so wrapped up in yourselves. I— Just *fuck* all of you!"

"Dana, we are all just as worried and hopeful as you." Blake's voice was steady and calm.

Dana's face contorted into an unpleasant smile, and she started to laugh. "You're so wrong about that." She shifted her gaze to me, and then beside me to Max, who had just stepped up. Her smile turned into a grimace. "You are both disgusting."

I felt stung as she looked directly at me.

I started to stutter out a response, but she got close to my face and said, "You're just a little slut from the South. You want everyone, and you can't have them. They don't *want* you."

Everyone hung on her every word.

"You don't...you don't even know me." My voice was not steady or calm.

"Shut up." She held a hand up in my direction and looked at Max. "If it wasn't for you, she'd be here tonight. Do you realize that? And that bitch—" she pointed to me "—would not be."

Dana stalked over to us, her gaze never leaving Max's.

"You know," she said, when she was face-to-face with him. Her voice was low, but everyone was listening hard. "You *know.* No one else here does, because I *kept* everyone's secrets. You know that's probably what she's off doing, right? Handling the situation?"

"Stop talking now." He said it firmly.

The air was thick and she stared at him for a long moment. Finally she walked out of the boathouse without saying another word. Johnny followed her.

The room filled with the immediate buzz of chatter that had been bound to follow her outburst. I felt sick and embarrassed. She so clearly hated and resented me. I didn't want to go back to that room. I wanted to go home. But I had no choice.

"I'm sorry about that," Max said. He didn't look at me, simply followed Johnny and Dana's lead by walking out of the boathouse. There was no reason for me to stay. After a five-minute search for my coat, I left, too.

I heard the screen door slam, and then footsteps. Johnny shouted after me when I was a few steps up. I turned, and he was coming up the stairs.

"Hey, you want me to walk you up?"

Not really. I was feeling sicker by the second, and really wanted to just dart from here to my room. I could hardly imagine saying very much at all. But I probably wasn't in a position to say no to people.

"Sure."

We walked in silence for a moment before he said, "So… did you have some fun at least, before the blowout?"

"Yeah, sure, it was fun." Though it was hard to think of anything else besides what Dana had said.

"People have been pretty messed up about her."

"Who, Dana?"

"Becca."

Obviously. I'm an idiot. "Right, right. Of course."

"Tensions run a little high when her name comes up."

"I'm sure. Yeah."

I didn't want to talk, and suddenly I didn't want to listen. What was it about this girl Becca? Everything I'd heard about her made it seem like she was some kind of goddess who enchanted people just by being around them. I mean, I understand that it's really awful to have a peer be missing and possibly dead…but it's like she was friends with everyone. It was like she'd been perfect.

I didn't want to go to my room, where Dana would inevitably be at some point. I was humiliated. I was sick. And to make matters worse, I felt cold pricks of rain start to fall into my hair.

A wave of sickness washed over me. We were only about fifty yards from the girls' dorm door. I wanted to run to it, but I couldn't.

"Well, I'm glad you came. We should, I don't know, hang out or something."

"Yeah sure. Um…thanks for walking me. I'll see you tomorrow or something." I gave a pitiful attempt at a smile and then flew through the door and up to my room.

When I got there, I took a deep breath. In almost that same instant, I was in the bathroom, getting close with the mouth of another toilet.

chapter 8 me

I WOKE UP BRIGHT AND EARLY AT TWO IN THE afternoon. Dana had made it her business to amble around as loudly as possible until she finally fell asleep. I had lain there for God knows how long with my eyes shut, pretending to sleep and trying not to move.

I was trembling and weak when I awoke, and I felt that putting my head in a vise might be a lot more preferable to the pounding it endured now. My churning stomach needed something in it or it was just going to shrivel into a raisin. But I really didn't feel like eating was going to go well. Even so, I made it down to the dining hall.

Sandwiches, soup, salad, chicken, pancakes…my stomach had all the options in the world and was rejecting even the thought of any of them. I groaned and turned to leave.

And then there was Max, walking in.

I gave a small smile. *God I hope I don't puke.*

"Hi." He looked uncomfortable.

"Hey."

"Did you just get here?"

I nodded. "Yes. Trying to decide what to eat." I looked around again at all the things I couldn't imagine putting down my throat and keeping there.

"Do you want to sit with me?"

A chill filled my chest. I felt so stupid for letting myself drink so much last night that I was screwing myself over to-day. "Sure."

We walked through the line together. I looked around me. I didn't want him to know how bad I was feeling. I really didn't want to give him the opportunity to picture me with my face in a toilet.

Potato soup. Nope. Would look the same going down as it would five minutes later.

Sandwich. Entirely too many textures.

Yogurt. Only one texture, but it was a nasty one.

Salad. That nail-polish-remover taste in the lettuce would remind me way too much of the alcohol directly.

Bread of any and all kind seemed out of the question. People always say bread and water is the way to go, but the very thought of either one of those things was absolutely revolting.

Chicken tenders. Maybe I could do that. Maybe. I grabbed them and a ginger ale, and sat at the nearest table.

I exhaled slowly and purposefully, trying to soothe my quivering stomach. I shut my eyes fast when I saw Max's cheeseburger. This was going to be tough.

"Did you have fun last night?" he asked. "Before Dana freaked out?"

"Yeah, up until then."

"Just…ignore everything she said. You're obviously not disgusting."

Only in this bizarre context could that give me the thrill of flattery.

"Thanks."

"I don't know why she attacked you like that."

I shrugged. "I don't, either."

I considered the chicken tenders, and took another bite. Oh, big mistake. The second it hit my throat I had to cough and swallow hard.

"You okay?"

I nodded vigorously. Too vigorously. "Mmm. Oh, yeah, I'm fine."

"Hey, so…" He looked uncomfortable. "I hope you didn't take anything Dana said to heart last night."

"I… No. I'm not even thinking about it." My stomach felt as though it was being pulled like taffy. "You know, I just remembered something I need to do. I'm sorry."

I fled from the hall like it was on fire. I jumped down the last four stairs of the staircase, and banged into a stall. I puked before I could get the door shut.

I was there for another fifteen minutes, my knees picking up God knows what off the floor, and my elbows turning red from being planted on the hard, plastic seat.

I wasn't sure if I was miserable about having to dart from the conversation right then, or if I was okay with that. It had sounded a lot like I was about to get rejected when I'd never even offered myself.

I didn't know. And before I could even begin to figure it out, the fluttering was back in my throat.

I slept until that night. Then of course, I could do nothing but sit up, wide-awake in my room. Dana read in her bed again, saying nothing about the night before, and all of Becca's pictures still stared down at me. I looked away from them and spent the next ten minutes trying to read the spine of Dana's book. Finally I saw what it was. It was called *Coping,* and was written by some doctor I couldn't see the name of. I felt a small tinge of pity.

A knock came on my door at ten-fifteen. I opened the door to find Madison and Julia looking very serious. I had a feeling I was going to start feeling sick again.

"What's up?"

"Would you mind coming over to our room for a minute?" Julia asked, as Madison looked at the floor.

"Okay." I followed them, sat down on one of the beds, and they sat across from me. "If you guys are getting a divorce, I know it's not about me."

"It's about Max and Johnny."

"We just think it's important for you to know a few things before your interest in either one of them goes any further."

I was baffled. "My interest in either one of them? I don't... What?"

Madison looked earnestly at me. "You already know Max was with Becca before she went missing. But what you might not know is that he was crazy in love with her. And so was Johnny."

Johnny had loved Becca?

Julia took over. "But Max and Becca were so in love. He said he wanted to marry her and everything. She tried to break up with him a hundred times, and he always begged for her back."

I found it hard to picture Max begging anyone for anything.

"If they were so in love, why did she try to break up with him so many times?"

They were silent for a few seconds, but then Madison spoke. "I really think they would have gotten married. And if—and when—she comes back...they'll definitely get back together."

"We just don't want you to get hurt," Julia explained.

"We don't want that at all."

"And if Johnny does have any interest in you, it's kind of weird."

My stomach was slowly plummeting. I didn't even know him. "Weird, why weird?"

"I mean…she was the new girl last year. Now you're here… in her room…."

"You even kind of look like her," Julia said. She observed me for a moment and clearly decided that if I did indeed look like Becca, I was a much less attractive version. "No wonder he likes you."

I froze. "I've only had a few conversations with him. I'm not trying to…anything."

"But we also don't want you to misread anything Max might say or do. He's protective of girls, so if he talks to you it's probably just him trying to make you feel better about how everyone is talking about you."

"Is everyone talking about me?"

I wanted to go home.

The two girls stared blankly at me.

"Look," I said, sparing them the duty of having to say yes, "I won't go near either of them."

"Do you promise?" Madison asked. "It's really for your own good."

"Yes. I'm— I've gotta go."

I went back into my room. I wished I could run farther. It seemed suddenly to be a horrible idea, sleeping in the school you go to. Everyone was everywhere, every second of every day. And in high school, that's pretty much the fastest way to lose your sanity.

I didn't even know what I wanted, and Madison and Julia were assuring me that anything I might consider was out of the question. I couldn't put one toe onto Becca's property.

Max could never like me. Johnny might, but I was supposed to know it was creepy. I got it. I wasn't going to start "going after" anyone. I never had, and I wasn't going to start now.

I sat down on my own bed, breathing hard. I looked straight across from me at all the many smiling faces of Becca, Becca and Max, Becca and Max kissing, Becca and Johnny, one of the three of them and Becca and the rest of her friends.

"Are you upset?"

I almost jumped at the sound of Dana's voice. "Yes. I'm upset."

"Why?"

"I'd rather not talk about it with you?"

Um. Obviously.

"Does it have to do with Max? I saw how you looked at him. You have feelings for him."

"No, okay, I don't."

"You better not, because—"

"Because he was madly in love with Becca—I get it, okay?"

"Is. He *is* in love with Becca. She's not gone. She's not dead. I wish everyone would try to *remember* that every once in a while." Dana threw down *Coping*. "Max and Becca are meant for each other...you couldn't even *begin* to understand! Anything she did...it was just— She'll come back and it'll be for him, not for anyone else!"

Dana had gone from less than zero to over a hundred in five seconds flat.

"I didn't mean to imply that she's definitely gone or...or anything!"

"Yes, you did!" Dana's eyes were wide and scary. She looked crazed. "And you don't even know her! I knew her, okay? She'll be *back*, nothing *happened* to her!"

"Okay!"

"No! She will! You have to understand that. And you'll

understand why no one will ever see you how they saw her, so you can just stop trying. Her hair? Her face? Her body? She's *physically* better than you. Her hair is shinier and lighter, she doesn't have stupid little freckles all over her face like you do, and she's taller than you."

I didn't even know what to say. This was baffling. She just went on and on.

"And that's just *physically*. But otherwise? Everybody loves her. She *started* everyone going down to the boathouse to have parties. She came up with that. She's *fun,* and you're *drab.* You and your hippie lifestyle—"

"*Hippie lifestyle?* Are you kidding?"

"Yes, you're all tan and your hair's all wavy, you're always wearing flip-flops and beat-up jeans—you're trying so hard to look like some kind of ad for Sex Wax. How much do you spend a year on self-tanner and highlights? How much of your life have you spent trying to look like you're not trying?"

"I…"

It was impossible to defend. This was crazy. For one small and pretty irrelevant thing, I actually *really* didn't use self-tanner. It was something my mom was always reprimanding me for. And as for my hair, it was the one thing I really liked about myself. I never highlighted it or colored it, and it always got lighter in the summer. But I couldn't insist that to a crazy person. I couldn't engage in this. *And* she was grief stricken. I wanted to understand her but she was making it impossible.

"Becca will come back," she threatened, "and then you'll see. If anyone is giving you any kind of second look right now, you'll see how quickly that goes away, because you could *never* compare to her. You'll never be as good as her. You'll never be as pretty. You'll never *have* what she *has*."

That was it. I whipped around, and my hands were moving of their own volition. I was pulling thumbtacks out of the wall and gathering the pictures of perfect little Becca and hurling them at Dana.

"Stop it!" Horror was filling her eyes, and seemingly paralyzing her where she stood. *"Becca put those there! You put them back!"* She was screaming now, reminding me of that scene in *Lord of the Rings* when that blonde girl goes from beautiful to a big computer-graphic monster.

"No! You take these. Put them up on your own damn wall if you want to. Put them in a box for when and if she comes to pick them up, but I am *not* going to stare at these pictures anymore." I threw the last of them on the floor and then threw the thumbtacks at her closet. It may have been the most violent act I'd ever made. "This is *my* bed. This is *my* shelf—" I picked up the remaining four picture frames "—and *this shit is not mine.*"

"You bitch. You fucking *bitch!*"

"I don't care what you think. I'm sorry you're worried about your friend. I really, *truly* am. But you will not belittle me and my life because of it."

I grabbed my wallet and key and left the room, slamming the door. I shouldn't have been surprised, but I was, that every single door along the hallway was closing as I walked out into it. Great. If everyone was talking about me, then now they could add *psycho* to the list of things wrong with me.

I had no idea whether it was too late to go check out my phone, but I needed to call someone. My mom. Leah. Emma. Someone.

I ran to the cell phone office. It was eight forty-five. I glanced out the doors. Dark already.

"Hi, I want to check out my phone, please." I handed him the checkout card I'd been given on my first day.

He handed me my phone. "Fifteen minutes."

"Okay."

I turned it on and darted out the side door into the court-yard. It was freaking cold, and my Florida-based wardrobe only made it colder. I called Home the second it turned on.

No answer. My desperation was starting to make my hairs stand on end. I needed someone to tell me that I was right.

But I had a bunch of voice mails.

The first one was from my mom:

"Hey, sweetie, I miss you already! I know you're going to have a *fantastic* time at Manderley. You really are. It's such a good school, you're going to get into a fabulous college, and oh, you're going to have so much fun. You're going to make so many friends there. Oh, gotta go, I think I'm getting pulled over. Call me sometime soon. Love you!"

She sounded so sure that I would do well here. I made sure not to delete the message and listened to the second one. It was from Leah, my best friend. The first few seconds was just a bunch of screaming, talking and laughing. Then finally:

"…give me the *phone*, Michael! Jeez! Okay, *finally!* It's all of us here—" she was interrupted by a bunch of people yelling their hellos into the phone "—and we just miss you *so* much! The senior cookout was at the A-Street Pier this year, and it's so freaking awesome! Rita's is giving out free desserts, and Mango Mangos is catering—I know you love their French fries and we just— Shut up! I'm trying to leave a message!" More laughing, and then my friend Emma took over the phone.

"Hey! Oh, my gosh, we miss you *so* much, seriously, it is *not* the same without you. Plus I don't think the guys know who to lust after now that you're gone—"

The phone exchanged hands again. My throat was tight, and there were chills going up and down my back. "It's totally true—" I recognized Jake's voice "—you were the hottest thing to ever happen to SAHS."

"*Any*way," Leah said, taking the phone back, "we miss you, and you would have loved this cookout it's so much fun. Not as much as if you were here though. Call me back! Or write to me on Facebook or something—jeez— I can't believe I haven't heard from you yet! Must be too busy with all your— Stop it! Okay, love you, bye!"

More laughing until they got the call to end. There was one more voice mail from home, left only an hour ago. It started with barking I recognized. Then I heard the small barely-familiar-with-a-phone voice of my little sister Lily.

"That was Jasper saying hello. He misses you lots, I can tell, and he's always sleeping in your bed! I think he's really sad every time someone comes to the door because it's not you. You have to come home soon so you can pet him and hug him, because he's really sad and missing you. He got a new collar and leash! I lost the other ones…but that's okay, because these are pink! Daddy let me pick them out, and Mommy thought it was silly because Jasper is a boy, but I think they look good with his black fur. He's really cute. Also another doggie moved in next door and Jasper is always talking to it. It's making Mommy irritated though, she says, because now they're always barking. But *I* said it's cute because it's like *101 Dalmatians* and they're doing the twilight bark. You know, when all the dogs talk before they go inside for bed? Anyway, Daddy is doing that thing with his finger that means 'wrap it up' so I have to go. Oh—wait, here's Daddy, he wants to talk, too. Bye!"

My eyes were burning now. "I just walked in, I'm not sure how long she's been talking or if it cut her off." I heard Lily in the background saying she had *just* called me. "Anyway, we miss you and can't wait until you come home. Love you, talk to you soon."

And that was it. I used to hear every one of those voices every day, and took them completely for granted. I couldn't even mentally utter the old saying about "knowing what you've got." I just missed them, even after this short period of time. I was so incredibly nostalgic for a life I knew I'd never, ever have again. But at this moment, I wanted nothing more than to give up on this stupid place and go back home. I looked at the weather app on my phone. It had been eighty-three degrees back home. The next two days were sunny, and the third had thunderstorms. I loved thunderstorms.

As for Manderley, the weather was anticipated to be overall gloomy, with a temperature of sixty the next day, with cold rains and a low of forty-three. Cold rains are really, really different than warm thunderstorms.

I tried home once more. When there was no answer, I left my own voice mail. "Hey, everyone, um…" Here it was. My opportunity. If I told my parents I hated it, they would let me come home. I could be home in forty-eight hours, sitting in the living room with my mom. She'd listen to my woes sympathetically and without judgment. I could be back at my high school in time for Homecoming. "I miss you all so, so much. I— It's…"

If I left, everyone would know why. If people talked about me, they'd say, *Remember that new girl? No, not Becca, the short one with the stupid freckles.*

Becca left here, alive or not, and left behind a legacy. I wasn't as good as her, only because she was so…whatever she was. If I walked out now, I'd be telling everyone they were right. If I left now, I'd be a coward who runs scared from the ghost of a girl who haunts the halls.

"Manderley is amazing. I can't wait until you can see it

in person. The classes are pretty hard, but not worse than I
thought they'd be. Love you all. Lily, give Jasper a paw-shake
and a hug for me, okay?" I briefly envisioned how good it
would feel just to scratch his ears and give him a squeeze.
"Love you. Miss you. I have to go turn my phone back in
now. I still love it by the way, thanks so much for getting it
for me." I was rambling. "Okay, bye now."

I texted each of my friends, giving them a brief and re-
spectively varied miss you, wish I was home, xoxo, and then
turned the phone off. It felt like saying goodbye to my visitors
and returning to my jail cell.

The only way I could think of to extend the visit would be
to go to the library, to the one computer equipped with the
ability to do anything but look up journal articles and other
scholarly things, and log on to Facebook for the first time
since I'd left home.

I really shouldn't have. It was just more of the same tortur-
ous happiness from my old life. My friends wrote to say they
missed me. It was really flattering and nice, but it just hurt.
It hadn't been long since I'd left, but it felt like it had been so
much longer. Leah wrote, Already forgotten about us, huh?
Ugh! Fine, go make your new friends…what do I care?
Haha, just kidding. Miss you, come visit!

I looked at the pictures from the cookout, and everything
else my friends had been up to lately. It was like digging into
my own flesh to find a bullet. I couldn't even get through
the whole album of all of my friends wearing sweatshirts with
shorts and flip-flops, still sporting sunburns at the cookout.
Leah had tagged me in one picture as an extra marshmallow
on a stick and her and Emma pouting.

I glanced at the other albums, of them just two days before,
swimming in Lucy's aunt's pool in the afternoon and then in
the hot tub at night.

Then I thought of something. I hesitantly typed her name into the search box. And then there she was.

Rebecca Normandy. Her profile was restricted so that I couldn't see anything but her profile pictures and the comments on her wall. It was really kind of disturbing. She'd been missing for almost five months, and there were still comments from the past few days, from people whose names I didn't recognize.

Miss you, beautiful.

I love you and miss you every day. Please come back soon.

XOXOOXO

Hey, remember that one time with the shoelaces and the Barbie? Oh, my God, the look on his face… Bahahaha come back, slut, I miss you!

They were all writing to her like she was checking her Facebook regularly. I wondered, with a pang, if she was. What had Dana suggested the other night? That she was off "handling" something.

I kept scrolling, and found Dana's most recent post: *I know you're not gone. I know it. So stop. Come back. Or at least contact me.*

There were tons more comments like those and like Dana's. It was creepy. Spooky.

And it made me really wonder what had happened. Maybe she wasn't even missing. Maybe everyone knew where she was, and she was just…hiding for some reason. That would be crazy…but maybe that's what it was.

But if she wasn't…what had happened? Blake had said something about a boat that went missing that night in the storm. Had Becca taken it out? She couldn't have. It was pitch-black down there at night, and in a storm? She could have just called a cab, like Blake had said, on the payphone in the lobby and…left.

To make my brain strain more, I clicked on her pictures. I could only see a few, but they were enough. In the one she had set as her default, Max was kissing her on the cheek, and she was smiling. In the next few, she just looked pretty. She looked like she was *trying* to look pretty, but she was undeniably succeeding. All the comments on her pictures confirmed it.

A sudden jab of uncharacteristic jealousy struck me. She'd been new at Manderley last year. How had she managed to make so many friends here, made such an impact, while I was greeted with only hesitance quickly followed by disinterest? Madison and Julia made some kind of an effort with me, and Johnny was nice. Max was…something. Blake was nice, too, I guessed. But Dana…

There was only a handful of people I'd even talked to, and all of them—except maybe for Cam, who rarely spoke—seemed morbidly and irreversibly affected by Becca. They all knew her. It's not like each of them talked only about her, but somehow that seemed more significant.

I don't know what happened to me, then. I was depressed about being away from home and jealous of Becca one moment, and then the next, something shifted in me. It was as if my skeleton turned to iron—I was strong, and I would not have my happiness and fate decided by some popular girl who had reigned before I got there.

It wasn't up to Becca or Dana how I lived my life.

chapter 9 becca

BECCA LEANED ON MAX, WITH HER DRINK IN hand. His arm was around her, tightened a little to keep her steady. He laughed at something Johnny said. Becca wasn't really paying attention. She was watching the way Johnny's muscles flexed when he moved his arms. He was too hot. But she couldn't go for him. She'd already gotten the ungettable.

Well. Almost gotten him. Tonight was the night to seal the deal. Madison and Julia had given her sympathy and said "not to feel too badly about him not wanting to get together officially, because really he just never does that."

Fuck that.

Becca's eyes slid involuntarily up Johnny's body and she flinched when she realized he was looking at her, too. She smiled and bit her bottom lip. Quickly she glanced up at Max, who had been taking a swig of his drink and didn't notice.

"Max," she said, readjusting her attention to him. "Let's go outside."

"Okay."

Johnny had already turned away when Becca looked back.

She grabbed his hand. "Lead the way."

Max guided her through the crowd, smiling and shaking his head at all of the "ooh's" and "get it, Holloway!" as they passed by.

Once they were outside, she gave him the look that always made boys kiss her.

It worked. He laid a hand on her jawbone and pulled her toward him. He was a good kisser. She should want this. But she felt like something was missing with him. She kissed him harder, hoping she could forget the thoughts in her mind.

She pulled away and smiled slyly. Then she yanked his arm and guided him away from the door and into the darkness behind the boathouse.

He silently allowed her to take him there. Then, in the darkness where she could pretend he was anyone, she kissed him hard. He kissed her back. So he *was* capable of not kissing just like a Nice Guy. She scratched his back, and all the way around the waistband of his boxers, which were a little higher than his slightly loose pants. She unbuttoned his top button. She could feel that he wanted it. And she was going to give it.

His grip on her waist tightened. She bit his lip and unzipped his pants, slowly dropping to her knees. She ran her hands up and down his legs, and kissed the sharp muscles of his hip. Then she did it.

A few minutes later, her lips were pink and so were Max's cheeks. She'd finished and then zipped and buttoned him back up.

"Becca..." Max said. He pulled her in toward him, and kissed her from her raw lips to her collarbone. Then he saw the look on her face. "Are you okay?"

"Yes," she said, as unconvincingly as she could.

"You're obviously not...what's wrong?"

She sighed, a tad theatrically. "Nothing…"

He looked her in the eyes and silently demanded an answer.

"I just…never do that sort of thing. And—" she intentionally let her breath quiver "—I just don't want you to think I'm a slut."

She'd used her sex appeal to get her anywhere she'd ever been in life so far. And this was not the first time she'd had this conversation.

"I don't."

"How could you *not?* I mean I'm not even your *girlfriend*…"

"I'm not going to tell anyone, if that's what you're worried about."

She was worried about exactly that. She *wanted* him to spread around how fantastically talented she was at…stuff.

"I appreciate that. But I don't care about what other people think. I care about what *you* think. And I want you to think I'm respectable. *God*…first we *did it* on my first night here, and now this? I'm so stupid."

Becca ran a hand through her long hair, swooping it to one side.

"No, you're not."

"Why would you like me?" She put on her cute voice.

He shrugged. "I just do."

That was not a good answer. She was used to guys falling at her feet and giving her laundry lists of reasons why they loved her.

She paused, and then tried to look sullen. "We just can't do this again. We can't do this until—I mean, unless we're official. I just can't live with myself."

Becca watched him decide what his next move was.

"If that's how you feel about it, I understand."

She nodded. Dammit. He wasn't going in for this.

★ ★ ★

Later that night, after Max had been too understanding and left her alone the rest of the night, Becca went up to her room to stumble out of her clothes and into a slip.

"You okay?" Dana asked from her bed.

Shut. Up. That was all Becca wanted to say. But instead she held up a hand and gave thumbs-up, her other hand putting pressure on her throbbing head.

"Should I get you some water? I have some Excedrin."

"Two." She held out a hand again, without looking. She heard Dana scrambling up and out of her bed to get the bottle.

"Here," said Dana, handing her a bottle of water and the pills.

"You don't have any *cold* water?"

"No, sorry."

Becca took the Excedrin. "Gimme another one."

"Another what?"

"Pill."

"You're really only supposed to take two, I think."

"Just *give* it to me, *Jesus.* You're not my mother, so don't baby me."

"Fine, I'm sorry." She put another pill in Becca's extended palm.

Becca downed that one, too. "What are you, mad now?"

"No...?"

"Okay, then."

"When was the last time you ate?" Dana asked sheepishly.

"Like...five hours ago."

"What did you have?"

"A salad. Why are you—?"

"Because you're not supposed to take that stuff on an empty stomach."

That was probably true. She didn't need to feel even sicker in the morning than she was already bound to.

"Fine."

Becca threw on a sweatshirt and then walked down to the always-open dining hall in bare feet and no bra. She looked like hell, and really hoped she wouldn't see anyone.

But of course, Johnny was sitting at a table in the middle of the hall, eating a sandwich.

He spotted her and smiled. "C'mere."

"Hey," she said.

"Hey. So where'd you and Max go off to earlier?"

"We were just talking." She eyed him, and ran a finger through her hair. "Where were you? You were gone when we came back in."

"Yeah, I mean the hottest girl at the party left, so I didn't see why I should be there anymore."

"Oh, yeah?" She smiled.

He nodded and took a sip of his Sprite.

"So are you and Max…"

"I'd have to be really stupid to go out with a guy already, wouldn't I?" She didn't want to think about how Max had rejected her earlier.

He shrugged. "Maybe. I think he likes you. He never talks about that kind of thing though."

"I don't care if he does."

One bagel and the rest of Johnny's Sprite later, he was walking her out of the dining hall. She suddenly didn't want to go up to sleep yet. Her headache was already gone, and she had a second wind of energy gusting through her.

"Hey, what's down that hallway?"

Johnny looked where she pointed. "Oh, that's…the staff room and a bunch of the teachers' offices."

She smiled and marched down the stairs.

"Where are you going?"

"Come on! I wanna see this 'staff room.'"

He followed her. "You're a crazy little girl, aren't you?"

She pulled open the heavy wooden doors that led to the darkened hallway. He closed them after they walked through.

Becca turned and could feel she was inches from him. She felt the light that slipped through the crack in the doors hit her face. She narrowed her eyes at him and whispered, "I'm not a little girl."

He gave a small moan as she looked up at him. She could see his eyes now. He made the tiniest movement toward her and she turned to run down the hallway, her bare feet tapping against the hardwood floors. She stopped in front of the double doors that had Staff Only written in gold.

He strode after her and pushed down on the handle to open one of the doors.

"I can't believe it's not locked." He held it open for her and then shut it behind them.

This room was also dark. There were flags around its perimeter and a long, darkly wooded meeting table in the middle, surrounded by chairs. There was an unlit fireplace, and a mantel beneath a large oil painting of the dean.

She took off her sweatshirt, aware that her slip rose a little as she did so. She tossed it on the ground.

"Well, if you'll please take your seat at the end of the table—" she gestured at the biggest chair "—this meeting can begin."

Johnny smiled and sat down where she'd indicated. She slid onto the table in front of him. Maybe it was the alcohol left in her system, but he was a lot more attractive than she'd noticed before.

"I think we both know why we're here." Johnny spoke smoothly.

Becca's heart leaped a little, but she remained composed. "I think I need reminding."

"Because," he said, slouched in his seat, "we've got a student here at Manderley who is just not behaving."

"I think I know who you're talking about."

"The miscreant who led poor Johnny Parker into the break-in of this—" he pounded on the desk and moved toward her "—very room."

"Really? Because as *I* see it, poor little Miss Normandy was influenced by this Mr. Parker."

He stood up, in between her legs. She leaned back, looking at him with all the sexy she could conjure.

Johnny effortlessly pulled her toward the edge of the table. She planted her feet on the armrests of the chair he'd vacated. He lifted the silky fabric and ran his hands along her skin, wrapping his touch around her hips and up her back. He sharpened his grip as he moved down to her thigh.

Becca's smile faded as *want* filled her chest and made it clench. It ran through her legs and made them close to shaking. It was in her head, making her dizzy and light-headed. She could hear her own breath in the still, dark room. She could hear his, too, and she saw that he was no longer looking clever.

His hands were gentle, and her muscles tensed as he ran his fingers farther up her leg. He came closer and kissed her neck, as Max had done earlier. It felt so different when Johnny did it. All Becca wanted now was for him to come even closer. And he did. He moved in and put his lips to her ear. His breath blew her hair just enough to send a tingle down her spine.

"What do you want, new girl?" His whisper was slow and deep.

"You," she said desperately. She wasn't in control. She was uninhibited and desperate for him.

With one hand still on her upper thigh, taunting her, he moved his other to her hair. He pulled it slightly, exposing more of her neck. She surrendered, leaning back with her eyes shut. Her breath came faster now. His hand moved just enough higher, and his lips moved down to her chest. He gently dropped her straps.

Less than two weeks since she'd lost her virginity, and her number had already doubled.

The following Monday, as Becca dawdled her way to English class, Johnny pulled on her arm and dragged her out the side door.

"What are you doing?" she asked.

"What are *you* doing?" Johnny looked livid. "You told me you weren't with Max!"

"I'm not!"

"Yes, you—" He paused, looking like he was trying to remember her exact wording. "But you're hooking up with him."

"What makes you say that?"

"He *told* me, Becca. In the locker room after practice."

A small thrill of satisfaction rolled through her. Finally, Max was bragging about her. "What did he say?"

"I asked him if you guys were a thing, and he shrugged and said, and I quote, 'we hooked up a few times.'"

That was not quite as flattering. But whatever.

She smiled. "So are you jealous?"

There was a flicker of movement in the corners of his mouth. "I'm not saying that. It's just not right. He's my best friend."

"Okay, sure, and if he's too stupid to snap me up…" She narrowed her eyes playfully.

"Stop that, Becca, come on."

"Stop what?"

"We had…" He looked around and lowered his voice even more. "We had sex and now this is just not right, I can't be—"

She rolled her eyes and leaned against the wall. "Oh, Johnny, you stop it. You're thinking way too hard. We're young. We only have two years left. Just *go* with it. No one's getting hurt. No one's going to get arrested or die. It's all good."

She could tell she was winning him over. But he still looked like he might argue.

"Look," she said, "is all this to say that you don't want to do it again?" Becca ran a hand through her hair and pushed herself off the wall. "Because I'm not going to stand here all day and beg for you."

She would not be rejected by both of them. If she walked away it would be her choice, not because he denied her.

He was silent for a moment, thinking. Her heart jumped as she realized he really might say no. She shook her head irritably and pushed past him. She got a few steps before he called her name. She hesitated and then kept walking.

"Becca…*Becca!*" He jogged up behind her. His hands on her shoulders stopped her.

He glanced around, and when he saw no one, he kissed her. It sent a shock through her. She hadn't felt anything like it. It was like no one had ever kissed her and meant it before. When he finally pulled away, she looked up at him. When she spoke, her voice wasn't strong or vital and controlling as it usually was. Her words weren't calculated and meant to get her to an end. Her voice was small and hopeful, and her words were nervous. "Can we go…somewhere?"

★ ★ ★

Later that night, Max came to Becca's door in the girls' hall. She opened the door to see Max looking hot, and the girls along the hallway looking out of their doors.

"I thought about what you said. And you're right."

Was he about to ask her out? She was practically still sweating from her rendezvous with Johnny. She gave a nervous flatten of her hair, and said, "Oh, yeah?"

He nodded. "So if you'll still do it, then…we can do it."

She felt everyone's eyes on her. "You want to be with me, is this what you're saying?"

"Yeah."

She smiled and pulled him into her room. "Dana, do you think you could…make yourself scarce for a little while?"

Dana hurried up and out the door. Becca shut it, and the flurry of chatter outside told her that what she was about to do was exactly what she had to.

chapter 10 me

ALMOST A WEEK HAD PASSED SINCE MY FREAK-
out at Dana, and neither one of us had said a word. She had
followed my snotty advice and put Becca's pictures all over
her own wall. I'd suffered the consequences of my own rage,
too, when I stepped on a thumbtack on the way to the bathroom one night.

I finished *To Kill a Mockingbird,* and completed my paper
on The Small Town Effect. I'd focused on the wildfire spread
of gossip and what it does in a small environment and to the
people within it. Somehow, I'd managed to get inspired. Go
figure.

All the other classes passed by in a haze of challenging
busywork. They were just the classes to get through until
Painting. When Max and I spoke, we talked about our as-
signments and other banal things like the weather. Of which
there was far too much. As I sat now, outside Dr. Morgan's
office, I watched cold, gray rain pour down in sheets outside.
It pounded on the windows, as though it was pleading to
come in. I didn't blame it. It was miserable out there.

My appointment to talk about college and "whatever else" had been at three-thirty, but it was three-forty now and I still hadn't been called in. Just as I glanced at the clock on the wall again (the only one I'd seen in the school so far), I heard a muffled shout coming from her office.

The secretary raised her eyebrows wordlessly and continued filing her papers.

Dr. Morgan's door flew open.

"I just *hate* this, I don't know why we're even pretending!" It was Dana. She stormed out and stopped dead in her tracks when she saw me.

She let out a groan, and her hands flew to her head in anger. Her fingers looked like they must be pressing dents into her skull. "Why are *you* here?"

I couldn't speak.

"Why?"

Dr. Morgan shuffled over to Dana. She put a hand on her arm, but Dana shrugged it off violently. "Stop! I want to be left alone! I want an empty room, I don't want to be with this stupid, *fake*—"

"Bite your tongue, Miss Veers."

"I *hate you!*" Dana spit at me. I stared at her in shock.

Dr. Morgan glanced at me, and then led a reluctant Dana back into her office. A moment after she shut the door, it opened again.

"Please come in." She gestured to me. I glanced at the secretary again, whose eyebrows were still raised, and who still filed wordlessly.

I walked into the room Dana was filling with negativity.

"Have a seat."

I sat.

"Very well," Dr. Morgan began. "Is there some kind of conflict between the two of you?"

"Nope," Dana said, simply.

"What is the problem?" Dr. Morgan looked to me.

"I...I don't know."

"There's no problem."

Dr. Morgan looked very seriously at her for a moment and then spoke.

"Miss Veers, I know this is an unspeakably hard time for you—" She stopped as Dana let out a derisive snort. She breathed and then started again. "As I say, I know it's difficult. But you cannot be angry because Becca's side of your room has been filled by a new student."

Dana didn't speak.

"I encourage you both to talk about what's bothering you, so that you can work through it."

Both of us? How was it not obvious that I had done nothing wrong?

I glanced at Dana, who was looking deadly. I stayed silent. Dr. Morgan waited at first, and then pulled out a date book.

"Dana, are you available at around four tomorrow afternoon?"

I looked at her. There was something in her expression besides fury. She looked worried. Nervous. A pang of pity struck me unexpectedly.

"Yes, four is fine."

Dr. Morgan scribbled in her book and Dana walked out without looking at me. The door shut quietly, but a sound rang through me as if she'd slammed it.

Dr. Morgan cleared her throat and looked at me. "How have things been since your arrival?"

"Um...fine."

"Really?" She raised her eyebrows.

"Really."

She waited for me to change my mind or go on. When I didn't, she cleared her throat.

"You know, it's a good idea to talk about how you're feeling to someone like me, especially when you're in a new place and don't know many people."

I hesitated. Nothing that was bothering me could come out sounding anything less than selfish and self-pitying.

I smiled and shrugged. "I'm good, I like it here."

She waited again, as she had when Dana had lied, and then carried on.

"Well, then, on to other business." She placed her glasses on her nose and looked down at a manila folder that must be mine. "You've been accepted to a few colleges already, I see?"

"Yes, Florida State University and Boston University."

She raised her eyebrows. "Two very different places. May I ask why you applied to each?"

"Boston is where my parents went. They met there and everything." I thought of the photo album filled with pictures from their four years there. It was what I imagined when I thought of college. It was so...I don't know, academic feeling. They had millions of pictures in front of big old buildings or in small, awful dorm rooms with big windows that looked out on a place filled with history. I imagined a grassy quad filled with studying students in scarves and BU sweatshirts, good-looking guys throwing perfectly spiraled footballs, and a slightly chilly wind carrying fallen leaves across the sidewalks that lead to brick dorms filled with first experiences.

Not that I'd thought about it very much.

"And why FSU?" Dr. Morgan asked, shaking me from my thoughts.

I shrugged. "I don't know. I just always planned to go there. It's where all of my friends are going and it's near home."

Then there were the thoughts that came to mind when I thought of going there. Palm trees and smooth, modern buildings. Hugely popular bands performing in the stadium. Still being able to tan in October.

It had always been the plan. But when I thought of it, it just felt like it would be too easy.

My friends and I would stay in our habits at school. I wouldn't make a whole other group of friends. I'd go home a lot. I'd have fun, but wouldn't try anything new. I had horrible images of myself graduating and sticking around, never seeing anything new. Never taking a risk.

"Which are you leaning toward, either one?"

"I've been planning on going to FSU."

"And what major are you considering currently?"

"I don't know yet."

She looked at me as if waiting for me to decide on one. When I gave a pitiful smile, she said, "All right, that's fine. Most people don't know at this stage anyway. You've got plenty of time."

"I wanted to talk to you, or whoever, about maybe a scholarship. I don't know if I have the grades or...I don't know, I guess I just wanted to ask about it."

"Well, the problem there is that scholarships are easiest to come by when you do have a major in mind." She squinted and then bent over to open a drawer behind her. She pulled from it a stapled packet. "Fill this out."

"What is it?"

"It's called Major Undecided. It's basically a test to find out where your interests really lie. I must encourage you to answer honestly. Take your time doing it. This could really help you. So don't look at it like homework. Look at it as a ticket to your decision."

I nodded. "I will."

"Well, if there's not anything else we need to discuss, then you're all set." She eyed me carefully. "And you're sure there's nothing else?"

"That's all for me." I stood, and then hesitated. "I mean, it's been difficult, in some ways. But that's just because I'm new. It's always hard to be new."

She nodded, waiting for me to go on.

"I just...I feel weird because I'm in Becca Normandy's room and I feel like everyone else feels weird about that, too. I'm not trying to take her place."

"Of course not."

"And Madison and Julia...I don't know if you know them, you probably do...well anyway, they were friends with Becca, and they keep asking me if I like Max Holloway—" my heart skipped a little on his name "—and I never said I did. And even if I did, it shouldn't be up to them what I do with it, right? I know it's kind of weird because Becca's his girlfriend...but if he liked me back, then would it be messed up of me to just go with it?"

"Don't worry about the other girls. They are going through something very traumatizing, and it's making them all think too hard. I must admit, I was afraid of what the repercussions might be when you arrived."

The idea that she had seen this coming startled me. "Really?"

"Of course. You *replaced*—" she did quotes with her fingers "—a student here whom a lot of other students cared for. Especially Dana, Madison, Julia, etc. I'm sure it's very difficult to feel welcoming of someone who wouldn't be here if their friend still was."

That was blunt.

"But what you must remember," Dr. Morgan went on, "is

that anything they do that is an effect of their own fluxing emotions has *nothing* to do with you."

When I left, I wasn't sure if I felt better or not.

Saturday afternoon, Blake invited me to go into town with her.

"Manderley is like being stuck in an attic. Dusty, cold, and you feel like you might be struck by lightning at any moment. Sometimes it's just nice to get out."

We wandered around Main Street for a little while, chatting about this and that, before deciding to get a bite to eat from a French café called Les Filles de Cuisine. I hoped it would taste anything like my mother's cooking.

I saw the menu had Orangina, like most of these American-ized places, and ordered it immediately.

"Blake?"

We both turned to see Madison and Julia coming in.

"Madison, Julia, hey." Blake sounded as tired of them as I was.

They pulled the other two-seater table up to ours. "I love this place," said Madison. "Their food is so good. I didn't think we'd be able to come though."

"Why?" I asked. For some stupid reason.

"Well…" Julia and she exchanged a look. "Last time we were here, Becca was with us."

"Oh," I said. "I'm sorry."

"That was where we sat last time…" Julia looked longingly at a table occupied by a couple. He said something to her, and she blushed.

"Aw, they are so cute," said Julia. "They even remind me of…"

"I know!" Madison exclaimed. "I was just going to say that! That day even."

Julia looked to us to explain. "We were here right after Christmas, and she was wearing that silver necklace Max gave her. Do you remember it, Blake?"

Blake stared at the menu on the table and said quietly, "Yes."

"It was from Tiffany & Co.," Julia explained to me. "He'd had her name engraved, and the date they got together."

"Oh, she looked so pretty that day. She had on those cute riding boots—they were the same ones Kate Middleton had been wearing in this one picture…well anyway, they were so cute."

The waiter came over and took our order. I ordered lobster bisque and Croque Monsieur. I hoped to God they'd stop talking about Becca when the waiter left. But no.

"When we were here that day, we were just talking, whatever, like we always did, and then Max came in. He just showed up. Johnny was with him, but he was in here talking to us. That was the day I realized Johnny had feelings for Becca."

Blake looked at her. "Do you think Becca ever had feelings for him?"

"Are you serious?" Julia scoffed and carried on. "Anyway, they sat on that bench there. They were there for like ten minutes. He looked at her necklace, and then they kissed… I was so jealous."

"Me, too," Madison said. "I want a boy to love me that much. He was always trying with her. He refused to let her go."

"He really fought for her."

"They were on their way to getting back together right before she…right before she went missing."

"They broke up?"

"Yes, for a little while. I don't like to talk about it," Madison said, as if it were her own breakup.

The Bobbsey Twins went silent, then began chattering on about where they thought she was. I shut them out until Julia said the words I had also thought.

"You know, I think Dana knows more than she lets on."

"Why do you say that?" asked Blake.

Julia nodded. "She's been acting so freaky and everything. I just think she knows something. Remember the night of her meltdown?"

"Oh, yeah, when she said 'You know' to Max? I think that meant something."

"Me, too."

"Speaking of Dana," said Madison, "what happened with you guys?"

"Yeah, we heard you screaming at each other."

I was afraid they'd ask me that. "She just kind of freaked out."

I didn't want to give specifics.

"She said you just started randomly throwing things at her."

"No." My cheeks were getting hot. "She was hurling insults at me, and so then I took down all of Becca's pictures and gave them to her."

Gave was a bit of a stretch....

"I just didn't want them up on my wall anymore. She's the one that wants them up, and I just feel weird looking at her pictures all the time since I didn't even know her. It makes me feel like I'm intruding on her space."

Neither of them looked like they knew what to say.

Blake shrugged. "It *was* weird. It's not a shrine, it's a dorm room in a school."

"That's not quite fair...." said Julia slowly.

"Sure it is, it's my side of the room now. She was being a bitch."

Everyone looked shocked. Blake smiled and took a sip of her drink. The other two changed the subject, and said nothing more about Becca for the rest of the meal.

"Thank God you called. Seriously, I've been desperate," Leah was saying into her end of the phone.

"What's wrong?" I asked.

"It's Michael."

Ah. Big surprise. Something was always happening with Michael. That's another thing I wasn't looking forward to at FSU—another four years of Ronnie-Sammi-esque drama. "What happened?"

"I am just *so* done with him. *So* done with him. He keeps acting superjealous, when I'm not even *doing* anything. I was with Emma yesterday and he got infuriated when I didn't answer his texts. It's so annoying."

I really hoped she *was* finished with him. If this continued on into college, and I really was her roommate, I'd absolutely kill myself. Or them.

"Just let go of him, Leah, seriously. You guys have been beyond finished for like three years."

"What do you mean?"

"I just mean, he's done everything you hate. He's read your texts, your Facebook messages, your emails, he's *followed you* when you left your *house*... How have you stayed with him?"

"I don't know. Because I love him? I really care about him. Ugh, I wish I could just let go, but it's so hard. How's your love life by the way?" she asked, brightening.

"Oh...um, nonexistent."

"Really? There's *no one* at all?"

"Really. Well. There's this guy...but..." Suddenly everything about Becca seemed like it was difficult to explain. I couldn't say that there was a missing girl and everyone misses her and it's really screwing up *my* life without sounding like a total jackass. Or maybe just thinking it made me one. "He's got a girlfriend."

"Aw, that's too bad. Does he love her?"

"Apparently."

"Aw. I'm sorry, that sucks. Well, is there anyone else you like?"

"Nope. I don't even really know anyone. Leah?" She was talking with the mouthpiece covered up.

"Can I call you back? Michael is here."

"Not really, I have to turn my phone—"

"Love you!"

And she was gone. I looked at my phone. It was nine already anyway. I sighed and stood up to return my phone to its own little jail cell.

I walked up to see that Max was returning his phone. I took a deep breath and walked toward him. He spotted me as he handed his phone over.

He smiled, and I smiled back. More backflips.

I said hi, and he said hi, and that was it. I could do nothing more to prolong the moment. I walked up the stairs and away from him.

That was all I could have done. Max and I had barely spoken. And all I'd gotten were reasons to avoid him.

When I arrived at my room, my heart still in my throat, I found my door locked. I hoped that meant Dana wasn't in the room. No such luck, however. She was there, looking as morbid as usual.

"Only five minutes after nine," she said, looking at her alarm clock. "Hmm."

"What?"

She sighed and set down her book. "Becca was never back this early. She used to stay out until the wee hours of the morning with Max."

"What makes you think I was with Max?" I thought of our brief encounter.

She laughed, and it did not suit her. "I just meant that *she* was always with Max. But I guess you can see now how you misunderstood."

I flushed pink. Dana stood and drifted into the bathroom. I wanted to smack her. My eyes scanned the wall of pictures, landing on one of Becca in a royal-blue shirt, her golden-blond hair in curls. She leaned back as Max kissed her. My heart fell.

I kicked off my shoes, and immediately stubbed my toe on that stupid Louis Vuitton suitcase. The pain that shot up my foot sent some kind of wave through me. I walked over to the bathroom and threw open the door. She had just tossed her shirt on the ground, and covered herself up as I walked in.

"I've had *enough.* You cannot talk to me like that and just expect me to take it. You don't know *me,* you just hate me because you miss your fucking friend. And I have *told* you that I understand, and that I sympathize. But you are just—"

"Oh, shut *up,* you're turning an ugly shade of red."

She smiled smugly at me and rolled her eyes, and I almost lost it. I envisioned slapping her hard and tossing an easy, "Who's red now, bitch?" over my shoulder as I left her to cry.

But instead I just steadied my breathing and stalked out.

chapter 17 *becca*

BECCA COULD NOT STOP THINKING ABOUT Johnny. How was that possible? What was drawing her to him? At first he had seemed so predictable and uninteresting. But now he was intriguing and desirable.

It had been three weeks since it happened, and time had only made her yearn for more of Johnny's touch, breath and whatever that strange power was that he had over her. Her wanting had made it nearly impossible to be with Max. She felt stone-cold. Nothing he did could rattle her. But every time she wanted something more with Johnny, she'd convince herself not to go toward him. After all, if she liked him, he could hurt her.

Then she'd stay with Max a little longer. At least until she really had Johnny.

But that didn't mean it was easy to stop talking to him in the meantime, or hooking a finger through his belt loop when they talked. She was doing that now, while the party surrounded them. As soon as she caught a glimpse of Max, she jumped away from Johnny as if he'd scalded her.

"Hey, baby," she said to Max, running over to him and then winding an arm around him. "You wanna do a body shot?"

He gave her a look. "No. Thanks though."

"But I do! Please, babe?" He said nothing, but laughed, and she smiled. She jumped onto a table next to her, shouted over the music to get the attention of the room. "Hey! Who wants to do a body shot off me?"

She pulled up her shirt to show her flat stomach, and smiled wider as her subjects cheered. She chose a random guy she didn't even know, and pulled him over to the beer pong table. She lay down, and laughed at the crowd around her. Someone poured a shot of tequila onto her stomach, sprinkled some salt on her chest, and then put a slice of lime from the dining hall into her mouth. The guy took the shot, and everyone clamored to be next. Becca looked at Max, who smiled and shook his head. He didn't look jealous enough. She glanced at Johnny, who did.

In short order, Becca had downed three shots and, finally, the room had begun to spin a little. She found that this was about how drunk she needed to be in order to feel affectionate toward Max and to forget about Johnny. Usually. But that became really hard as she looked up and saw that Johnny was dancing with that girl Susan.

Susan? Really? That poor ditz was only *trying* to be like Becca. Suddenly her mousy blond hair was up in a spunky ponytail *just like Becca's,* and her glasses were gone, and her boobs were in a real bra instead of a sports bra. Oh, and she'd picked up smoking Camel Lights, *just like Becca.*

Becca stood quickly, momentarily losing her balance, and took two shots right in a row. They burned, and she looked to see what they were. Hundred-proof vodka.

Twenty minutes later, it was kicking her ass.

She spotted Johnny about twenty feet away, and ambled over to him.

"I think I had too much stuff," she said.

"What did you have? You didn't accept anything from Ricky, right?"

"No, no…I just had some shots of that." She pointed indiscriminately. "I didn't know it was hundred proof."

She wanted to lean on him. To feel his arm around her, making her feel safe. From what, she didn't know. But he always made her feel better.

"Johnny…*Johnny.*"

"Yeah?"

"We should be, you know, like…" She pointed between them. "Together or whatever."

He looked at her, and she wanted to reach up and kiss him.

"We can't."

"Not ever? Not even if I break up? I mean with Max. If I break up with him, why couldn't *we* be, then?" Those shots were tangling her tongue.

"Because that's almost as bad as what we're doing now." His voice was low. "He'd never forgive me if he found out. So even if we were legit together, it would be wrong."

The words sank in, and her eyes began to burn. She turned away, not wanting him to see her wipe her eyes. She found Max.

She stumbled up to him. "Dance with me?"

She pulled him into the group of people dancing, careful to stay within Johnny's eyeshot. Becca grinded into Max's leg, and ran her hands along his neck.

"I like you so much. I'm so glad we're together."

She kissed him, and then turned around so her back was on his chest and her hand still on his neck. Johnny looked at her and quickly turned away.

"We should go somewhere," said Becca, tugging on Max's collar. "I want you so bad right now."

He hesitated, and then gave a nod. "Okay, let's go."

She pulled him down so she could talk into his ear. "Why don't you go to the supply room and I'll meet you there? It'll be less obvious, and we won't get interrupted."

He shrugged. "Okay, whatever."

She waited for him to go, and then tapped Susan on the shoulder. "Hey, Susie! Love your hair!"

"Thanks!"

"No problem." Then she pulled Johnny toward her and said as quietly as she could so that he could hear, "Meet me in the supply room in three minutes."

"What? Becca, no—"

She nodded and went off to meet Max.

"Mmm," she said, when she closed the door behind her. "You look so sexy right now."

"You, too. Come here."

She had to make this fast, so everything would happen at just the right time. She pulled him close to her. "I want you *now*."

He lifted her easily, and she leaned on one of the shelves. Only a minute later, they were in the throes of passion and Johnny walked in. Becca screamed and pulled Max closer.

"Whoa, sorry," Johnny said, and then he closed the door. But not before giving Becca the look she'd been hoping for.

Jealousy.

"Are you going to the Halloween Ball?" Becca buffed her nails and idly made conversation with Dana.

Becca was not entirely sure how to feel about Dana. Ever since she'd been hanging out with her, Dana was getting attention. No one seemed to notice that it was *entirely* because of

Becca, and that clearly that meant that she held all the power in the school. All they seemed to notice was Dana.

She was pretty, and lately she had more confidence. Becca knew better than anyone that this was a dynamic duo of traits. Dana was also pretty quiet, but had been sent here after some kind of weird bipolar flip out at a teacher at her old school. Becca had zoned out while Dana was telling her.

"Oh…no, I don't have a date."

"Do you *want* to go?"

"Maybe…I've never been."

"Oh, that's pathetic. You've been here since freshman year and you haven't been?"

Dana shook her head.

"I'm going to get you a date."

"No, I don't want a pity date, really."

"You're already getting *my* pity. I'm just going to ask Johnny if he wants to take you."

That would only make Becca look less interested. Maybe then he'd actually try to go for her.

"Johnny Parker?"

"Yup." That way he wouldn't get a *real* date.

"He'd never want to go with me probably. He's gorgeous and smart and everything. He could get anyone."

"Okay, yeah, obviously, but that's why I'm setting it up. He'll go with you."

A smile stretched across Dana's face, and her eyebrows flickered a little. "That'd be cool, I guess—but only if he wants to go."

"Meanwhile," she said with a sigh, "Max and I are just madly in love."

She did this often with Dana. She would sit down and talk at her, making her relationship sound perfect, and the rest of her life sound enviable. She would never tell Dana that she, too, had bad experiences in her past that had landed her here. She definitely wouldn't tell her about the one thing that had pretty much bought her ticket.

As far as Dana or anyone else for the rest of her life needed to know, Becca was perfect and her life was charmed.

"That's good that everything is good with you guys," Dana said, and took a sip from a glass of water she had next to her bed.

"It is good. We're getting pretty serious. I'm a little worried he likes me *too* much."

Lie.

"Really?"

There was a knock on the door.

"Can you get that?" Becca looked hopefully at Dana.

Dana pulled open the door to reveal Madison and Julia.

They both cooed a hello, and Becca smiled superficially. "Come on in—I was just telling Dana about how Max might be falling too hard for me."

"You think so?" Madison asked eagerly, sitting down in Becca's chair.

Julia sat on the desk, partially obscuring Dana.

"Yes, I'm totally serious. He pulled me out of the party the other night at the boathouse, and told me he had to talk to me…he was worried I was going to leave him for some other guy, you know, and then he took my hand—" she smiled as she watched everyone's eyes get bigger "—and told me he never wanted us to end."

Lie.

Madison and Julia aahed together.

"That is so sweet," Madison said, her hand over her heart.

"I know. He says this kind of thing all the time. And about how, like, he wants to get married one day and we'll have a big house on a beach that *doesn't* suck like this one."

Lie.

They laughed. Dana looked down at her fingers and said nothing. Whatever, Becca thought, she's not the most important one to pass the information along to anyway. Madison and Julia were bound to tell everyone how completely all about her he was.

Dana didn't matter at all.

chapter 12 me

I'D TAKEN TO SPENDING EVEN LESS TIME IN MY room than before. Rather than be in there, I even studied on the way to the senior study room.

"Look at you, getting your homework done."

I looked up from my book. I'd been reading and walking, and hadn't noticed Johnny walking toward me.

"Yes, I actually *do* my homework," I said. Johnny was never to be seen with any assigned books or even a pencil. I constantly felt I was going to discover he was just a maintenance guy masquerading as a student.

"I do homework. I just do it last minute. That way I spend as little time on it as possible." He smiled, and leaned against the wall.

I laughed.

He smiled. "So, new girl, you want to go to the ball with me?"

If I'd been a cartoon, my eyes would have popped out of my head and I'd have done a double take. "Are you... What?"

There was no real reason why I shouldn't. He was hot. He

was nice to me. Everyone told me to stay away from him and Max, but since Max had almost completely ignored me lately, all of my hopes in that direction had died.

When I hesitated, Johnny said, "You're not with anyone, right?"

"No, no, I'm not...."

"It can be just as friends if you want. I just think it would be fun to go with you." He shrugged.

I scrambled for an answer. "Um. Okay. Sure. Yes. Let's do it."

"Four kinds of 'yes,' that'll work."

I gave a nervous laugh, thinking now about what people would say when they found out. I liked the idea of rebelling against them, but I wasn't usually a rebel—and therefore wasn't sure I had the stomach for it.

"All right, you go do your homework. I'll talk to you about the plan later."

An hour after I arrived in the study room, the door opened. All at once my heart jumped out of my chest, and my stomach melted into my shoes.

"Hey," said Max. "You are here. Blake said you might be." He shut the door behind him. "I've been looking for you everywhere."

It felt like another dream. "You, um, you have?"

He nodded. "I even asked Dana if you were in your room. She didn't give me an answer though. Just glared at me."

"Well, I'm here," I said, unnecessarily.

Max sat down in the chair opposite me. "What are you reading?"

"Taming of the Shrew."

"Ha, I can relate to that guy's struggle." He cleared his throat. "We haven't really talked in a while."

"Yeah, I know." My heartbeat accelerated.

"I, um…I wanted to ask you if maybe you'd want to go with me to the ball?"

I froze. I was so shocked that I couldn't help but be honest. "We've hardly ever even talked."

"I know, I know." He shifted his weight. "I know. But I thought you might want to go with me anyway." He shook his head slightly, as if his words hadn't come out properly.

I could tell Johnny to forget it. It'd be mean. But I wanted to.

"Unless you're already going with someone," he added.

"I am." The disappointment was tingling in my every nerve. If only I hadn't run into Johnny. Why had I said yes?

"Ah. I'm not surprised."

I didn't know what to say. My chest was constricted, and no words would come to my mind besides profane ones.

"But we should be friends. You know? I just wanted to go as friends anyway." He straightened up.

"Right, friends, sure. We can still do that without the ball. Right?"

"Yeah. So I'll see you soon. The ball I guess." He gave a small smile and turned to go.

"Yeah. I'll see you then."

"You mind if I ask who you're going with?"

"Johnny Parker."

His face drained of expression.

"Are you guys together?"

"No, not at all."

He nodded. "All right, well, I'll see you around."

I wanted to scream. I wanted to kick something. He'd asked me. Max asked *me*. And I'd said no. But then he'd said he wanted to go as friends. My brain was doing cartwheels. I dragged my feet back to my room. There was no way I could keep reading.

★ ★ ★

"Oh, my God, you're going with *Johnny?*"

Madison and Julia burst into my room without knocking and spewed the question at me.

Dana, who was of course reading a book and pretending I wasn't in the room, glared at me. "Johnny Parker?"

"Of *course* Johnny Parker," said Madison.

Dana was still staring at me blankly, but with that look in her eye I'd seen in Dr. Morgan's office.

"I'm so glad you're not upset that Max didn't ask you. I mean, he is still totally in love with Becca." Julia sat down on my desk and looked pityingly at me.

"He did ask me," I said, enjoying the looks on their faces. "But I had already said yes to Johnny."

Dana was still staring at me.

Neither Madison nor Julia said anything right away. Finally Julia smiled, and said, "I mean, we did tell you not to go after him. His feelings for Becca... I mean..."

I breathed deeply. "I didn't go after him. And also it doesn't really matter. He's no one's property."

Another brief silence, and then Madison said, "Great! That's so great. Um, so, what are you going as?"

"I have no idea. I was thinking I might have to have my mom send me something I have at home, I have no clue what I'm gonna wear."

Madison smiled. "I'm sure you'll figure something out. You have two weeks after all."

"Could you guys finish up or go somewhere else? I'm going to sleep." Dana said it without apology.

Madison and Julia left with a quick goodbye to me.

As soon as they were gone, Dana asked, "You need a costume for the Halloween Ball?"

"I don't have anything yet, no." My tone was short and

sharp, and I dug through my dresser drawer to find my pajamas.

"I might have something you can use."

"No, thanks."

"No really," she said earnestly, her face paler than I'd ever seen it. "I think it'll suit you. And I'm not going."

I wasn't sure if this was an olive branch she was extending or a trap. But I couldn't imagine how it could be the latter.

Dana pulled something from her closet. "Here, it's a Marilyn Monroe dress." She shrugged. "Wear it if you want to. "

I hesitated and then took the package. "If I can't find anything else."

Two weeks later, Halloween night

It was 6:57 p.m. Four hours ago, I'd been in the front hall, waiting for the last shipment of mail to come in. There was no package for me. That meant no Snow White costume. I'd ordered it forever ago *and* paid for faster shipping.

After digging through my closet for an hour and trying to assemble something, I had to give up. Anything I'd do would look stupid and incredibly homemade. I didn't even have a nice dress to wear.

And then Dana reminded me of her offer. I took her up on it, and wore her extra costume. I had no choice. It was that or go as Daisy Duke.

"Dammit," I muttered, looking everywhere for the white sandals I'd set out. Finally I found them, underneath a pillow I had tossed aside in my search for them.

Dana was still in the room, silently watching me scurry. "You look good."

I swiped aside my sandy-not-platinum-blond hair from my eyes and threw on my coat for the walk to the dining hall.

I was confident. I felt good about myself for the first time in a while. I looked pretty good, if I did say so myself, and hoped Max would think so. I cringed a little as I wondered if he'd gotten another date. I cringed again at the fact that Johnny, my actual date, was not the one that I thought of first.

And what about Dana? Maybe she wasn't so bad after all. She had probably just lashed out because of her grief and was now trying to make up for it. I could forgive the awful things she'd said if she was trying to make up for them.

Johnny was waiting for me outside the dorm door.

"You look great," he said.

"You haven't even seen my costume yet." I smiled. "But thanks, you look good, too." He was wearing a normal tuxedo. I'd heard that that was what most of the guys did. We walked down the stairs. "I'm sorry I'm late. It's a fatal flaw of mine."

"No problem, that's a flaw in most girls." He smiled and gave me a wink.

The dining hall looked odd now that it had been cleared of its tables, chairs, food and surly employees. It was now darker than I'd ever seen it, with blue lights darting around the ceiling and walls while bass-heavy music filled the air and shook the marble floors. Everyone in costumes, in a place that should be familiar but was not, made it seem surreal. In the dim light it wasn't obvious who anyone really was. There were people in masks left and right, people with blood pouring from drawn-on wounds, zombies, ghosts, princesses, aliens and then me. I turned and jumped when I saw that Johnny had put on a Jason mask.

"God, that's awful," I said, laying a hand over my chest.

I couldn't see his face, but he had paused and was looking at me. "Are you taking off your coat?"

"Not yet, I'm freezing."

It wasn't strictly true. The problem was that I suddenly had no desire to unveil my costume. The dress was revealing and I had no confidence in it. It had not really struck me that I'd have to wear the costume in front of everyone. They'd think I was being a show-off—or trying to be. Someone else would probably even be wearing the same dress, and I'd pale in comparison. It felt more and more like the worst idea. Everyone already looked at me like I was an idiot. What would they do when they saw my dark blond hair barely holding a curl and a dress that gaped a little where bigger boobs should be?

"You're going to get hot in here."

"Oh, I'll be fine."

Johnny shrugged and led me through the crowd. My heart skipped as I laid eyes on Max. He was wearing a suit that looked prohibitionist-era, and it suited him perfectly. I smiled and waved at him, noticing that he was with Cam and Blake.

"Why are you wearing your coat? It's sweltering!" Blake said, after giving me a hug.

"Is it? I'm just so cold."

She nodded and then started talking to Johnny. Max looked at me.

I scrambled for something to say. "No date?"

He shook his head. "Nah. Didn't ask anyone. Except you, that is."

My stomach twisted. "Oh, I see. I like your costume."

"I don't know if I like yours."

"Why?"

He gave me a look. "I haven't seen it yet."

"Oh!" I laughed. Maybe I didn't need to be so nervous.

I took off my coat and revealed my dress. His smile vanished, and his jaw tightened.

Blake gasped, hand over her mouth, and she looked at Max.

"What?" I asked, my arms closed tightly over my chest. "I look stupid?"

I should have known it was worse than that.

Suddenly everyone was looking at me. Max looked like stone, and Johnny looked like the floor had fallen out from under him.

I looked to Blake.

"*What* is the matter?"

Max walked over to me and put his hand on my wrist tightly. "What is wrong with you? Why would you *do* that?" He let go. "Take it off. That's not your fucking dress."

He turned and walked out. Anyone who had been watching us was looking at me in shock or following him with their eyes.

Blake came close to me, so everyone else that was listening wouldn't hear her. "That's what…that's what she wore last year."

Blake must have seen the comprehension dawn on my face. She shook her head apologetically. "It's just that…for a minute it looked like…it looked like she was… It would be like her to show up like that."

I was dizzy. I had no words. I wanted to scream louder than I ever had, and without my permission, tears had begun to fall down my cheeks. All I could do was breathlessly look from Blake, who pitied me, to Johnny, who just looked concerned, and then to Madison and Julia who had just come up. Madison looked hesitant and worried. Julia looked shocked.

I ran out of the dining hall, ignoring Blake calling my name.

I burst in, and panted at Dana.

"Why would you *do* that to me?"

"Do what?" Dana spoke quietly, as if she hadn't just fed me to the wolves. "Oh, by the way," she reached under her bed, "this came for you last week."

She threw a white package onto my bed. It was from Costume Warehouse.

I wanted to cry. My throat was constricted and my knees weak. Where would people go with this? Would they start to think I was some kind of crazy person, desperate to be like *her?* Did they already think that?

"What did I *do* to you?" My eyes were burning. "Or to anyone else? I didn't know she was missing when I accepted this spot at school! It's not like I intentionally tried to replace her!"

She shrugged and set down her book. "I think it's good everyone finally saw you for what you are."

"Saw me for— And *what is that,* Dana? What is it that I really am?"

"You want to be her. You're trying to be her. Now everyone knows that about you."

"I don't *want* to be her!" My voice was strong, but I felt it might give out at any second.

"Why wouldn't you?" She looked challengingly at me.

I breathed deeply, never taking my gaze from her empty black eyes. "I didn't know her. I don't want to be her. I don't want what she had."

"What, to be beloved by everyone? To have Max deeply in love with you? To have Johnny wanting you?" She cocked her head.

I did like Max. I had gone to the ball with Johnny. I shook my head. I didn't want to think that she might be right. *Was* I just going after what had made Becca happy?

"No, I don't!" I said, trying to sound stronger than I was. "I don't want that. What I want is to be back *home!*"

"Then leave. Who would care? Who would even notice if you did leave?"

I shook my head. "Shut up. Please, just shut up."

"I will if you stop trying to steal the identity of a girl you couldn't be an eighth of if you sold your very *soul* to the devil."

"I'm *not* trying to!" My face was hot, and all my words came out in sputters.

She sighed deeply and shook her head. "That's fine. You'll know when she comes back."

I threw the door back open, not knowing where I was going to run to. I heard Dana's taunting voice as I closed the door: "And she'll be back soon...."

When the library was locked, for what ungodly reason I could not imagine, I ran to the only place I could think of. The boathouse.

I flew from Manderley into the raw, gusting air. The surrounding trees had dropped their dead leaves, which now crunched under my feet and swirled around in the wind like in a cartoon. One big gust of wind set me backward in my trek by a few inches and made me shut my eyes as much as I could and still see.

The waves were like a million dead, gnarly hands throwing themselves onto the sand and trying to bring whatever they could back with them into the darkness. The sand was prickling me in the legs, as if warning me that the waves were after me. I pushed and walked through the boathouse door. The threatening sounds from outside died a little. I gave one big shake and clutched my arms with my hands to keep warm.

I felt around for the light switch before realizing it was just a beaded cord that hung from an exposed lightbulb. I pulled it, and tried to convince myself that anything I heard was the ocean and not waves of cockroaches and mice shuffling across the two inches of dust on the floor. The boathouse felt a lot more sinister when I was there by myself. I could see now that the walls were covered in dust and spiderwebs, and that the windows were so covered in grime that you wouldn't be able to see out of them even if it was light outside.

My sandals clunked with every step on the hollow-sounding wood beneath them as I made my way to the couch. I'd just wait until Dana was probably asleep and then go back up. She was usually in bed by eleven, so I'd just wait until... dammit. Once again, I had no idea what time it was. I needed a watch.

I sat on the couch and got a throat full of dust. I waved it away from my face. There was a thick blanket—or maybe it was one of those rugs that are easily mistaken for blankets—folded on the armrest. I grabbed it and wrapped it around myself. It was almost as cold as I was. I lay down, curled up as tightly as I could, and tried not to think.

But I couldn't help it. All I could think of was Manderley. Why did I leave home? I should have just been honest and told my parents I didn't want to leave. My friends were probably all at Lucy's house, where her parents had funded every snack imaginable, and where losing at Apples to Apples was anyone's biggest concern. Rather than being here, where everyone was straight out of a Lifetime milk carton movie.

That wasn't very nice. I didn't mean that.

But even without its zombie students, the ones milling in the dining hall right now, Manderley itself was cold and austere. It was nothing like the proud and exciting hallowed building I'd imagined at that early age.

I'd been here for two months now, and it's not like I knew *no one,* but it did seem I'd only gained them as friends by luck. I was like the unwanted new stepsister who was suddenly supposed to be accepted as part of the family. Like everyone had been perfectly content before I came along, and now I was making Manderley a little bit too cramped.

Nobody wanted to know me. And I was not the type to get down on myself like that. There was a distinct message from everyone here to me: *we don't like you.*

I could go this year without friends. Fine. I could quiet the part of my brain that told me how different it would be if I were still back home. But I was constantly being re-minded that it wasn't good that I was here, and that I might as well leave. And Becca was here, too, *everywhere,* even though she was nowhere. I heard people talk about her all the time. Everyone wondered what had happened. Everyone had a theory. Everyone had questions. Everyone had to talk about it all the time.

I'd made the right choice when I decided to go to FSU. I didn't have what it took to be a risk taker. I was a small-town girl, who couldn't handle the real world.

I lay there, getting colder every second, and tried to do that thing my mom taught me about breathing in and counting slowly to three and then breathing out and slowly counting to three. It should steady my breathing and relax me, appar-ently. Instead, it just meant that I was breathing slower than my thoughts were coming.

I didn't want to be ungrateful. I didn't want to *not* be able to make the best of it here. I hated hating my situation, but I couldn't help it. I felt like I was trying to wear someone else's clothes, and they didn't fit. I gave an audible scoff as I realized I *was* in Becca's clothes right now. It was darkly funny, and then it was spooky.

Maybe this was all my fault. I'd made the mistake of liking Max—something that was starting to feel embarrassing *and* blasphemous—and now I'd shown up at the only school-wide occasion so far and worn Becca's dress. I wanted to undo it. But I couldn't.

In…one, two, three.

Out...one, two, three.

In...

"Get out of my dress."

I blinked. I looked around the room, and saw her. Becca Normandy, smoking a cigarette and looking as cool as we've always been told cigarettes don't make you, and leaning on her crossed legs.

I couldn't breathe. I couldn't talk. She was...she was here. She was...here. My throat was tight from the shock. That feeling of chills running down my back wouldn't go away. I couldn't ask what she was doing here—all I could do was see her. Her blond hair, so much lighter and softer than mine, had light reflecting off it that made her look practically ethereal. I wouldn't have thought that was possible in this musty room.

She was staring at me, and I felt like she could see everything about me. Everything I'd ever been or thought.

I opened my mouth, and she rolled her eyes.

"I don't even want to hear it. You're a cheap imitation of me. You're *dirty* blonde. You're muscle-skinny, not a waif. You own *moccasins*." She stood, and stamped out her cigarette. "That dress looks terrible on you. You know that, right?"

She looked at me amusedly through narrowed eyes, and turned her head. I still couldn't speak.

"*That* is why everyone was asking what you were wearing. It's not that they didn't know you were supposed to be Marilyn Monroe, or even that they were so shocked that you would try to copy *me*. It's because you were filling it out so badly you made it look like a sleeveless muumuu." She exhaled noisily. "I have only one question for you."

Becca crouched at the side of the couch. She was painfully beautiful, the ideal kind of pretty that doesn't fear a magnified mirror. She didn't seem to have any flaws at all. Not an eyelash was out of place. Her teeth were toothpaste-ad white.

Under her eyes there were no circles. She wafted the scent of alcohol and menthol cigarettes in my direction, but it mingled with her perfume and made her whole image tie together in some kind of strange, unusual beauty. It was like she waited for me to notice these things before moving on.

"I want to ask you...what made you think you could have him?" She smiled a little, and briefly allowed a line to come between her eyebrows. "Haven't you heard everyone? Max is in love with me. He's *in love* with me. I'm that one he'll never forget. I'm the one he let get away. *I* am the girl that boys never, ever get over. If I don't come back or want him back and he marries someone else, even, his future wife will have to come to terms with the fact that he's never going to get over me. Sure he might continue living, but *I*—" she bit her lip "—I am what made him *live*. I am his light. I am his excitement. I was the bells, the light, the *darkness* and the melody in his life. You? You could only ever hope to be—" her nose wrinkled as she tried to think of what I could hope to be "—a butter knife. You might be practical and useful, but you're just a blank, dull, staring thing that's there to serve a purpose. And any reflection of me that might be in you is distorted and ugly. You are nothing more."

My heart pounded, and my face was hot. My body trembled. I could hear the ocean. When I noticed it, she did, too, and held up a finger.

"You hear that? The water? No one knows if it ate me alive or not." She said it with a singsong voice like she was keeping a secret from a child, saying the last few words with a seductive, dripping relish. It was like the whole thing was a game to her. "Doesn't that already make me more interesting than you? If or when I come back...can you imagine it?" She rocked backward onto her heels, a smile stretching across her face. "I could walk up there right now, take back Max, and

have a world of people who know me and love me thrilled to
see my pretty face again."

I was colder than ever, and her words were making my head
spin. I felt like I was being hypnotized.

"And what will that mean for you?" she went on. "No
one here likes you. They all whisper about you. Not because
you're interesting, mind you, but because you're just this sad
little thing who wishes she was better. Everyone can see that."
She suddenly adopted a look of sympathy. "Your friends back
home don't even miss you, do they? You've barely heard from
them, I bet. Is that right?"

I had thought this before but refused to believe it.

"Well," she went on, "it looks like no one really needs you
at all, do they?"

She laughed, and as she did, chills ran from my toes to
the back of my neck. I could hear voices. Becca looked up,
toward the door. The light went out. I gasped, and finally
felt in control of my body again. I heard the door slam open.
My heart pounded. I was sitting up and the blanket had fallen
and gathered at my feet on the dusty floor, and I didn't even
know since when.

The ocean was crashing outside, and my ears filled with the
pounding of that and my heartbeat. I felt paralyzed, unable
to stop my fingernails from digging painfully into the rough
upholstery of the couch.

Noise was still coming from somewhere by the door, but I
had no idea of its source. Then, quite suddenly, the light came
back on.

And beneath the bulb stood Max.

chapter 13 me

NOTHING WAS MAKING SENSE.

He saw me, and I watched as he inhaled sharply with surprise. "What are you doing down here? I went up to your room, but you weren't there—I looked in the study room... why did you come down here?"

I could hardly speak. "I came down here to... I was just... I had to get out of my room and...and—what are you doing here?"

Words were tumbling fast from my mouth before I could form them. I stood, on weak legs, and looked around for Becca. She was nowhere. I glanced at the floor, where Becca had stamped out her cigarette. There it was. I resisted the urge to pick it up and see if it was still hot.

"We just wanted to come down and hang out I guess...are you okay?"

"What?" I whispered to myself as I looked at it. I looked helplessly back at Max.

His expression became one of concern, and he stepped back

to open the door. He spoke to someone outside. "Just one second, I think I see a rat."

I heard a few girls shriek. Max walked over to me. "I'm really sorry about earlier, Blake told me she told you…" He trailed off, as he saw the expression on my face. "What's going on? Something else is wrong."

"I don't kn–know, I just…I can't. I—" I was trying to gain control of myself, but I couldn't breathe. It was like that feeling you get when you're sobbing so hard that your lungs take in breaths you're not prepared for.

"Come with me."

And I did. He put his hand on my lower back and guided me.

I trusted him. I didn't care where we were going or who was outside, I felt better that he was there. That was crazy, since I didn't even know him, but it's how I felt.

My static breathing slowed some, and I could take deep breaths. I coughed some of the dust out of my lungs as I walked outside. The usual people were there—Madison and Julia, clutching each other's arms as I walked out hand in hand with Max, Blake, wearing a glittering tiara, and Cam in a gold crown. There must have been some kind of king and queen thing like at homecoming. They both looked at me with concern, and then to Max. Johnny also looked at him and asked, "She okay?"

I gave an embarrassed shrug and waved away their concern. "I'm fine. Not feeling well." Other people whose names I kept forgetting were there, all talking to each other and looking at me like I'd just been dragged from the sand beneath their feet. I couldn't look at them. I realized, as I looked ashamedly down at my feet, that they were bare. I didn't remember when I'd taken off my shoes. I remembered Becca's words about how everyone talked about me because I was just a "sad little thing." This was a perfect example, I supposed.

Lonely, friendless, barefoot new girl, with no identity more specific than that. They'd never see me as anything but that. And I was really starting to fear that maybe that's all I was. I'd always been the star of my own story. But not at Manderley.

Max said nothing, only giving a nod to the others, and then directing me firmly up the stairs.

"You're freezing," he said, when his warm hands touched my cold skin. He put his coat around my shoulders. "Not to be too cliché or anything."

I clutched the jacket closer and summoned a faint smile but said nothing. He led me inside and to the library, which was open.

"This was locked earlier, that's the whole reason I went down to the boathouse."

"Shouldn't have been. But I don't know, I've never tried to break into the library in the middle of a ball before." Max gave me a small smile and gestured for me to go in.

He led me to the senior study room, and then turned on the fire.

"You want to sit?"

I nodded and sat on the couch. He sat across from me in a chair.

"So…" he said. "What happened down there? You looked like you'd seen a ghost."

I cringed and stared into the flames. "I didn't even think about whether anyone would be going there tonight."

"How long were you down there?"

I shrugged. I really didn't know.

"I was rude, I'm sorry."

"No, please—" I didn't want him to explain it.

"But Blake told you?"

"Yes. She told me. I didn't know when I—" Furious humiliation filled my chest. "Dana suggested it."

"I figured it was something like that."

I tried to smile, but it didn't work, and I just ended up taking a deep breath and looking at him. "I don't know what everyone's problem is. I realize I could never compare to B-Becca." I had never sounded so pitiful. I'd never talked about myself like this. I'd never *felt* like this. "But everyone could stop telling me…Dana yelled at me about it the other day…."

I wanted to be honest, but instead I was just coming off as whiny. I didn't feel like I could explain quite what it had felt like when Dana had said what she had. Or what dream or ghost Becca had just told me.

"You're nothing like her."

"Yeah, I get that." My bitterness was not fully disguised. I bit the inside of my cheek anxiously. The whole "you're not better or worse, you're just different" response was not making me feel any more confident. "I don't know. I just wanted to get away for a little while, I guess. And then I fell asleep or something."

Or something. That was the only explanation. But it had been so incredibly vivid. Her smoke had made me cough. I'd smelled her. I'd heard her voice. Can you do all that in a dream? Obviously so, I guessed, but it still left me with a creepy feeling. But her cigarette had been on the ground…it could have just been left there from some other time, I supposed. But…

"It just felt like she was there," I said out loud, without meaning to. I quickly looked up at Max.

"What?" he asked sharply.

I shook my head, regretting what I was about to say. "I

don't know. I fell asleep. I had a d-dream or whatever...and she was there. Becca was there."

There was a pause. "You've never even met her."

"Obviously. It was strange. I could hear her talking to me, and she was just...right here." I held my hand in front of me to show how near to me her stupid, flawless skin had been. "She was chilly...just icy. The way she spoke, that is. And she smelled like...she smelled like cigarettes and liquor...but then this perfume that sort of made the other smells more agreeable."

Max's jaw clenched. "What was she saying?"

I shook my head. "Nothing important."

"Tell me anyway."

"I don't even remember. I just know I was startled when you... I could have sworn the light had been on when I fell asleep."

"It's an old boathouse. It hasn't been used in years, I'm sure the wiring is just faulty."

I bent over onto my knees, mentally exhausted. I heard Max rise, and then felt him next to me. He pulled me by my shoulders so that he was holding me against his chest. He was warm, and I was cold.

"You're fine."

I wished I could believe him. The silence that came between us was comforting and still. He ran his hand over my hair for a few minutes, until we both finally drifted to sleep. It was the best rest I'd had since before I found out I was going to Manderley.

I awoke hours later to Max whispering my name and giving my shoulder a light squeeze.

"We should go," he said quietly. "If we're caught out of bed like this, we'll get in trouble."

The idea of getting in trouble had been appealing since I arrived. Getting expelled and having to go back home seemed like a win-win for me. But all of a sudden it didn't sound so good.

We walked out into the silent halls, and walked to the girls' dorm door. He didn't say anything, and neither did I. Somehow it wasn't awkward at all.

When we arrived at the door, I glanced at Max and smiled nervously.

"Thanks," I said. "For…you know, whatever."

He smiled back. "Don't worry about it. I hope you feel better."

"I do."

The moment changed, suddenly, as we both knew we were finished talking. He leaned in and put a hand on my neck, then kissed my cheek. I felt it turn hot.

I opened the door to go, and then spewed the question I hadn't even known I was going to ask.

"Do you think…she might have been there?"

His face turned to stone. "No, of course not. Just a dream."

We caught eyes. He looked very serious, and he looked like he was going to say something and then changed his mind. He held up his hand and said, "I'll see you later on."

I wished I hadn't asked. But it was too late.

chapter 14 becca

THE NIGHT OF THE HALLOWEEN BALL. *FINALLY.*

Becca had ordered her Marilyn Monroe dress online a month ago, and couldn't wait to wear it. Now finally, her hair was curled, the red lipstick on, the beauty mark in place, and the eyeliner had given her that sultry look. She looked in the mirror and seethed.

She was just bland, bland and more bland. Plain hair, plain skin, plain eyes, plain everything. She was boring to look at. Not like Dana, who looked like Cleopatra even though she'd been talked into going to the ball dressed as a witch.

Dana had asked Becca to help her get ready. So now her hair was straightened, her eyes were rimmed with dark liner and she was wearing the same red lipstick as Becca. But she looked too good. And Becca was torn between making her look good to show how she, Becca, could turn an ugly duckling into a swan, and making her look worse.

"Almost finished," Becca said, grabbing her eye shadow kit. Green. She filled the blush brush with it and powdered it onto

Dana's face. She couldn't go all-out green, but just enough to take her pristine skin to a slightly sickly level.

"What are you doing? Is that green?"

"You are a witch don't forget."

Now, one more thing and Dana would be finished.

Becca drew a big spot on her nose and used other colors from her eye shadow kit to make it look as wartlike as she could.

"Okay, you're all set."

"Can I look?" Dana said, standing. It was hard not to laugh as she smiled, having no idea there was a big black dot on her face.

"Um, sure." She really hoped Dana didn't object. She still looked good, but hopefully with the green tinge and wart, she'd look at least a little less pretty than Becca.

But Dana just laughed when she looked in the mirror. "I look like a witch, that's for sure." Her smile ruined the ugliness.

"Come on, we have to go." Becca turned and marched out of the bathroom. She dropped her things off on her bed, and they were on their way.

Tonight, Becca was determined to make everyone sure that Max and she were in love. She knew exactly how.

When she met him in the dining hall, she smiled broadly.

"You look very handsome." Becca reached up and kissed him on the cheek.

Max smiled, too, and kissed her back. "You, too."

"Although it's kind of a vague costume. Who are you again, just anyone from the fifties?"

He looked down at his suit. "I guess."

"If you weren't wearing a fedora it would be impossible to tell."

He laughed and put an arm around her. "Let's go."

They were stopped and asked to place their vote for king and queen at the door. Becca voted for herself and Max. She leaned over to him and saw that he was voting for Cam and Blake.

"What are you doing? Vote for *us!*"

"You can't vote for yourself, that's stupid."

"Everyone is going to."

"No, I'm not voting for us." He laughed and dropped it in the box.

Her plan wouldn't work if they didn't win. She seethed quietly and dropped in her own ballot.

"Do you think we're going to win?" she asked happily a moment later, squeezing his arm. "I hope we do. I really do. We are the cutest couple, obviously."

"I wouldn't get your hopes up, usually it's a senior couple who gets it."

"Well, I'm not giving up hope. Everyone knows we're perfect together, so…"

Max was barely listening to her prattle on. But Johnny had caught her eye. She looked away quickly, and pulled Max on.

"*God,* Max, can you just *stop?*"

"Am I really the one that needs to stop?"

"What do you expect from me, to be standing by your side all night and never talking to anyone else? Seriously, Max. I can *talk* to other people. That's what I was doing. Talking. I don't see why you can't trust me."

Her heart was pounding. She'd been around the back of a column with Johnny. She'd known it was risky, but she couldn't help it. Not that anything had happened. Johnny had refused, saying it was "wrong" or whatever. She couldn't believe he was still saying it.

Every time she was around him, she wanted more and more to just end it with Max and find a way to be with Johnny.

Max shook his head and bit the inside of his lip. Becca knew when he was really mad. And he was getting there.

"This is so embarrassing, to be arguing outside the dance." Becca sighed. She didn't even care anymore.

"You know what you're doing, Becca."

She stared at him. "What does that even mean? *Ugh,* I'm not going to sit here and try to figure out riddles."

"I realize you're flirtatious. You flit around the party like the social butterfly you long to be so *badly,* charming everyone left and right. All I'm asking is that you stay away from Johnny, seeing as he's my best friend, and that with other people you just keep your hands to yourself. You always take it too far."

Becca tightened her jaw with resolve. His words had scalded her. The "social butterfly" she "longed to be so badly"? Was he serious? How *dare* he imply that she's just some kind of desperate, friendless fool?

There was a pang in her chest as she hoped it was only Max who saw her that way.

"I do not 'always take it too far.'" She repeated his words in a nasty tone. "And don't suggest that I'm just some kind of jackass around Johnny. He flirts with me just as much as I do with him. God, it's not like he just wishes I would back off him."

She couldn't bear the thought of Johnny hating when she was all over him. Max didn't know what Johnny said when they were alone. And she couldn't tell him.

"Are you serious? It's just not okay to flirt with everyone around you all the time."

"You're *so* annoying. Just an insecure little boy."

He didn't freak out. He didn't yell back. He just looked at her, and laughed.

Panic rose quickly in her chest. *He* couldn't break up with *her.* She couldn't let him. They were about to win king and queen. Maybe later she could end things, but not right now. *Not right now.*

"Something has to change." His voice was emotionless.

"Max! Max, *please!*" She couldn't get herself to cry, but she was really trying. She took his hand. He tried to pull it away, but she wouldn't let him. "Look at me."

She yanked his arm and gazed sweetly at him, working in as much worry and desperation as she could into her blue eyes. Time for the last resort.

She'd have to phrase it just right. "But…I mean, I lost my *virginity* to you…and now you're just…" She looked as emotional as she could.

He froze.

On the inside, she smiled. Bingo. Yeah, she'd told him she wasn't a virgin, just in case this sort of moment arose.

He sighed, and looked out to the great hall, clearly trying to decide what to do or think. "You said I wasn't your first."

"I didn't mean to say that. I'm sorry. I'm sorry. *Shit!*"

"Is that true?"

She paused. "Yes, it's true."

Max clearly didn't know how to react. After a moment, he said, "Why would you tell me I wasn't?"

"Because I didn't want you to stay with me because you felt guilty or anything." In fact, she was one hundred percent sure that was why he'd stayed with her anyway. Lucky her that he wasn't *usually* the type to get drunk and sleep with the new girl everyone else wanted already.

"I wouldn't. I liked you."

"*Liked.*"

He breathed in deeply. "Like. But you're acting different lately. I don't know if this is who you are or what. Stop trying so hard, just act like yourself again."

How many times had her mother begged her to be herself again? It was fruitless. Useless. There was no point in begging Becca to stop or change or be someone nicer or easier to be around. This was Becca. And that was all.

The only person who'd ever thought she could really change, apart from her hopeful mother, was Dr. Winthrop. He told her it wasn't her fault, and that if she just took this, this and that medicine for the rest of her freaking life then her moods would level out.

Screw that. She wasn't going to do it.

Dr. Winthrop had tried to talk her through her "compulsive lying" and her "pathological desire" to do what she thought would make people like her, instead of what was right. *You have to control yourself,* he'd said. *Or someone else will get hurt again.*

She shivered and pushed the memory from her mind.

"Or maybe this *is* you," he added after a moment.

She was realizing now that she couldn't let him go. She liked being the golden couple. She liked being enviable, she always had. What would she do without him? No one else could give her what Max could.

The music faded quickly in the dining hall. "And now it's time for the reveal of Halloween King and Queen."

Cheering. Quieting. Drum roll. Max looked Becca in the eyes the whole time.

"Maxwell Holloway and Rebecca Normandy!"

She tried to mask her delight, but he knew how important it was to her.

"Come on, your highness," she said, grabbing his arm. "Let's go claim our crowns."

They walked onto the stage. Everyone cheered.

"Would either of you like to say anything to your public?"

Max shrugged. "Thanks to everyone for voting for me, I'm really flattered, thank you." He gave an insincere but winning smile and handed the microphone back to Professor Crawley.

Becca took it. "I'd actually like to take a moment to say something if I could."

"Sure, go ahead."

Max looked at her nervously. She smiled.

"First of all, I just want to say thank you to all of you… you've all welcomed me to Manderley and I couldn't be happier to know each and every one of you." *Gag.* "And as for you, Max, I just have one thing to say to you."

Everyone was quiet as they listened to her. She took her time and smiled at Max, gazing at him as earnestly as she could. "I love *you.*"

A bunch of the girls gasped and then there was applause. She knew exactly what she was doing.

"Oh, he's embarrassed." She wrapped an arm around his waist. "I'm sorry, baby."

"Kiss her!" said a voice in the audience.

She smiled. Max tightened his jaw and looked down at her, his eyes furiously questioning her. He kissed her quickly, and she pulled him in for a real kiss. He was mad, and she knew it. She didn't care.

More clamor from their onlookers.

"Thank you so much." She handed the microphone back, curtsied and dragged Max behind her by the hand.

He left after that.

"That was *so* cute, Becca!" Madison said, running up to her. "I can't believe you didn't tell us he said he loved you! Oh, my *God!*" She waved a hand in front of her face.

That was definitely the implication in the way she'd said it. But it was easy to claim as an accidental inflection.

"Yeah, it's really sweet. Look, don't tell anyone, but I'm sneaking into the boys' dorms."

Julia's jaw dropped. "Are you serious?"

"Everyone's down here, so no one will even notice." She tried to ignore the pounding in her chest. She had to look happy and cool and confident. "Besides, Max and I need to celebrate." She smiled, but it faltered as she saw Johnny by the entrance. She didn't look back at her friends, but went to him.

For once she was lost for words as she looked at him. She hadn't thought about him when she'd done what she just did. It hadn't occurred to her that he might care.

After not looking at her for what felt like a very long time, he spoke.

"You guys...you're saying *that* now?"

She shook her head, but didn't know what to say.

He finally looked at her, and the look in his eyes made her heart skip. "Do you love him, Becca? Really?"

"I—I don't know."

For the first time in she didn't know how long, she felt her eyes brim with real tears. She took a deep, steadying breath. She did know that she *didn't* love Max. Her stomach clenched. Why *was* she staying with Max? Was it worth it?

Johnny nodded once and walked past her toward the dorms. She called his name, but he didn't turn. She looked around to see if anyone had seen. No one seemed to have.

That was why she was staying with Max—because Johnny could walk away. And when he did, she would feel like this.

Becca flew down the stairs and into the bathroom. The tears were threatening again; her heart and throat were hot and sore from being in knots. She was on the brink of letting it out when she came upon two girls.

"Becca! That was so sweet! Are you—are you okay?"

It took everything she had to look blasé. "Am I okay? Yes, I'm okay. Just...freshening up before I go to Max's room." She smiled and tried to blink the tears away.

She looked in the mirror and wiped any running mascara from under her eyes. She looked pitiful, she thought. The crown looked like it was making fun of her. She left the bathroom and the two girls, whatever their names were, and went up the stairs toward Max.

What was his room number? He'd said something about it the other day because his parents had sent a letter to the wrong room. They sent it to eight. He was in...ugh, for *once* she wished she'd listened to him. Eighteen? Twenty-eight? It was one of those two. She'd just have to try both.

She found door eighteen. She knocked. No response. She tried the knob, and it was open. She peered in and saw an empty, messy room.

Door twenty-eight. No answer. Locked.

Dammit. Was it...maybe *his* room was number eight?

She found it and knocked. She shouldn't be here. She should be trying to fix things with Johnny. She was on the brink of running when Max opened the door.

Becca reminded herself that this was the way to be happy. To have who everyone wanted. And not risk real heartbreak.

She threw her arms around Max. "Oh, thank God you opened the door. I've been looking everywhere!"

"Becca, what are you *doing?*"

"I'm so *sorry.* I...I just..."

He stepped back, throwing her arms from him. "Stop."

"I love you. And I mean it." The words sounded unnatural. It was the first time she'd said it to anyone. He still looked livid, but she could see in his eyes that he was working to understand what she'd said. She took his hand to squeeze it for emphasis. The emotions from a moment before were threatening to come back.

"I *do*...and I know you don't believe me, Max. But I do. I just...don't know what to do with it. I've never been in love before. I just don't know how to act." She let go of his hand and stepped backward. She felt herself mean the words she said. But not toward Max. "I'm so sorry. I guess I just hoped you'd say it if I did that." Her voice was small. She wasn't this person. Why was she feeling like this? "I feel like everyone knows you don't like me that much and it's so embarrassing." Becca drew her eyebrows together, and let her hands drop to her sides.

Her knees felt week. She succumbed to it and sat down. She stared at the floor and tightened her jaw. This wasn't where she wanted to be. Not with Max, not on his floor, not in love with someone she feared wouldn't love her, too.

"Becca, I'm sorry. I can't...say that back to you."

She shook her head. "I don't need you to. I shouldn't have said it."

There was silence while she breathed deeply and tried to keep the tears at bay. She was using every muscle in her body to not scream and burst into shuddering, pathetic tears.

"What should we do now?" he asked. "Are we..."

"I want to stay with you," she said. "I'm really sorry."

"If we do, you can't do things like that."

She nodded and tightened her stomach. "I know."

chapter 15 me

IT WAS THE FIRST DAY WE HAD PAINTING SINCE Halloween. It'd be the first time I'd seen Max since he walked me to my dorm. I tried hard not to wonder what it would be like, where our conversations would go now. We'd fallen asleep in each other's arms, as lame as that sounds, and now... how were we going to act? How was I going to make an idiot out of myself this time instead of being cool and collected?

I shivered as I thought of Becca. She probably wouldn't feel nervous at all. She'd probably smile and toss her ribbonlike hair over her porcelain shoulder and say something clever and seductive. I imagined myself trying it, and cringed with my own embarrassment.

All I'd wanted to do was get under everyone's skin, and just tell them what had happened. But I didn't. I kept it to myself.

A tall, lean boy with Ray-Ban glasses walked in. The girls in the class stopped talking immediately as they took in his good looks. He scooted the glasses up his head.

"Hey, guys," he said as he set down a laptop bag. "I'm Isaac. Frank—Professor Crawley—is my uncle, and he had a family thing he needed to do this week, so I'm covering for him. I, incidentally, am thrilled to be avoiding the family thing. So we'll have fun this week. Just so you know, I'm not just some random nephew, either. I just graduated from Corcoran in D.C. with a bachelor of fine arts. I'll be headed back in a year to get started on my master's."

The class was silent. The girls were still gaping, and the guys were sizing him up. Max walked in and took his seat next to me while Isaac dug through his laptop bag for the attendance.

"Who's that?" Max asked me.

I nearly seized up. "Uh. Professor Crawley's son. No, I mean nephew. He just graduated college and he's covering for Crawley."

I didn't need to be so stupid when I talked to Max. It would be nice if just sometimes, I could say things without stumbling through them.

Max nodded.

Once we were given our assignment, which was to paint abstractly using at least two different kinds of brushstrokes, the classroom was buzzing with whispered conversation. Most of it about how hot our sub was. Max was listening to headphones and furrowing his brow at his painting. After half an hour passed, I came to terms with the fact that we wouldn't be talking today.

I was just laying Cadmium Red Light to the underside of a Cerulean blue stroke when Isaac approached me.

"That's awesome."

"Mine?"

Isaac nodded and squinted as he leaned in to look at my colors. "That's really awesome. I gotta say, I usually hate the look of colors straight out of the tube, but you're doing something really interesting here. Is there any kind of inspiration for this? Like, what's going through your mind as you do this?"

Max. Just a whole lot of Max. "Nothing really. I'm just… painting I guess."

Isaac looked at me through narrowed eyes, chewing on the end of his Ray-Bans. "Are you in love?"

I noticed now that the whole class was listening. Even Max had taken off his headphones.

"Love? No, not at all. *God* no." Slick.

"I see…a lot of torture here. All these reds…the Alizarin with the Cadmium, especially over here," he indicated a sharp, narrow line in the corner. "This is amazing. You really have a gift."

"Oh…no, I don't even paint. This doesn't even look abstract like it's supposed to. It's just…a mess."

He raised his eyebrows and smiled. "It doesn't matter. It's *working*."

I was flattered and was brimming with pride, but I couldn't enjoy it. I could feel everyone's eyes on me, and could practically hear their loathing thoughts about me.

"Looks like you're a painter now." He smiled and winked.

I smiled back. "Thanks."

As Isaac walked around, the classroom's eyes shifted from me to my painting, I imagined then. They probably all wanted to see what Isaac had been gushing about. They'd probably decide there was nothing special about it, and that they couldn't see what the fuss was over.

I wished I had my phone and could listen to music. Then I could ignore the whispers, and at least try to escape.

"It *is* good."

I turned to see Max looking at my canvas. Isaac's question about love burned in my ears. I almost didn't want Max to look too hard. If he did, he might see the truth.

"Thank you. I don't even…" I waved a hand at it. "It's not even a big deal."

I directed my gaze back to my canvas, for fear of saying something else dumb.

Later, Max and I were at the washing station, cleaning our brushes when Susan came over to us and draped her arms over our shoulders. She had a group of girls watching whatever performance she was about to put on.

"So, are you two tortured lovebirds now?" She looked at Max. "Doesn't that seem a bit idiotic given the *circumstances?*"

"Hey, Susan?" said Max. "Why don't you fuck off?"

I could tell the words bit at her, but she smiled and moved her long straight hair from her face. "I'm sorry, does it bother you when I stand here and touch you? That's true, that's in-appropriate. Considering Becca, and all. I'll back off." She stepped backward, looking smug. "Take the hint, *new girl.* Stop trying to copy his girlfriend. It's *weird.*"

Max shook his head at her. "You're just a fucking rip-off."

"Rip-off? Me? How you figure?"

"Because we all saw you before Becca got here, and we all see you now. Your hair, your jewelry, your shoes…and didn't you pick up smoking sometime last year? And what was it you smoked? That's right. Camel Lights. Same as Becca."

The fire in his eyes intimidated me. He was fighting for Becca, and she wasn't even here. I wanted everyone to be wrong when they said how much he loved her. But maybe he really did.

"Yeah, I heard you beat the living shit out of Johnny over the summer. I saw the scar he's got on his cheekbone now. Doesn't scare me—what are you gonna do, hit me?"

I looked around for Isaac. He was talking on his phone in the corner. Crawley wouldn't have let this conversation carry on.

"I'm not going to hit you. You just need to stop."

"Oh," she said, laughing, "right, you wouldn't hit a girl. Maybe you'd just *kill me*."

There was a collective response in the classroom. Gasps, *whoas* and whispers.

"Don't fucking talk to me." Max's eyes were hard, and the veins in his hand were pumping

"If you didn't kill her, and she is still out there, I wouldn't be surprised if she's keepings tabs on what you're doing with this one." Susan pointed lazily at me.

I laughed. This was just too much. "And that wouldn't make *Becca* the psycho?"

Max looked at me, and for a second I thought he might yell at me. But then he took my brushes and his and threw them into his locker.

"Is all your other stuff packed up?" he asked me.

"Yes." I would have said it even if it hadn't been.

He took my hand and pulled me from the room. It was quieter in the halls, even though I knew classes were about to let out and fill them up again.

Max pulled me into an empty classroom and shut the door. The gray light from outside put an eerie filter on the room.

"I'm sorry." Max sat down on one of the desks.

"Sorry...why are you sorry?"

"Because that's not okay. How Susan was acting...it's messed up. I hate when people talk to you like that. I don't like when they talk to you about her at all."

"It's okay."

"*No*. It's not." He stood and came toward me. "You're not her. You're you."

I couldn't summon any words. He was so close to me now that I could feel his warmth. I could barely feel the cold of the chalkboard I leaned on.

He put a hand on my hip, and another on my waist. His eyes were boring into mine. They still held the same fire they had when he was talking to Susan about Becca. His hands tightened on me, and I wondered for a moment if maybe that fire wasn't about Becca at all. Maybe it was for me.

Before I could talk myself out of it, his lips were on mine. My mind went blank. My body went numb. I faded into him, letting my bag fall to the floor. I didn't care if someone walked in. I didn't care if anyone saw.

If Becca was alive or Becca was dead, I would have kissed him in front of her.

chapter 16 becca

"STOP ACTING LIKE YOU DON'T WANT TO TALK to me." Becca was sitting on the step in front of the boathouse, smoking a cigarette when Johnny walked up. She'd slipped him a note and told him to meet her here.

Johnny sighed and looked at her. "You know I do."

"Then why have you barely talked to me since Halloween?"

"You know *why.*"

"Yes, but you shouldn't be so stupid. You should talk to me again." She stood and moved a little closer to him. "I've missed you."

I need him to say it back, she thought. *Please say you've missed me, too....*

He looked at her for a moment before saying it. "I have, too. I've missed you, too."

He looked her in the eyes, and she thought she'd fall apart. She had worked so hard to stay away from him, and to wait for him to come to her. But the whole time she had, she knew she was doing the right thing. Johnny didn't seem to have any trouble not talking to her. And that was exactly *why* she couldn't give in first.

But now she couldn't help it. Not after what she'd just found out.

"Good," she said. "I have some good news."

"What?"

"Didn't you say you were going to have to stay at Mander-ley over the Thanksgiving break? Your parents are doing something, right?"

"Yeah, jeez, how did you remember that?"

She shrugged. "Well, I'm staying, too. And Max is going home."

Becca watched his eyes for a response. He looked back at her, and let out a deep breath. "That's…not good."

She raised an eyebrow. "No?"

There was the flicker of a smile on his face. "Becca, we can't…"

"Look, I don't want to hear it. Just…if you want to…then meet me here at nine on the Friday he leaves."

She tried to look cool and collected, and then walked away without looking back.

The Friday finally came. She said goodbye to Max. And she sat, tapping her foot for the last hour before she was supposed to meet Johnny. What if he didn't show? She tried to think of other things, but she couldn't. Finally it was ten minutes to nine. She was out the door.

This was no time to arrive fashionably late, much as she might want to.

The trek down to the boathouse was a tense one. She tried to sing the lyrics to a song in her head, to keep her mind off her fears, but it did nothing.

Down the steps. Across the sand. Open the door. Pull on the light. No one there.

Her stomach fell, and she walked to the couch. She couldn't believe it. No one had ever rejected her. Ever. This was why she'd chosen Max. Because he could just hook up with her and act enough like a couple. He didn't have to put his arm around her or kiss her in front of everyone. She just had to tell all the girls that he was in love with her and pretend that there was something behind the scenes besides sex. She could look beloved, and have the guy everyone wanted, because he was so passive that he didn't care who he had. She was hot enough. She knew that was all it was.

But Johnny could resist her, where she could not resist him. And that was killing her.

The door swung open. Her heart leaped. It was Johnny. She wanted to smile from ear to ear, but she couldn't. That wasn't like her.

He closed the door behind him and turned off the light. She couldn't see him, but she could feel the cast of moonlight on her. He walked right to her and kissed her. They fell backward onto the couch, and he pulled off his shirt before pulling off hers.

"I thought you weren't going to come," she whispered.

"I couldn't stay away."

"I don't understand why you can't just say you're sorry."

"Okay, I'm sorry."

"Like you mean it."

Johnny laughed and glared at her. "I'm so sorry. I'll never call you by your full name again."

"Good."

Becca and Johnny were lying in his bed. His roommate

had gone home for Thanksgiving, and Becca had snuck in an hour ago. There was hardly anyone on the hall.

She flipped over and propped herself up on her elbows. "Tell me something, Johnny."

"Tell you what?"

"Something. Anything. Tell me something no one knows."

He raised his eyebrows. "I don't really have any secrets."

She gave him a look.

"Fine," he said, thinking. "I've always wanted to join the Marines."

"Why?"

He shrugged. "I don't know. I've got two cousins in the Marines and they love it. I mean, it's a good thing to do, and it's gotta be such a thrill."

"No...you can't do that. You'll die!"

"Hopefully not. Max always talks about it, too."

"Don't talk about Max."

They were silent for a few seconds. They both knew that what they were doing was wrong. But for this one weekend, they were playing pretend.

"Why don't you just become a doctor or something? Save lives but don't risk your own."

"I don't know. It's just something I've always thought about doing. If I were to do it, it would be the most independent choice I'll have ever made. My parents want me to do the typical follow-in-your-dad's-footsteps thing, and I don't."

"I don't accept." She draped herself over his stomach. "You'll have to just become a rich doctor and I'll stay at home with my Pomeranians. I'll leave the house, sure, but only to go to happy hour."

He laughed. "Not Pomeranians. German shepherds. Labs. Something else. None of those yappy little cotton balls."

"We'll just have to see." She smiled, and then looked very

seriously at him. "Like, what if something happened to me? What if I died tragically or was kidnapped or something?"

"What about it?"

"Well, I mean would you cry? Would you weep uncontrollably and go insane with missing me?"

"Yes, I'd probably never take a happy breath again."

"Good."

"What about you?"

"Don't be stupid, Johnny." She gave him a devilish smile. "Now kiss me."

chapter 17 me

A FEW WEEKS PASSED. MAX AND I MET ALMOST
every night. No one had seen us. No one knew but us. We
hadn't said aloud that we were keeping it to ourselves, but
that's what we were doing. We never spoke about Becca. But
we were the only ones.

The rumor had circled around to my ears that Becca was
pregnant. That she was off being pregnant and waiting to give
birth. Everyone seemed to assume that if she was doing this,
she was giving up the baby for adoption.

"Do you really believe that's where she is?" I asked Blake,
as we sat in the dining hall one evening, when someone had
already brought it up again. For once, there was decent food—
Wisconsin Cheddar Beer Soup. I was on my third bowl.

She took a sip from her Sprite and shrugged. "I don't know.
Dana seems to know more than she lets on. That's all I know."

"Maybe that's what she knows." My chest hardened as I
envisioned her coming back and presenting a child to Max.

"Well…let's see. If it *is* that…then she would have to have
gotten pregnant like…April or May. And then she'd be having

the baby in like…January or February. Right?" She counted off the months on her fingers.

"So you think that's something she'd do? Just not contact anyone here?"

"I would have thought she'd talk to *someone*. But I don't know. She was hard to figure out. And who knows, maybe she *has* contacted someone but told them not to tell anyone. They'd probably listen to her."

I nodded.

"It's just really weird. It's like…how can she possibly be alive? But then…how can she be dead?"

"No one really seems to think that, though, do they? That she's dead?"

"I don't think anyone knows what to think. She's so unpredictable that she could be doing anything. She could come back at any moment. But then, the cops have pretty much given up."

She looked over my shoulder, and for a moment I thought I was going to turn and see Her. But it was Max.

He nodded a hello to Blake, and then looked at me.

"I know you're eating, but I'd like to talk to you, if you want to come sit with me. I know it's rude."

"Yeah, that's fine. We can go now."

I stood up with my tray, and said goodbye to Blake. She gave me a questioning look that I had to ignore.

I followed him, my heart pounding the whole way, to a table. His jacket was slung over the back of the chair he sat in. I sat, too.

"I just want to talk to you, I guess." He looked at me with hardened eyes. "How are you doing? I mean really, is everything okay?"

"Sure, everything is fine, why?"

"Don't lie to me. You can tell me if anything is up."

"Everything is good."

He took a deep breath. "I know this is probably a really stupid..." He shifted his weight. "You're not hooking up with Johnny Parker, are you?"

It was so unexpected that I laughed. "*What?* No, of course not, why?"

He looked a little relieved. "People are just saying that. Dana...I guess Dana noticed you leaving your room a lot. And you went to the ball with him."

I scoffed. "For like ten seconds."

"Yeah, sorry about that."

"It's fine."

He was silent for a few seconds, and then said, "How's Dana acting? I mean, she treating you okay?"

I laughed before I could stop myself. "I mean, she sent me to the wolves of Halloween in a dress made of raw meat, and since then has barely spoken to me, but yeah, she's treating me fine."

"She been okay since then?"

"I guess...she just kind of ignores me."

Dana had been pretty silent since Halloween. She hadn't told me I was a terrible excuse for a human being or insisted I was a waste of space or anything, so that was...nice, I guess.

"You have to tell me if she starts acting weird. You have to."

"Okay, I will."

"Promise?"

"Promise."

That Friday, Blake convinced me to go down to the boathouse with everyone again.

"It'll be fun! I *promise.* I'll punch Dana right in the face if she freaks again. Plus, almost everyone fun is staying here instead of going home for Thanksgiving." She shrugged. "Senior year. I guess people don't want to miss out."

She promised to walk down with me, so she'd meet me outside my door at eleven. At ten-fifty, I was putting on my makeup and trying to slow my thudding heartbeat. Dana's bed was empty still; she must be at the boathouse. Max would be there. I couldn't kiss him or show anyone what we were, but I still wanted to look good. I did what I could, and then met Blake in the hall.

"You ready to go have fun?" she asked, smiling.

"Of course," I responded automatically. I took a step, but she grabbed my wrist.

"Hold on, let's go in your room for a second."

"Why?"

"No reason."

I opened the door and let her in. She pulled a flask from her handbag and took some of whatever was in it. She held it out to me.

I downed a few sips myself. This is exactly the kind of private school bad-influencing that everyone talks about. I didn't know if I felt included, or like a sucker. But tonight I wanted to feel a little less…just less. I wanted to see Max. I wanted to see him and not feel the inevitable glares of Susan and whoever else wanted to say horrible things to me. I knew it wasn't right to gain confidence this way. But as I felt the burn in my throat and under my tongue, I almost felt the nerves fall into submission.

One hour later

Max walked in. It was raining, and his dark hair was clinging to his eyebrows. He looked around the room before locking eyes with me. I couldn't look away. I couldn't even get myself to smile and wave geekily like I usually do. I just looked back at him until someone went up to him and diverted his attention. I turned back to Blake, and saw that she was watching me with narrowed eyes.

"What?"

She smiled. "What was *that?*"

"What was what? Nothing. Huh?" I was incapable of lying or playing it cool in these situations. I just turned lobster-red and stuttered like that.

She pulled me closer and said, "Oh, my God, you're...are you..." She looked around and mouthed, *"With Max?"*

"No! Oh, no, that would be so *stupid,* I mean I'm under siege enough as it is. Plus he's in love with Becca. And she's... I mean I could never compete with her. Not that I'm trying to. You know what I mean."

Her mouth hung open in a smile and she didn't break my gaze as she handed me her drink. "Have some."

"No, really, I'm—"

She put it up to my mouth and I laughed as I swallowed and then wiped my cheeks.

"First yesterday at dinner, and now that look—are you hooking up with him?" Blake asked, her eyes filled with eagerness.

I tried to say I wasn't, but I couldn't stop smiling.

Blake stood up and pulled me to her, squealing. "Oh, my God, that's awesome. I thought he was just going to mope around forever."

That stung a little. It shouldn't have, but it did. "Well, I guess not. *Please* don't tell anyone."

"Oh, please, I was going to tell *you* not to tell anyone."

We laughed and then she pulled me over to the couch. She recruited people to play cards, while I waited. I took a sip of my drink and then realized Dana was staring at me. Her already dark eyes seemed darker than ever. She was right where Blake and I had been standing. Had she heard us talking? Would…would she care?

"Okay, Ace is high!" Blake sat down next to me.

Dana couldn't have heard me. She would have said something. She was always willing to embarrass me.

She must not have heard.

"You know what we haven't done in the longest time?" Madison, who always got more confident with a few too many drinks in her, was standing on a box and commanding attention from the room. "Seven Minutes in Heaven."

I laughed, thinking it was a joke, but it wasn't. Everyone whooped in agreement and seemed excited. At my high school, this had been a very lame thing to play and was found only in Judy Blume books and nineties teen movies. It had always seemed so stupid. But now that I glanced at Max, who was loosened up enough to smile—no easy feat it seemed—the game might not be so dumb.

"There should be a notebook behind you," Madison said. I realized she was talking to me.

"Where?"

"In the supply closet. Just look on the shelves. Does anyone have a pen?"

I went in and started feeling around the shelves for a notebook. I jumped when my fingers landed on something cold. I thought it was a bug, but upon closer investigation, I saw that it was a silver necklace. I pushed it back on the shelf. I found the spiral notebook, which was covered in dust, and pulled it out.

"Here it is, Madison," I said, wiping it clean.

"Okay, write your name in it with this pen and then pass it along." She tossed me a red ink pen.

I opened to the first page, and saw a list of names already

there. My eyes immediately went to Becca's. The names were all in different handwriting, so it was easy to presume she had written her own. It was odd to look at it. She wrote in sort of half-cursive. Also in red ink. I wondered, briefly, if she had used the pen I held now.

I flipped to the next page and wrote my name at the top, before handing it to Ricky, who was next to me.

A few minutes later, the paper was filled with names, and Julia had cut it apart and put the strips into a coffee can.

"I'll draw, since Cam and I aren't playing," Blake said. She took the can and began feeling around for two choice pieces of paper. "First up, Ricky and Susan!" There was a lot of cheering, and then they disappeared into the supply closet. Cam kept time on his watch, and everyone laughed and talked loudly until the seven minutes were up.

Every time she dove her hand into the can of names, I held my breath until neither my name nor Max's was spoken. After Ricky and Susan came two girls I didn't know, who agreed to go in together and got a lot of attention for it. After a few more rounds, though, Blake called Max's name.

"Max!" She smiled at him, and he shook his head.

He said something to her I couldn't hear, but she shrugged and then called my name.

Unlike the whooping that had gone before our names, there was a sharp and collective intake of breath mixed in with the drunken chatter of those who had not heard.

I didn't know whether to stand or laugh or refuse or what. There was no reason to say no—everyone else had gone in willingly. Finally, Max stood and walked past me. For a second I thought he was just going to walk right out and away to avoid causing more gossip. But he didn't. He opened the storage closet door and looked at me.

"After you."

I didn't look at anyone before going in. I wished the volume would rise again so my heart pounding wouldn't be the only sound in the room. I followed him in, and he pulled on the light. It was so dim it looked like it might die while we were in there.

"I knew I'd end up with you in here."

His voice startled me. When I processed what he'd said, I immediately took it to mean that he had been dreading it. That was the self-deprecating pessimist in me.

"How did you know?" My voice sounded small and uncool.

"Because I didn't put my name in the can. And I know Blake." He hesitated. "And Blake knows me."

My heart skipped before melting into my stomach. "Oh," I whispered back. We were both speaking low. It was very quiet on the other side of the door.

"And she didn't pull *your* name out of the hat, either."

"No?"

He shook his hair, which was dry and soft-looking now. "No. She had Julia's in her hand."

He took a step toward me, and put his hand on the shelf behind me. He smelled like clean laundry and soap. It felt so different to not be in secret—there was only a door between thirty people and us, all assuming they knew what was happening.

It was taking almost more control than I had not to reach a hand out and touch him. The air between us was tight and seemed to be pulling us closer.

I heard Blake's voice, but not what she said, and then the stereo turned on. It was a Mutemath song I couldn't place.

"Did Blake assume too much, or was she right to send you in here? I mean…people are going to talk."

The light hit his eyes, giving them the appearance of being

lit from behind. He looked at me, and I nodded dumbly. "I'm starting to really not care what they think of me."

Then his mouth was on mine. His hand was in my hair. His body, lean and strong, was pressing into mine. All I could hear was the music outside, and all I could feel was him. I wasn't worried about what anyone thought, including him. I was unselfconscious for the first time since the last time we'd met.

I ran my hand up his shirt and felt his impossibly perfect body. His skin was warm and soft, but he held me and kissed me with strength. He lifted me up a little, and I flattened my hand on the shelf for support. It landed on the cold necklace I'd found earlier.

I wanted to stay there forever. I could imagine passing hours this way. But that couldn't happen. Because the next second, the closet was filled with light, and Dana stood in the doorway. My feet landed on the floor and my hand swatted the necklace there, too. Dana's eyes darted down to it, and she shoved past us to get to it. She picked it up slowly, examining it and then closing it in her fist.

"This is it," she said. "This is the proof. Becca's back. Or she will be soon."

Max looked at her, and then at the silver chain in her hand. Some kind of realization washed over him.

chapter 18 me

JOHNNY WAS STANDING BEHIND DANA IN THE
doorway, and he was looking at Max like he'd killed someone.

"What is *wrong* with you, man?" he exploded.

Max raised his eyebrows and then walked out of the closet.
I didn't move.

"What's wrong with me?"

Johnny threw a hand up at me. "Her? *Really?* After what
you had—don't you think it's a little messed up to just be…
doing that?"

Something recoiled in my core. Johnny had always been
nice to me. Why would he say that?

Dana shot him a look that he ignored.

Max lifted his chin a little and looked at Johnny. "You
wanna talk to *me* about that? Are you sure?"

"Oh, I'm sure."

Max pushed him hard. Johnny stumbled back.

"Outside." Max's voice rose on the word.

Johnny went out the door, and Max followed. Then so did

everyone else. A few people went to the shut curtains, and others went outside. I pushed through them into the night air.

I felt like I should say something. Like I could somehow get them to stop.

"—after *everything* with Becca, you really think you can talk to me about this?" Max yelled at Johnny.

"That's exactly my point, Max! You're supposed to be in love with Becca, remember?"

"And where is she, Johnny? She's not here."

"That makes it okay? You're just doing whatever you want, and you don't care anymore about her feelings? She *loved* you, Max!" I could hear the ire rising in Johnny's voice.

"That's bullshit and you *know it!*"

"It's because of you she's gone, you know. Because of *you!*"

Max, who'd had his back turned to Johnny, turned toward him and pushed him again. This time with enough force to knock him to the sand. Johnny recovered quickly.

"Don't mess with me, Max, I got a *lot* of shit to take out on someone, it doesn't matter to me if it's you or not."

Max gave a laugh and shook his head. "Yeah? *You* got shit to take out on *me? Do it.*"

They looked at each other, rain still coming down. It started to pour harder, but neither of them seemed to notice. Johnny balled his fists and hesitated. He didn't want to hit Max. I could tell.

But Max was done hesitating. With a solid punch to the jaw he hit Johnny, who stumbled backward but caught himself. He swung at Max and made loud contact. Max didn't miss a beat, grabbing at Johnny and throwing him onto the ground. Johnny pulled on Max's shirt, ripping it so it hung wet and loose. Max yanked it off, revealing a sweating, tight body. His muscles rippled as he held Johnny down and punched him hard in the face.

Cam ran forward and pulled Max off Johnny, shouting at them to stop. The rain got heavier. Max spit blood onto the sand. Dana, who had been crouched on the ground over Johnny, ran to Max.

She slapped him across the face. He didn't move.

"You," she said, "are so *messed up*. And this?" She pulled out the necklace. "This is *proof* that she's coming back. And you know what that means."

"I think that's a bit optimistic."

Fury seemed to run down her spine as she said, "When you say things like that, Max—" she took a deep breath "—you really make me think you know more than you pretend to."

He smiled, and I saw his teeth were covered in blood. "Yeah, Dana? *You* want to talk about that?"

She breathed quickly and then went back to Johnny, who was now standing and looking furiously at Max.

Max looked at me and then walked up the stairs without saying another word.

I felt like my world had fallen in. I'd been a fool to think that any part of this place was mine.

Things got worse over the next month. Not only were the days some of the shortest I'd seen, but the cold was getting colder by every minute. It hadn't snowed. It had only rained icy, gray droplets. The building was cold everywhere. I was constantly in a sweatshirt, and if I'd had my way, I'd be in gloves, boots and a hat 24/7. But that's just simply not the way to look attractive or to live down your reputation as a pariah.

Susan, who had been polite enough to ignore me at the last party I went to, was now glaring at me and laughing every time she saw me in the hallways or in class. Like she knew something I didn't. Which I was sure she did.

Every time I heard whispers of "she," I was sure they were

either talking about Becca or about me. Sometimes I was so sure, I felt like I should say something. But what could I say?

I didn't know what everyone's *problem* with me was. I had merely gotten accepted to the school. It wasn't *my* fault that I was replacing—or *not* replacing—the girl who had vacated my spot. Plus, so many people seemed so sure she'd be back. And if so, then what was the big deal?

Ever since the party, rumors and whispers had begun swarming through the hallways like locusts.

Becca is pregnant.

Becca will be back soon.

That *new girl* is a psycho and is trying to take Becca's place.

Becca's dead. And maybe Max killed her.

I couldn't even wrap my mind around any of the suggestions. If Max loved her, he wouldn't have killed her. And of course he didn't, because that's just…crazy.

But then…he didn't seem to be having that much trouble moving on. He didn't seem overly troubled. He wasn't pouting or weeping in dark corners. Then again, he really didn't seem the type who would, even if his heart was broken. Also…it's not like he wanted to be with me like he'd been with her.

What surprised me was where my mind spent most of its time. I didn't spend all of my time feeling embarrassed or put upon because everyone talked about me. I didn't wonder so much about where Becca was or when and if she'd return. All I could do was think of Max, and our seven minutes.

The rumors about us had begun to circulate, too. Questions of whether or not we were together and what we had done in that supply closet were on everyone's minds. Meanwhile, they still bandied around the idea that Johnny and I were hooking up on the side. It was a complicated web of rumors, and I couldn't figure out why anyone cared.

Max and I didn't discuss what had happened, or what

everyone thought of us. We talked in class and acknowledged each other in the hallways. But that was about it, until early December. I was in the painting studio, finishing up a still life that I *hated,* when Max walked in.

I paused my computer at a Zero 7 chorus and said, "Hey."

"Hey. You doing the still life, too?"

"Yeah, this one's pretty hard. I thought it'd be easier, but it's just not."

We had to paint a still life lit by candles instead of by angled lighting. It made the contrasts stronger, but the tones had to be just right.

Max looked at my painting. "Pfft."

"What?"

He pointed at it. "I don't think you have any room to say that this is hard for you."

I laughed, not knowing what to say.

"Sorry that everyone is talking about—" he pointed vaguely between himself and me "—you know."

"Oh, it's fine. Are you—is it bothering you?"

He shook his head. "No."

A shiver went down my body, and suddenly I wasn't as tired as I had been.

"So, really, you're doing all right? Everyone talking isn't driving you crazy?"

"It's okay, really. It's only another six months, anyway, right?"

He nodded. "Yeah, it's not that long. I don't know why...I don't know why I'm so worried about you."

"What? What do you mean?"

"I want you to be okay. And it...really pisses me off whenever I hear anyone talking about you or comparing you to her."

That feeling snuck up my spine again. The one that made me feel inferior to Her.

He went on. "I don't think it's fair that they do that. There's *nothing* wrong with you. Nothing wrong with you being here or...or anything."

I took a breath. "Thank you."

"I don't think she's coming back."

I wanted to ask him if it was because he thought she was dead. But instead I just asked, "Why not?"

"I just don't. I don't want anything to have happened to her. We got into a fight that night, so everyone thinks I—" He had been staring at a place on the floor, but now he looked at me. "You know...I didn't do anything to her, right?"

"Right. Of course." I didn't know why I believed him, but I did. Maybe that made me the dumb girl in the horror movie who willingly takes the hand of her killer, but I did.

"And I don't consider myself to be her 'property.'"

"I should hope not." I looked at the floor and then summoned some courage. "But if you don't, then why do you suddenly care so much about not letting anyone know we've been hooking up? Sometimes you're all willy-nilly with it, and then you get paranoid. I don't get it. You don't seem like the type of guy who concerns himself too much with how other people see him."

"I can't just *be* with you. I can't just get with the next girl that comes along after my girlfriend dies."

I raised my eyebrows. "The next girl who comes along?"

"I didn't—"

"No, you know what? I'm sorry, but I can't keep being this anonymous replacement for *her.* Because I'm not. I'm just not."

"I don't think you're a replacement for her. It's just difficult. Everyone either thinks she's lurking around a corner waiting to come back, or they think she's off having my *kid,* or they think she's dead and that *maybe* I killed her." His voice had gotten louder. "It's kind of hard to just be with you now. Not to mention the fact that she kind of ruined my desire to be with anyone right now. I'm sorry. It's just not going to happen."

In the pit of my chest, something had been growing stronger and stronger. And the more time that passed at Manderley Academy, the more it reared its head and breathed hot fire. It ran through me, keeping me from feeling sad and lonely—which could have easily happened—and instead drove me to get quietly more and more sure of myself.

After my conversation with Max, I packed up my oil paints and left. My painting was fine. It was just me who was nitpicking at the details in it. I walked up to Blake's room.

"Let's start drinking."

These were the first words out of my mouth when I saw her. I hadn't been sure about going to the last party of the semester, but now I definitely was going. She laughed at first in surprise, but then narrowed her eyes and asked if I was okay.

"I'm great, I just want to have fun. Let's go do our makeup!"

Blake grabbed two Gatorades and a water bottle full of clear whatever, and we went into my room. Dana sat on her bed, filling the air with gloom.

"Want a shot?" I asked her. Blake smiled when Dana glared at me. I rolled my eyes and walked into the bathroom. We set up my laptop and turned on iTunes. I had no new music of course, since I was not allowed to connect to the internet.

This place was practically primitive.

We each downed the liquor in the water bottle, and half an hour later we were dizzy and laughing hysterically about I-don't-even-know-what.

"Oh, my God, that's hilarious," said Blake, who was sitting in the empty tub. "So tell me. Did you guys ever...you know...."

I bit my lower lip and took another swig. I nodded.

"No *way,* really? How was he? I know Becca said he had a big—"

We both started laughing again. I noticed that the door to my bedroom was not completely closed, so I crawled over and shut it.

"Yeah, it's definitely, um...fun. He's good. You know. Awesome."

Blake snorted and then knocked the soap into her lap. She put it back, still laughing. The door in my room slammed shut, shaking the door in the bathroom. We ignored it.

"Well, what exactly happened tonight?"

I told her that Max and I had talked and he'd been a dick, and gave me a speech about how it was never going to happen.

"I don't even know where it came from, really. We were talking...she came up...and then all of a sudden he was telling me he couldn't give me what he gave her."

She furrowed her eyebrows. "It's weird. He acts way different around you than he ever did around her. Like...he seeks you out. He wants to talk to *you.* He laughs around *you.* I swear I'm not sure I ever saw him smile before this year."

I shrugged. "Maybe he goes for that whole painful relationship thing. Maybe it's some kind of masochistic thing."

She sneered, and handed me the bottle. "Way less hot than hair-pulling."

We laughed again, and then both squealed when our newly decided favorite song came on.

Blake glanced at her watch. "It's almost eleven, let's start getting ready."

★ ★ ★

Everyone was in good spirits tonight. Including me. Even the dreaded, freezing walk down to the boathouse was okay. Blake and I kept making too much noise and shushing each other and ourselves—so there was little time to worry about the chilly air.

The music inside the boathouse was loud, and everyone was laughing and flirting. Maybe it had always been this way, and I'd just been too self-conscious and worried about everything that I hadn't enjoyed it. Whatever it was about that night, I ended up being bolder than I'd ever been.

"You know what we should do?" I shouted across the beer pong table. "We should— Wait, Blake," I whispered in her ear.

She nodded and then laughed.

"Okay," I continued, "we should play strip beer pong." I smiled and bit my bottom lip.

Our opponents, Cam and Johnny, laughed and said that that sounded like a fantastic idea. Johnny had apologized to me earlier in the night, and in my current mood, it had been no problem. The dragon in my chest just seethed a little flame, and then relaxed, waiting for the right time to really explode.

"So every time we make one, you have to take something off," said Blake.

Johnny smiled. "And vice versa."

"Well, that's just not going to matter, because we're not going to give you a chance."

"Oh-ho!" Cam exclaimed. "It's our shot first." He threw it and made it in the middle cup. The crowd around us, which had grown considerably since Blake's and my announcement, whooped.

Dana, who looked constantly on the verge of exploding

herself, was sitting straight up in a chair against the wall and staring at Johnny.

Whatever.

Johnny missed. I made mine. Blake made hers. We got the balls back. However long later, however, Blake and I were both in our bras. I could kind of see how easy it would be to rope in these people and herd them like cattle. I get too drunk, I act fun and a little slutty—and suddenly their hearts are mine. No one was talking about Becca.

I was about to take my shot when the boathouse door opened. I'd almost known it'd be him.

The music kept pounding, but the chatter died for a few seconds when he came in. I shot the ball and made it. Johnny sighed and took off his shirt. I didn't want to, but I glanced at his body as he did so. It was a good body. So I guess I wanted to.

I averted my eyes, and unfortunately locked eyes with Dana. She stood and walked over to me, pushed Blake out of the way, and then slapped me hard across the face.

My chest burned. The room was silent but for the music.

Max and Johnny were on her like bouncers, each taking an arm. But still no one spoke.

"I think you know what that's for." Her words were icy and sharp.

"I—I…" My cowardice was back.

"You need me to clarify?" She squirmed in the clutches of her restrainers. "How about you stop *fucking* him?"

Everyone was looking at me. Waiting for me to confirm or deny with words or with a reaction. I let my face be blank. I would be strong. I had to be. I wasn't going to slap her back. But I had to do something.

"Stop fucking him?" I took a step toward her, feeling the dragon in my chest open its jaws. "Maybe when I'm dead."

I didn't look anyone in the eyes but her. Hers widened and then narrowed.

I grabbed my shirt and walked out. Blake followed me, and we walked to our rooms in silence.

It was snowing. The small snowflakes were accumulating on the ground, creating a soft, delicate blanket. It was the first time I'd seen snow. It seemed appropriate that I should see it now.

For I had never felt colder.

chapter 19 me

IT WAS CHRISTMAS EVE, AND I'D ALREADY GOTTEN my first present: I could take off my sweatshirt and squint in the sunlight. I was standing at the arrivals loop at Jacksonville International Airport. Any moment now, my dad would be rounding into sight in my mom's robin's-egg-blue convertible, and I could feel like I was at home again. I could try to forget everything that had happened at Manderley, and pretend—like I had to—that everything was great.

My bag was weighing on my shoulder, the guy next to me was blowing cigarette smoke so directly in my face that it felt intentional, and it still was a little too cold to be in only jeans and a tank top, but I didn't care. I didn't notice any of that. All I could do was snap my gum anxiously, until I finally saw the car.

There was Dad, and there was Jasper.

A grin stretched across my face as I pulled open the door. "Hi!" I waved to my dad. "Oh, Jasper!" He jumped on me, his tail wagging so hard it shook the rest of his body.

I threw my bag and Jasper into the backseat and took a deep breath as I put on my seat belt. I was still smiling like a fool.

"Hey, honey," my dad said, giving me a hug and a kiss on the cheek.

"Hi! Oh, my God, I'm so happy to be home."

"How do you like it? You glad you went up there?"

I nodded and considered how I was going to make it seem like I was in any way glad I'd left Florida for New Hampshire. But before I had to decide how to do that, Dad started to drive and then had to slam on the brakes as someone nearly lurched into us.

"Come on!" My dad laid on the horn. "Sorry, honey. Right. Well, I'm glad you like it up there. You wish you'd done all four years there?"

"Nah."

"And you're here for what, a week?"

"I have to go back January second."

"That's all they give ya? Doesn't feel like long enough."

"I know."

I was soon distracted from the conversation as we drove over the familiar bridge and I could feel the crispy, almost wet breeze on my face. I leaned back and closed my eyes. The sun was hot on my eyelids, but the wind whipping around the convertible was cold. I'd never been more comfortable.

My dad turned up the Eagles on the radio, and Jasper panted in the seat behind me, possibly the only one who understood how incredibly refreshing this car ride was.

An hour later I was sitting at the counter eating my mom's steaming hot popovers, smeared with butter and raspberry jelly, and sacrificing little bits to Jasper at my feet.

"So tell me all about it," my mother said as she leaned on the counter across from me, some flour in her hair. She'd been baking all afternoon, which was clear from the dining room filled with every type of Christmas cookie and four loaves of bread.

I shuddered. I couldn't tell my mom anything.

"What do you want to know?"

"Well, I already know they aren't feeding you enough." She looked at my arms and gave them a squeeze. "Look at that, no healthy fat on your little bones. You're too skinny, *mon petite chou!*"

"The food is just kind of…prisonlike. It's not a big deal, I still eat."

"Uh-huh." She moved a piece of hair from her eye, putting more flour in it. "I'll send you care packages. I hadn't thought of it—I'd assumed the food would be five-star!"

Ha. "Not quite."

"Okay, so what about your friends? Do you like any boys? You would tell me if you had a boyfriend, no?"

I felt myself blush, and I wished I hadn't. It wasn't the normal, coy kind of blushing. My face was hot because I was filled with guilt and resentment. Max and I hadn't spoken at all since I said…what I said to Dana…and everyone else within earshot.

"Ooh!" she shrilled. "Tell me!"

"I kind of…there's a guy I'm sort of talking to…"

"What's his name?"

"Max Holloway."

"What's he look like—do you have any pictures?"

I didn't want to show her his Facebook. It was riddled with pictures of Her. That she'd tagged. In *her* albums.

"No, I don't. But he's really, really cute. You'd like him. He's the type of guy you always say are *a-dor-ah-bleh*." I imitated her accent.

"He is dark-haired? Is he tall?"

I smiled. "Yes, he is. Light blue eyes. His hair comes down

about to his eyebrows, and he's got a really straight nose." I was caught in a stare and came to, only to find my mother looking smugly at me.

"You like him a lot. I can tell."

"I mean…it's complicated."

"Why isn't he your boyfriend? He likes you, surely." She looked as though she was ready to turn on him.

"He has a girlfriend."

It was the easiest answer that had any truth to it. I didn't know why, but I didn't want to tell her about Becca. Maybe the reason was that I would never get sympathy from an out-sider for being jealous of a girl who had gone missing. But my mom nodded in understanding and turned around to pull out yet another baking sheet. I slipped another bite to Jasper. A second later, I heard the front door open, and looked up to see my best friend.

"Leah!" I screeched as she walked into the kitchen. I prac-tically leaped on her as if we'd been separated by a century instead of only a few hundred miles.

She squeezed me back. "I'm so happy to see you! Michael came, too, he's outside talking to his mom."

Small drop in my stomach.

"Michael?"

"Yeah…we're back together."

My jaw dropped. "Are you serious?" My smile ebbed a little. "But you texted me like a week ago and said—"

"We're working through it. Plus he's the best kisser ever."

My little sister screamed with delight.

"Oh, sorry," Leah said to my mother, and slapped her hand over her mouth.

"That's fine, that's fine," my mom said, and smiled down at the onion she was chopping.

I loved that we were getting ready for dinner and the sun

still hadn't set. It was really, really good to be home. But something was different. It was still my house, but suddenly I felt like a guest. A welcome guest, for sure, but definitely a guest.

The house was the same, something that thrilled me and simultaneously seemed inexplicably strange. I'd only been gone a few months, but it felt weird that everything had just carried on without me. My house was my memory, something I'd always be able to conjure up, even when I was ancient and couldn't recognize the back of my hand. But when I wasn't there, it still existed. The doors still slapped and thudded open and shut, flies were still smacked on the outside porch, the fridge still emptied and filled, and my bed was never surprised that I didn't come back.

All without my mind and me holding it together.

Michael, who had a mop of curly brown hair and teeth that looked almost *too* straight, walked into my kitchen and greeted my parents, and then smiled at me.

"'Ey, girl!" He wrapped his arms around me and shook me. "I've missed you!"

"Michael!" I feigned excitement. Michael and I had never really gotten along. That's what happens when you make my best friend cry hundreds of times. It really irritated me that she'd brought him to my house on Christmas Eve. But if she hadn't, I felt kind of certain she would have just not come. I always tried to rationalize this trait of hers.

Whatever it was that had changed in me lately had no patience for it.

He put his arm around her, and she held his hand. Leah cooed as he kissed her on the tip of the nose.

Yuck.

"Hey, so you're at Manderley Academy, right?" Michael said, adjusting his attention to me.

"Yeah, it's in—"

"I know where it is," he interrupted in that…way of his. "Didn't some girl go missing from there?"

I felt shaken as my two worlds collided. My mom turned. "Missing? What happened? Did you know her?" She looked at me.

"N–no."

"Yeah, she was hot in those missing photos, too. If she had a boyfriend, I bet he's pissed he didn't hang on to her."

Leah thudded him in the chest. "Mikey, shut up. She's missing, it seems wrong to talk about her like that."

"Hang on to her?" I repeated his words. "She's *missing,* she's not flitting around the world with some other guy."

I couldn't believe I was defending her. But somehow, she felt like mine to think bad things about. Certainly not Michael's.

"Whatever, I'm just saying she's hot. She's been missing since the end of last year. I read it online somewhere. She's probably dead."

"Oh, my God," Leah said, ignoring Michael's more ominous prediction, "that's just so incredibly *General Hospital.*"

"She's got some friend, Diana or something—"

"Dana," I corrected, automatically.

"Yeah, Dana—she was hot, too—said that she didn't know where the girl was but she was sure she was still out there. She's all over interviews online."

I felt light-headed. It was too strange to hear my best friend's annoying douche of a boyfriend talking about Becca and Dana.

"That's so weird. Is everyone freaking out at your school, then?" Leah's eyes were wide.

I nodded. "Yeah, everyone's really worried."

"That's just awful. That poor girl." My mom clucked her

tongue and started moving the cookies from the tray to a cooling rack. "I hope they find her. Her poor friends, they must be so worried! Oh, and if she *did* have a boyfriend…that must be just the worst kind of worry— Oh! The corn bread! I'd nearly forgotten it."

I wanted to press the reset button, and make it so Michael had never come. It would have made things infinitely better for a thousand reasons, but right now his little bit of online stalker info was making me feel nauseous.

"Look!" Lily ran over to me and presented me with the drawing she'd had her nose to for at least ten minutes.

I crouched down to her level, thankful for a change in subject. "What have we got here?"

It was the most tactful way of asking an easily offended child like Lily what on earth she'd been trying to depict with the four free crayons she'd smuggled out of Harry's Restaurant and Pub.

"Jasper," she said, pointing to the thickly drawn figure that took up a third of the page. He looked like a horse. "And that's me." She pointed to a squat little girl with a crown on her head. "That's the house, and that's Mommy and Daddy."

"Where am I?"

She stretched her mouth out to either side and looked guilty. "Um…" She ran into the other room with a red crayon, and came back a moment later with a stick figure drawn in on the backside of the sheet. "You were just here on the other side. Because you're not here anymore."

Ouch.

I smiled, feeling as separated from my old life as the little crayon me, and put an arm around her. "That is an excellent drawing. It should definitely go on the fridge."

I pinned it up with a magnet and all the other drawings.

★ ★ ★

An hour and a half later we had finished eating my mom's best Christmas Eve food (chili, corn bread and—less happily—green beans) and were watching *It's a Wonderful Life*. We watched it every year. Even Lily could be heard whispering some of the lines to herself in her small falsetto voice as she played with toys by the Christmas tree.

The sun had finally set, and there was a slight chill wrapping the blanket around my feet. Jasper was curled up next to me, breathing quietly. Michael and Leah were sitting next to me on the sectional sofa, holding hands and whispering things to each other too often and stifling giggles. My parents were in their respective chairs. My dad was falling asleep, as he almost always did during movies, and my mom was sipping on her warm—and spiked—apple cider.

I thought about Michael and Leah. Just about anyone who didn't know the intricacies of their roller-coaster romance might look at them now and think they were in love. Maybe that's what it had been for Becca and Max. Maybe they weren't as in love as everyone thought they were. Maybe they weren't blissful and bound for a lifetime of happiness. Maybe everyone had been wrong. The thought lifted my heavy heart for a second before it fell again.

Because what if *I* was wrong? Maybe Michael and Leah were what love was. They always came back to each other, no matter how bad they were for one another. They chose to forget the wrongs of before and stay together. It *was* their choice. There must be some reason they got back together and stayed with each other through thick and thin.

Was that love, or were they just emotionally destroying each other? My phone buzzed on the cushion under me. It was a text from Max.

Watching *It's a Wonderful Life*...you said you watch that every Christmas, too, right?

I clicked off my phone's screen, feeling an unexpected urge to cry. It was stupid, and I knew it. But suddenly I felt the weight of realizing that no one had ever felt that way about me. No one had ever not been able to stay away from me. Whether Michael and Leah were true love personified or not, they always came back to each other. And even if Max hadn't loved Becca like everyone said, then it made no difference. Something had kept him magnetized to her. Something, it was to be assumed, other than her beauty and charm.

Michael and Leah whispered things to each other, not meant for anyone else to hear. Suddenly I couldn't help but imagine Max and Becca sitting next to me instead of them.

Jasper jerked in his sleep, bringing me back into the room and its reality. I looked back at the screen. It was the part where Jimmy Stewart is sitting at the bar, and the weight of his entire life seems to fall on his shoulders.

I texted Max back.

Yeah, I'm watching it now. I miss—

I backspaced over the last two words, shaking my head and feeling embarrassed for myself, and pressed Send.

I didn't know what else to say.

Leah giggled next to me at something Michael said. I fixed my eyes on the screen.

It was like nothing could satisfy me. At school all I wanted was to come home, and once I finally got there, my best friend was an entirely different person and seemed barely happy to see me. Meanwhile my family was the same as always, my dog was the same, my sister was a little taller and everything had carried on.

I felt like Jimmy Stewart's character. I had stepped away from my life, too. But unlike him, when I came back it was like it barely mattered that I'd been gone. He comes back to a town taken over by the evil Mr. Potter, and I come back to St. Augustine, a town unchanged. Not that it should have turned into Potterville by the time I came back, but…still.

Instead it felt like Becca had left her life, and *I* was the one to come see what life was like without her in it. It was a lot different than my life without me. Without Becca, her friends talked constantly about her, the school had a picture of her on the wall in the hall, and I, the *new* new girl, couldn't get away from being compared to her. And always unfavorably.

I fought, once again, to forget what Becca—dream Becca or whatever—had said about my friends not caring that I was gone. It was a dream, for God's sake. I couldn't set so much by it.

More unbelievably than anything, I couldn't get my head out of Manderley. I had been sure that when I came home I'd never want to leave again. But instead it just felt like exactly what it was: a week back at my house, before I'd return to my new life. Back to my roommate. Back to my routine. Back to my…well…back to Max.

I watched the movie, before finally falling asleep with my arm around Jasper.

New Year's Eve

"Another glass?" My dad, as flushed in the cheeks as I was, handed me a glass of champagne.

"Sure!" I took it, and had a bubbly sip.

Our house was buzzing. Every year, my parents invited over their oldest friends, Rick and Sarah, with their dalmatian, Pongo, a few of my friends, and my aunt Tammy and her husband, George. This year Lily got to have a friend sleep over, so the two of them were running rampant through the house with Pongo and Jasper. Everyone in charge of them was too tipsy to do anything but make sure they didn't topple down any stairs or anything.

Leah was paying me a little more attention this time, probably since Emma was here. Emma kept smacking her on the arm and holding out a finger to reprimand her every time she and Michael got too intimate. I asked her if this was something that happened often. Emma rolled her eyes and mouthed, *Oh, my God, yes.*

Then we'd laughed, and I was glad to find that I wasn't the only one who thought Leah was being annoying.

I finally felt at home. I felt warmly toward everyone who walked in the door and everything was ten times funnier. I was really at home again, and happy to be there. I'd gotten over everything I'd felt on Christmas Eve.

Just in time to leave.

"Come take a picture!" Leah pulled on my arm. "We've been calling you!"

"Okay, I'm coming!" I laughed.

My mom ushered us over. She was wearing black leggings and a cowl-neck sweater. She had on the pearl earrings my dad had given her for Christmas. Dad had also gotten her a brand-new camera, and she'd been shutter-happy ever since she got it. On Christmas morning, she'd photographed every present being opened, and every reaction—slowing down the process considerably. Though hers when she'd actually *opened* the camera had been the one really worth recording. Up until then, she'd been using a camera that still took double As and made every picture so pixilated it looked like a mosaic.

She'd used her new camera to document almost everything. I even walked past her room and spotted a weary-looking Jasper sitting on the couch in my parents' room with a Santa hat on, and my mother—wielding the camera—saying, "*Assieds-tu!* Stay...sta—*stay,* Jasper!"

"Get together, ladies!" she said now, throwing her head back and standing an unfamiliar-with-newfangled-camera distance away from the screen. "Okay, one, two…"

Jasper jumped up and barked, as if he wanted to be in another picture. The flash caught us reacting down at the dog, and the next picture was of us laughing about it. I couldn't remember the last time I'd felt like this. I was surrounded by people who used my name, who liked me, and who never compared me to Becca Normandy.

"You, too, Barbara," my dad said, taking the camera from her.

"Oh, I can't, I'll look even *older* next to these," she said, gesturing at Emma, Leah and me, "beautiful, *young,* faces!"

"You look gorgeous," Leah said, putting an arm around her and pulling her in for the picture.

My dad smiled. "One, two, three, say *New Year's Eve!*"

"New Year's Eve!" we all said together.

"Me, too!" Lily said, and then stood in front of us, hands on her hips.

It carried on like this for most of the night, everyone taking turns with the new camera. At some point during the evening, Lily and her friend had paraded in Jasper and Pongo. The dogs were wearing some of Lily's princess dresses from her dress-up trunk, panting wildly and obliviously.

A game of charades was attempted, but could not be taken seriously by anyone, and no one seemed to notice or mind. When it came time for the ball to drop, we all counted down from ten together, and had the ceremonial hugs and kisses to celebrate midnight.

Michael and Leah kissed well into the New Year. Emma and I squeezed each other and gave a quick peck before blowing into and rattling our noisemakers.

A few minutes later, I was coming out of the bathroom in the upstairs hallway and I ran into Michael.

"*God,* Michael, don't just lurk around like that. It's creepy."

He shrugged. "How are you doing up at Manderley?"

I straightened up, surprised at what seemed to be a genuine interest in my life. "Um…pretty good. It's hard being new. But I expected that."

"Yeah, but you're probably popular."

I scoffed and wavered a little in my heels. "Oh, yeah? Is that what you see when you see me? Popularity material?"

He looked me up and down and then pushed himself off the wall he'd been leaning on. "You're hot as shit. That usually does it for girls."

It was dark, so I couldn't totally see his face, but he didn't sound like he was kidding.

"Ha," I said anyway, "right, well. Yeah, thanks, Michael."

I started to walk down the hallway, but he grabbed me by the elbow. I tried to shake him off.

"Please don't make this weird, Mike."

He pulled me toward him and kissed me. I pushed him back, pulling my mouth away and finally stomping on his foot with my heel.

"What the hell is your problem?" he asked.

"*My* problem? You're *kidding* me!"

I stormed off, and down the steps. I walked up to Leah. "I need to talk to you."

"Why's your lipstick so smeared?" She looked over my shoulder. I followed her eye line to see Michael limping and pink in the face. Not just from blushing, but from my lipstick.

"I *need* to talk to you," I repeated. But she didn't look like she was going to listen. She was angry and ready to yell.

"Leah, calm down, you don't know—" Emma tried to reach for her, but Leah shrugged out of her grip.

"Please—" I started, but she put a hand in my face.

"Do not," she said, *"talk to me."*

I swatted at her hand. "Are you joking? You *really* think— are you fucking *kidding* me?"

She stormed out of the house, Michael on her heels. I followed them both.

"Leah!" I shouted. "You cannot seriously think what you seem to be thinking."

"I don't know what to expect from you anymore!" She cracked her knuckles like she did when she was nervous. "You know, Michael said you always seemed to want him, but I thought that couldn't possibly be true. Yeah, you always seemed to like him, but I didn't think you'd ever *try* anything. Frankly, I didn't think you'd have the *guts*."

"If by that you mean that I can't even stomach the *thought* of it, then no, I do not have the guts."

"Whatever, it just figures that you'd do it and immediately come to talk to me about it. You are such a *coward*."

I was baffled. I shook my head in disbelief. "What exactly are you criticizing me for? The fact that you think your best friend betrayed you, the fact that I'm too big a wimp to do that or the fact that I'm a little bitch because I'm too honest? Well, throw this on top of everything you're mad about. Your so-called best friend—" I pointed to myself "—thinks your boyfriend is a disgusting, smarmy sleazeball."

"Don't you even—"

"Oh, I'm not done!" My voice rang through the night air. "I think that smarm is contagious, because you've obviously caught it. What kind of a dumb girl *are* you, that you believe your *dick* of a boyfriend before you believe your *best friend*?" I turned to leave, but then added, "And when you *do* realize you're wrong? Do *not* even bother trying to make up with me. We're done."

I didn't know why, but somehow I felt better. I had no place in this world, and in some way that was freeing. It meant I had no allegiance.

chapter 20 becca

IT WAS CHRISTMAS BREAK. BECCA HAD PLAYED sweet with Max for a tortuous two months, and kept him with her. By now she'd really convinced everyone around her that they were madly, incurably in love. Including, hopefully, Max.

Max, though still *with* Becca, was clearly growing less enchanted with her. It didn't seem to matter, however, because his parents wanted to meet her, and had invited her for New Year's weekend. Her own parents were more than willing to let her go, since they wanted to spend even less time with her than did Max.

Assholes.

He'd gotten her a Polaroid camera for Christmas. It was one of the old ones that spit out a square picture with the white frame. He remembered that she had mentioned something about how they were the best cameras and always resulted in the best pictures. He gave it to her early so she could take pictures at the boathouse before Winter Break. She'd gotten him a watch because boys like watches. She'd had the back engraved to say *Max and Becca, for the rest of time.*

Now it was New Year's, and she sat at the dining room table with Max and his parents, who had introduced themselves as Mr. and Mrs. Holloway. He had a six-year-old brother who had eaten earlier, and she hadn't met him yet.

She'd hoped they wouldn't be the Mr. and Mrs. type and more the first-name type who'd joke around and tell her she was so pretty and she could just be charming with them. She could do that. But these parents were like *her* parents. And *her* parents didn't approve of her at all, and seemed not to find her charming.

That was it. She'd be the person she knew her parents wished she had been. All she needed to do was say the opposite of what she really felt.

After a few pleasantries and most of the meal, Mrs. Holloway laid down her fork and asked, "So, Rebecca, what brought you to Manderley?"

"Public school got to be too much, I suppose." She dabbed at her mouth with her napkin. "The people there were just not the type that I like to surround myself with."

Or she didn't like who she had become there. Either or.

Mrs. Holloway nodded. "That is a big problem in public schools these days. That's why we just had to send Maxwell to Manderley."

Becca nodded. "I'm so glad you did." She looked across to Max with a smile. He gave a small smile back.

More silence.

"What do you like to do, Rebecca?" Mr. Holloway asked.

She hated when people asked her this kind of question. She didn't really have any hobbies or anything. "Um...I used to horseback ride when I was little. And now...I don't know, I guess I hang out with my friends?" She shrugged.

Max's parents exchanged a quick glance.

"And your father is Mason Normandy of Normandy and Associates, is he?"

"Yes."

"My brother went to school at Yale with your father. I mentioned that Max was going to have a friend come to visit, and when I said your name, his first question was if you were Mason's daughter."

"Fancy that," she said with a convincing smile. That was *not* fancy, that was awful. She didn't want their parents meeting or talking or anything. Her two worlds could not combine.

"Do you plan on going into law yourself?"

God no. "Maybe, but I'm not sure yet. I'm not tying myself down to any decisions yet."

Mrs. Holloway piped up again. "Do you have any idea what you would like to do?"

Becca took a moment to read Mrs. Holloway. "I'm very interested in volunteering at charity organizations."

She'd never volunteered to do anything unpleasant in her life. Her most concrete plan was to marry rich. And judging by the expanse of this house, Max was a perfect candidate.

"That's very honorable. I'm involved in some myself." Mrs. Holloway sipped her wine. "I find it very fulfilling."

How could anyone find that fulfilling? But who cared, the parents were totally eating up her lies.

"Max, you're awfully quiet," said Becca.

"I'm just letting you all get to know each other."

"He's so polite, don't you think?" She looked from Mr. to Mrs. Holloway. "You're *never* this quiet at school. Especially on the weekends."

Max's gaze lurched to her. She knew things about him she could spill if she wanted to. He knew that.

"The weekends?" Mrs. Holloway looked curiously at her son.

"She means when we all hang out and aren't in class. Have to be quiet in class."

"Oh, that's not all I mean!" She smiled at him. "You can get pretty rowdy at our parties."

"Parties?" asked Mrs. Holloway.

She could see a stab of panic behind his eyes. It's not like he really ever did anything wrong, but if his parents were anything like hers, they wouldn't want to hear about association with anyone that they might consider to be a bad influence. Except, at this point, Becca's parents knew she was the bad influence.

Becca had come to Max's with the intention of solidifying their relationship. Clearly going home with him was a step in the direction of staying together. But suddenly she didn't care anymore.

"I don't get 'rowdy.'"

"Sure you do! Remember that time—oh, that's probably not good table talk."

"Go on." Mr. Holloway looked stern.

"Well, I don't really know too much. I don't drink or do drugs or anything, so I usually leave early."

"Are you implying that Max *does?*" Mr. Holloway asked. His wife was silent, looking wide-eyed at whoever spoke.

Becca waved a hand. "Of course not." She sounded as unconvincing as she could.

Max was staring daggers at her, but she ignored it, and took a bite of her mashed potatoes. "These potatoes are so great."

"Good, I'm glad you enjoyed them. If you'll excuse me." Mrs. Holloway stood and walked out of the room looking a little emotional.

Mr. Holloway followed her without saying a word.

Becca finally locked eyes with Max.

"What's the matter with you?" His voice was low and quiet.

"You had better stay with me or I'll tell them everything."

He shook his head in disbelief. "Go right ahead."

"You have to stay with me. I'll tell Dr. Morgan, the headmaster *and* your parents that I'm concerned about you and your abusive tendencies, your drug use and your drinking. Let's not forget you practically *raped* me."

She raised her voice on the last two words, and he shushed her quickly. She immediately felt guilty.

"Just stop. You're not freaking me out in the way you're hoping to, Becca. I'm okay with losing you, but I don't need you to lie to my parents on the way there."

She threw her napkin on her plate, infuriated by his condescension. "I've been at this school one semester and I've already got everyone under my thumb."

"So?"

The question hung in the air. Becca didn't have an answer. Nothing besides, *because I hoped it would make me happy.*

"Max, come here." Mr. Holloway's voice was low and resonating, and without shouting he managed to be heard startlingly from another room.

Max stood. "You're insane, you know that?"

"Ha!" She crossed her arms in an effort to look stronger than she felt. "That's not what everyone *else* will think!"

He left the room, looking kind of hot all mad like that. A moment later she could just barely hear the muffled conversation he was having with his parents behind a closed door down the hall.

She tiptoed toward the sound, and tried to hear.

"What are you doing?"

Becca jumped, and turned to see the small figure of what must be Max's little brother. *"Shh."*

"Why?"

She spoke through gritted teeth. "Can you just *hush?*"

She tried to listen again, but all she could hear were the low, resonating tones of firm-sounding adult voices.

"Are you eavesdropping?"

"Shh!" She pulled the little boy back into the dining room by his arm.

"Ouch!" he whined, wrenching his arm away. "Stop it!"

Panic rose in her chest. "Quiet! You can't tell them I was listening."

"I'm *going* to!" He started to run from her but she grabbed the back of his shirt.

"Stop, Nick!" That was his name, right?

He was pulling away from her. She thought quickly. The next thing either of them knew, she had tipped a delicate-looking vase off a pedestal by the door, and it shattered into a million little pieces on the hardwood floor.

"Oh, *no,* Nick!" She elevated her voice. In a few seconds, the other Holloways appeared on the scene.

Mrs. Holloway gasped and emitted a tiny whimper.

Mr. Holloway looked to Becca. "What happened?"

"She did it!" Nick pointed desperately at her, tears welling in his eyes.

Becca shook her head with a pitying smile at Nick. "No, we had just met and Nick said he wanted to play. The next minute, he had run into the vase."

"She pulled on my arm!"

"I *tried* to stop him in time, but I just couldn't!" This time Max was looking directly at her, but she refused to look back. "I'm *so* sorry, Mr. and Mrs. Holloway."

She hung her head, fake worry etched in every feature of her face.

"It's all right. Nick, go straight to your room and stay there. You're not having Michael over tomorrow night."

"But, *Dad—*"

"Your mother bought that vase in Germany when she was a teenager. You've been told before to be careful, and you continue to roughhouse. There is no excuse. Upstairs. *Now.*"

"I should have kept a better eye." Becca looked earnestly at Mr. Holloway.

He put a hand up. "Rebecca, you don't need to apologize again."

"Okay." She nodded.

"We're going outside," said Max, taking Becca by the waist. He led her to the backyard.

"It's freezing, what are we doing out here?" She was wearing a skimpy black dress.

"I'm done with you. And I'd like to have this conversation away from my family. You've already treated them to enough of my personal life tonight."

"I know. I just don't know how to keep you, Max!"

"Did you think blackmailing me was really going to do that?"

"It's not! I realize that. It's just that I feel you slipping away...you're only with me because you feel guilty."

He raised his eyebrows. "I have not been with you for that reason. And I don't intend to. So just stop."

"Then why, Max?" Tears were in her eyes. "Why would you be with me?"

"I'm not doing this with you." He paused. "When's your flight?"

She stared back at him, her eyes wide and her heart pounding. She'd gone too far. She was going to lose him now. She considered standing here and fighting, but she didn't want to. Not only would it end in more humiliation, but if they didn't get back together, she'd be...free. To be with whomever she wanted....

"I'll change it to tomorrow morning."

He sighed. "I'm sorry, Becca."

"No. You're not."

She went inside, stormed up to the guest room, and stayed there for the rest of New Year's Eve.

Facebook relationship status: Single. Status update: I'm sorry it had to end. But it did.

Pfft.

Five days later, back at Manderley

"It's just really difficult right now," Becca said, hiccupping through tears she was lucky to conjure.

Dana nodded sympathetically from her bed. "I'm sure it is."

"I didn't *want* to have to end things with Max. But I just… we were way too serious for our age. You know, like, if we'd met—" she sniffed "—when we're like twenty-something? Things would be totally different."

She looked mournfully down at a Polaroid of the two of them taken right before Christmas. He stood behind her with his arms around her shoulders. She was laughing and looking off to her left. She remembered that she'd been laughing at something Johnny said.

She looked at Max's beautiful face and her own. She was not attractive when she smiled for real. She never had thought so.

Becca did not return it to the bulletin board with all the rest of her pictures. She threw it into the suitcase under her bed with all of the other things she didn't want to think about.

"I don't know what I'd do without you, Dana. You're the only one who really seems to care."

"That's not true, everyone cares."

"But not as much as you do."

★ ★ ★

Tonight was the night. She was going to do what she could to start getting Johnny *for real*.

She had done her best to look good, which wasn't as effective as she would have liked. She had ignored Max so far, even though she had felt his gaze on her more than once.

"Hey, Becks!" Johnny shouted to her from across the boathouse.

Her heart skipped when she saw him smile at her.

"What?" She sipped through her straw and looked at him through the crowd of girls surrounding her. They always flocked to her. She loved it.

"Wanna be my partner?"

He was standing by the beer pong table she'd thought to throw together on her first night at Manderley, constructed out of wood and cinder blocks.

She shrugged. *"Fine."*

Becca walked over to Johnny and the table, glancing at Max. He was talking to Cameron, and Blake was staring right at her. Becca narrowed her eyes. Blake smiled back.

Bitch. If it wasn't for Becca, she might not have Cam. How dare she be so obnoxious.

The other team took the first shot. One miss. Two misses. Becca could still feel Blake's eyes on her.

"Ladies first." Johnny handed her a ball.

She tossed it at the triangle of red Solo cups. It bounced off a rim and into the water. She'd played enough that she should be good.

Out of the corner of her eye, she saw Blake shake her head and interrupt Cam and Max's conversation. Becca wished she could hear it.

Johnny took his shot, and made it, too. "Ha! That's both, we go again."

Blake finished what she was telling Max, and he looked at her.

"It's your shot, babe."

Becca took the ball. Max walked toward her.

"Let me talk to you for a second," he said, walking right past Becca, and out the door.

She rolled her eyes. "Here—um, Susan, come play for me." The next second, she was out the door.

Max jumped in, without preamble. "Do you have a thing with Johnny?"

She stood, feeling shocked. No words came to her.

"Just fucking tell me, Becca. I do not have any patience right now for this."

"Wow, you are so untrusting it's unbelievable."

"If you are? If you've been hooking up with my best friend all along, I just need to know."

She smiled. "Let me guess, Blake told you that?"

His expression told her she was right.

"Okay, well, you know what? That's because Cam has been coming on to me since day *one*." She held up a finger.

"Oh, shut *up,* that's not true."

"I don't care if you believe me. It's just the explanation. If you *want* to feel like your best friend and I have been lying to you, then fine. Makes no difference to me."

And she went back inside. Max never followed. She marched up to Dana. She wanted to be around someone she knew liked her.

An hour later, Becca was buckled over with her hand on her knees. She could see her breath in the air. "*That* was so… *funny!*"

Dana was laughing, too. "Not *that* funny, just…" She fell into giggles.

They walked down to the dock. "If you fall," said Becca, "I'm going to freak out. I can't swim, and so I can't save you."

Dana waved her hand. "I'll be fine." But then she stumbled, almost doing exactly what they were afraid of. Becca caught her by the shoulder.

"Oh, my *God,* see? You almost *died!*"

They got to the end, still laughing, and sat to dangle their feet over the edge.

"I'm…so drunk." Dana took a swig of Coke.

"I'm not drunk enough," Becca responded with a sip of her bottle, which was filled with rum. "I can tell because I'm cold."

They laughed, and then fell silent.

"So," said Becca, "tell me a secret." She loved saying this to people. They almost always had something to tell her.

Dana squinted out into the darkness, her face lit only by the safety lights at the end of the dock. She sighed and closed her eyes. "I'm in love with Johnny Parker."

Becca froze, her smile falling, and then took a burning gulp of the rum. "Really."

Dana nodded, swaying a little in her drunken dizziness. "He's…strong and…I don't know, I guess I feel safe around him." She laughed and looked down at her knees. "It's probably stupid."

"N-no, it's not." It wasn't stupid at all. Becca had thought the same thing.

"I haven't really ever…liked a guy like I like him. I've… It's been since I got here. Ninth grade. That's when I first had a crush on him." She looked to Becca. "And you know, I don't think I ever would have really talked to him if it wasn't for you. You kept throwing us together. It wasn't on purpose?"

"No."

She nodded. "I thought it was just psychic of—" she hiccupped "—of you."

"Nope. Luck."

"I couldn't even believe he knew my name or anything. But he did." She shook her head, and furrowed her brows at a spot off in the distance. "Can I trust you, Becca?"

She'd been asked that before. She couldn't say for sure that she was trustworthy. She'd only ever been out for herself. Even when that messed up everything.

But she wanted to be better than that. She had to be. If she wasn't, if she didn't try to change in some way, then what was the point in running away and coming here at all?

Woo, thought Becca, *this rum is working now.*

"Of course you can trust me."

Dana took a few deep breaths and then took the bottle from Becca's hands. She took another swig and then said, "I've never told anyone this."

"Okay."

"I… When I was in eighth grade, something happened. It's why—it's why I'm here at all. I didn't tell my parents the extent of it. Just said I didn't want to be in my town anymore. They'd always wanted me to come here anyway, so they didn't have a problem with it." She took another deep breath. "I was actually very popular back at home. I was the girl with the squad of girlfriends and boys being all about me. Yeah, we were all like thirteen, but whatever. I was voted *Most Likely to be Prom Queen.*"

Becca listened intently. "Wow, that's…"

"Yeah, so…I was popular or whatever. I was happy."

"I'm trying to figure out how this has a bad ending." Becca laughed, even though she knew it was headed somewhere not funny at all.

"I was at my friend Hannah's for a sleepover one night. She

was asleep. We'd hung out with her parents and their family friend, Tom, who was like…I don't know, late twenties maybe. It was one of the first times I ever got drunk." She held up the bottle. "And I had a little too much. Everyone was drinking, and everyone was having fun before bed. It was a good night. I got pretty dizzy and then fell asleep. Um. When I woke up, I was in the guest bedroom, which was barely lit, and Tom was on…top of me. It took me a few seconds to realize what was happening, but…then I realized I was naked. I tried to push him off, but he wouldn't stop. Then he put it in, or whatever. And it was… I don't know that anything has ever hurt so badly."

Becca's heart was pounding. She was in shock.

Dana continued. "Finally he was done, and all I could do was go back into Hannah's room and try to sleep. I woke up the next morning and he was in bed with us, with his hand on my leg." She shook her head and chewed the inside of her lip. "The insult on top of injury was that Hannah had been all casual like, *'Did you guys hook up?'*"

"Jesus."

"Yeah. So then she told everyone I'd had sex with this older guy, and I couldn't bring myself to tell anyone the truth. I felt embarrassed or something. Which is so stupid, because it wasn't my fault. But I just couldn't. And then time passed and there wouldn't be any way to prove it anyway. So I just gave up."

Becca's breath was caught in her throat.

"I'm so sorry." It came out as a whisper.

Becca didn't even know if it was just Dana she was talking to. She was imagining that girl…the small girl with red hair. Lulu. Becca couldn't even pretend to herself that she didn't remember her name. It had been her fault.

It was Becca's first year at McDaniel High School—tenth

grade. Her middle school had been seventh through ninth grades. And for her, her tenth-grade year was the year she became pretty. For the longest time, it seemed to her then, she had been too skinny with big hands and feet. She'd been pale and had straight light hair. Her skin had been clean, but her braces had made that irrelevant. Her chest had been as flat as her butt and her stomach. But now she had a clean slate, where she only knew some of the people around her, and she was completely different. Her mom finally let her get contacts. Her braces came off. Her boobs started to grow in—enough to wear a padded bra, anyway. She was suddenly tall, thin, blonde and pretty.

She was suddenly Becca Normandy. Not Rebecca, anymore. Becca.

It was right after the Homecoming football game, which was a week before the Homecoming dance. She didn't have a date, but she'd certainly become more popular lately. She'd gotten her friend, Lulu, to come along to the game, even though she didn't want to.

"Oh, come *on,*" Becca had said, "it'll be fun! I bet you'll even get a date! What if we both do?"

So Lulu had come. By the end of the game, they'd been chatted up by some of the Most Sought After senior boys. They invited the two girls to a party at the quarterback's house. Everyone knew Jake Lanter hadn't found his date yet. He'd just dumped his cheerleader girlfriend.

Becca begged Lulu to go with her. "*Please!* They invited us both, there's no way this isn't, like, our beginning of popularity."

Lulu finally gave in, reluctantly lying to her mother and saying she was staying at Becca's for the night. Becca called her mother and told her she'd be at Lulu's. Classic.

It was almost two in the morning, and Becca was on her

fifth Smirnoff Ice. It was enough to make her loopy—she'd never had anything much before. Just sips of her parents' merlot when they weren't looking. And that had been just…awful. Nothing like these bottles full of sugar.

Jake, the god of Hotness, Popularity and the ticket to Becca's happiness, walked over to her. He was probably about five inches taller than her, and very intimidating. He smiled, his eyes narrowed.

"You're so hot," he said, then biting his lip. "How come I've never heard of you?"

She shrugged. "I don't know."

She knew why, of course. It was because she hadn't been "so hot" until recently. The braces coming off had really tipped her into the attractive zone.

"You know, my friend Eric has a crush on your friend Lulu."

She looked at the guy he indicated. He was talking to a nervous-looking Lulu. She couldn't help but think smugly that Jake was hotter.

"Does he really?" she asked. "She probably likes him, too."

Lulu would have killed her for saying it. But Becca had said it before she could stop herself.

He looked over at the pair. "Thing is, she looks a little nervous. Don't you think she looks nervous?"

She nodded. "She probably is." She hoped *she* didn't sound nervous.

"So here's what we're gonna do. Slip this into her drink." He handed her a small Ziploc bag with a tiny bit of white powder in it.

She shook her head, but he smiled.

"Baby," he said, putting his hand on her cheek. "It's nothing bad, come on. You can trust me. Hey, I mean, I'd offer you some, but you don't look nervous at all. You're cool. You probably know *just* what to do. Don't you?"

Jake kissed her on the neck and pulled her close. Her heart pounded, not only with the thrill of being pursued by the quarterback, but with the unhappy thought that she *didn't* know just what to do.

"I can't...she's my friend, I don't want to give her anything without telling—"

He rolled his eyes, and she cowered under his growing agitation. He looked at her. "Okay, listen. It's called Delastor. It's just gonna stop her from thinking too much. Does your friend worry a lot?"

Yes. That was Lulu. It had only been with Becca's begging that they ended up here at all. And look at them—two football players were talking to them. It was a good thing Becca had done the thinking for Lulu. Maybe this was just one more time she needed that.

"I'll do it."

"Good," said Jake. "Do that, and then find me. We'll have fun."

She nodded and smiled. "Okay."

He walked away, and she grabbed another Smirnoff Ice. Watermelon—that was Lulu's favorite flavor. She had pajamas with watermelons all over them.

With shaking hands, Becca poured in the white powder. It was just going to make her relax. That was all it'd do. What's the worst that could happen? She fell asleep?

To Becca, who was fourteen and had seen little of the world, this seemed completely reasonable.

She handed the drink to Lulu. "Here," she said, giving a small smile to Eric. "Drink this. We should cheers to...our first Homecoming game."

Lulu didn't argue. She didn't have any reason to mistrust

Becca. She drank hers and waited for Lulu to finish—Becca got a small flip in her stomach when she imagined telling Jake that not only had she done it, but she'd made sure Lulu drank the whole thing.

When she told him, he smiled and pulled her outside and onto the trampoline. Almost everyone was asleep or hooking up. After some preamble that Becca had now blocked out, she and Jake were making out hard core. She wanted to enjoy it. She *did* enjoy the fact that it was *Jake* doing it. But he was rough, and never gentle. His tongue stabbed into her mouth harshly and without consideration of what she was doing. He pulled her hair a little too hard, but she was too afraid to say anything.

It was only with the strength she had in the core of herself that she was able to tell him that she wouldn't have sex with him. He did exactly what she'd feared when he tossed her aside muttering that she wasn't worth all that.

She sat there for a little while, feeling sorry for herself and hoping he'd come apologize. She tried hard not to cry from the embarrassment, and failed. Finally she wiped off her tears, and went inside to find Lulu. She'd pay for a damn cab. All she wanted was to go home and watch something with a happy ending. She remembered that her dad had just bought her Thin Mints.

She pulled open the sliding door. She walked past a couple grinding on the sofa, illuminated by the blue light of the TV screen. She opened a bedroom door and found people smoking weed. She opened another and found a bunch of sleeping bodies—none of them Lulu's. She went upstairs and hesitated. The only room up there had noise coming from it. Banging. She didn't want to open the door. But after looking everywhere else in the house, she knew Lulu was either gone or in that room. She opened the door and saw Lulu's naked, limp body. Her red-haired head was repeatedly hitting the headboard as Eric, the narrow-hipped boy with pimples on his back, thrust against her again and again.

The bag of white powder came into her mind.

"Eric! *Eric,* stop! What are you doing?"

He ignored her, and kept moving. She watched the scene with horror, even stepping forward and trying to pull on his arm. He shook her off and kept going. She said Lulu's name, but she only responded with the slightest opening of her eyes.

Becca didn't know what to do. Wait? Leave? No, those were wrong and unthinkable. Call the police? No. She was drunk. Everyone was. Everyone would hate her. She couldn't be the girl who got everyone in trouble.

And what about...what about the fact that she'd been the one to give the drug? Whatever it had been—she'd heard of the date rape drug—had that been it? But Jake had said some weird name...she'd never heard it before.

"What are you standing there for, sweetie? You wanna join? I'd rather fuck you than her anyway."

Eric's words stung. Not only was he raping—God, was that what she was watching?—her friend Lulu, but he was insulting her.

Becca shrank onto the floor and covered her eyes. She tried to block out the sounds—the quiet, sinister sounds—and waited for the last pound and the groan from Eric. She heard him get off the squeaking mattress, exhale loudly and pull his pants on. She heard the jingle of his belt buckle, and then he walked past her and shut the door.

Then there was silence in the room.

She carried Lulu out to the curb, which took all of her strength—even with how light Lulu was—where they waited for a very expensive cab. She found the spare key under a flowerpot on Lulu's front step, and took her up to her room.

By that point, Lulu was awake enough to walk some. When Becca left Lulu's room, Lulu was whimpering softly. She was in pain.

Becca walked the next mile to her own bed, where she lay awake for the rest of the night.

The truth came out. Eric got in trouble. Everyone but Lulu insisted that they'd seen Becca slip something in her drink. She got away unscathed by the law, but she was a social outcast. And she knew she deserved it.

"Becca?" Dana put a hand on her shoulder.

Becca looked into her narrow, dark eyes, and shuddered. "I'm so sorry that happened to you."

She could tell Dana didn't quite want to say it was okay, but wanted to seem undramatic.

"Come on," said Becca, standing up. "Let's go up to our room. I've got a movie with a happy ending we can watch on my computer."

chapter 21 me

I KNEW SOMETHING WAS DIFFERENT THE SECOND I stepped off the bus at Manderley. Everyone was talking very importantly to each other, and I was getting a lot of looks. More than ever. At the end of a break it makes sense for there to be an excited, catching-up buzz about the school.

This wasn't that.

It got weirder when I walked through the doors and saw a line that ended in Dana, Madison and Julia sitting at a table. Madison had a cash box, Julia was taking money, and Dana was handing out T-shirts. They were pink with black writing and had a picture on them I couldn't make out from where I was standing.

I dropped my phone off at the office and walked over to the line. All of them watched me as I approached.

"I'm not butting or anything," I explained, a bit uselessly, to some of the waiting students as I walked past.

I looked at one of the shirts Dana handed to a girl. The picture was of Becca, I could see now, and I read the words.

FIND BECCA

Dana had boxes of the shirts behind her. "Do you want one?"

It took me a moment to realize she was talking to me.

"You can even have one for free," she offered, not sounding generous at all.

I shook my head and looked around to see that I was being swallowed by a sea of pink. Everyone around me was either wearing or holding a pink shirt. I walked quickly from the table and toward the stairs. I stopped when I saw Max. He was holding a shirt and looking a little dazed.

"Max."

He tried to smile, but barely pulled it off. His jaw was clenched tightly again. "Come here."

He pulled me in for a hug. I didn't stop him, even in light of how uncertain everything was with him. He put his cheek to my hair and didn't let go for a few seconds.

"What's going on?" I asked. I never wanted to let go of him, but something had clearly happened.

"You didn't hear, then?"

I shook my head. My heart was beating fast. "No, hear what? What's happening?"

He hesitated. "They think...Becca's alive." He looked hopeful and regretful all at once.

"Why? Who thinks so?"

"Her Facebook...she had a status update, and it said she was alive. And...it was right after there was a sighting of someone who looked like her."

"What?" I was breathless suddenly. Everything was going to change. Would they kick me out? Would she come back? "Where? What did it say?"

"They saw her here in town somewhere. The status just confirmed that it was her...I don't know."

Blake and Cam approached us a moment later, neither of them holding pink shirts.

"Can you believe this?" Blake asked, looking only at Max.

"No."

"I don't even know what to think. I guess we'll hear more at the assembly. They're holding it tonight instead of tomorrow." She looked at me. "How are you?"

"I'm fine." My voice was much higher than usual. "What time's the assembly?"

"Eight-thirty. Come in uniform." Cam winked at me, apparently remembering my first assembly.

I smiled weakly. "I should go get situated. That's only an hour from now."

I needed to breathe, and to stop feeling that a seventeen-year-old missing girl being alive and well was a bad thing.

"Okay," Max said, "meet me outside of the auditorium at eight twenty-five."

I hated myself for getting excited by his willingness to meet me in public and that he wasn't ignoring me. Maybe I was being Dumb Girl. But I couldn't care.

Max paused and looked at me, like we'd never see each other again.

"What's wrong?"

"Nothing. I'm just... Never mind, I'll see you in a few minutes."

As soon as I walked away, I heard Blake start talking quickly and quietly to the other two.

I arrived at my room only to find that the few pictures I'd pinned to my bulletin board last semester had been taken down and put on my bed. So had the thumbtacks. All but the four tacks that held up an eleven-by-seventeen poster pinned in their place. It was a poster printed with the same picture and bold words as were on the T-shirt I still clutched absent-mindedly. I threw it on the floor and took down the poster.

I gathered the thumbtacks Dana had intentionally scattered evenly all over my comforter and put them back up with the pictures. Including some of the new ones from the break. My mom had pulled into the driveway just before I left with my dad and Jasper, yelling for us to wait, and then handed me an envelope of pictures she'd just gotten printed for me.

I pinned up some of those, mostly the ones from New Year's Eve—before it had gone sour—and tried to stop my throat from tightening with the desire to jump right back on a plane. I'd made the decision to come back. I had no choice.

I unpacked my bag, my heart still pounding. I felt guilty for every selfish thought that crossed through my mind as I imagined what it would mean for me if Becca came back. It was good that she might not be dead. Good.

I jumped when a little while later there was a knock on the door. I was expecting Becca at every turn now.

"Come in."

Madison and Julia floated in, both wearing expressions of great sympathy.

"This must be hard for you." Madison sat down on Dana's bed, moving the poster carefully out of the way.

"Why do you think that?"

Julia looked to Madison and then to me. "Becca coming back? You like Max…right?"

"No."

"Sweetie, I'm sorry but…" Madison ignored me, and laid a hand on her chest, over her heart. "I'm your friend. *We* are your friends. But we know Max. We know Becca. And… we just don't want you to have your heart broken by surprise when Max goes back to her."

"And chances are…" Julia trailed off.

"Maybe he won't." I tried to sound more confident than I felt. "And we're not even, like, together, so if he wants to be with someone that's not... I mean he's allowed to do whatever he wants."

She shrugged. "Look, we're just trying to look out for you. If you don't want our help then just say so."

I didn't know what to say. But I figured the only way to get them to stop feeling sorry for me was to agree.

I nodded. "You're probably right. I'll try not to get too close."

"*Good*. Because he *really* loves her," Madison said, smiling sadly at me.

Okay, *got it*.

"You guys going down to the assembly now? It's soon, isn't it? I'm meeting Max—" I paused as Julia raised her eyebrows. "I'm meeting Max out front of the auditorium."

"We'll walk down with you, sure! Don't forget your uniform." Madison couldn't quite pull it off like Cam without sounding a little mean.

I grabbed my Manderley polo and khaki skirt from the closet, and they stepped outside. To talk about me, I was sure, rather than out of some sense of my privacy.

I was out in a few seconds, and we walked down the stairs silently. I felt relieved when I saw Max.

He nodded a hello to the other girls, and then looked to me. I stepped toward him. He shook his head slightly, looking around, and held open the door for us instead of taking it. I was sure Madison and Julia were exchanging yet another look behind my back.

We walked into the dim auditorium. No one was talking, but everyone watched as we found a place to sit. Soon after we did, the house lights dimmed down to nothing, and Professor Crawley took the podium.

"Welcome back, students. I hope everyone had a good Winter Break. Classes will start up tomorrow as usual, at 8:00 a.m. I want to ask you all to remind yourselves of the rules, and to make sure you ready yourself for school and to shake off the holiday mentality." He cleared his throat, and carried on with a reminder of what those rules were. I checked off the ones in my head that I'd broken.

Most of them.

The room was filled with the anticipation of what *exactly* had happened concerning Becca. But we had to wait a full forty-five minutes before all of the administration had spoken and Crawley had taken the microphone again. The room stiffened and went silent.

"There's been a…progression with the Rebecca Normandy case. I'm sure most of you already know, at least those of you who knew her, but for those of you who do not, Dana Veers is here—once again—to explain. Miss Veers?"

She took the stage, looking even slighter than ever, squinting in the stage lights. "Hi. I think a lot of you bought the T-shirts we've been selling outside, and I was glad to find that many of you took our suggestion to buy more than one and to send them to your friends and family members. We want to increase awareness everywhere we can, and the more people who wear her picture the better. Becca Normandy is *alive,* everyone."

Cheers immediately broke out. Max was still and silent, as was I. Professor Crawley made a movement toward Dana, but then allowed her to go on when she gave him a scathing look.

"Make it quick," he said, his voice carrying just enough to get to the microphone.

"As some of you know, Becca updated her Facebook with the following—*I am alive, and I will be back to Manderley soon.*

Love you, Max." I felt him stiffen next to me. She went on. "I don't know when she'll be back, but obviously she will be. Because of this update, her parents have funded advertising in newspapers and magazines nationwide. She has become an icon in news stories practically overnight, and I'm sure it'll be no time until she's back. So what I'm saying is, tell your friends and family to keep an eye out for her. All of the money from the T-shirts is going to the cause."

She stepped down, to applause. Professor Crawley took the podium over again. "Actually, in line with that, there is no way to know if this posting was really by Becca or not. The police are searching, but please, I implore you not to get your hopes—"

But Professor Crawley could hardly be heard. Everyone in the auditorium was talking noisily.

It stayed like that through dinner. I sat at a table with Cam, Blake, Max and some others I barely knew. Most of them were talking about Becca. I was poking at my spaghetti and meatballs, and Max was staring at his meat loaf.

I tried to formulate a million different questions and things to say before landing on, "What do you think?"

We couldn't be heard over everyone else.

He shrugged. "I don't know."

"Where would she have *been* all this time?"

"I don't know."

I waited for him to say something else. When he didn't, I took a deep breath. "Max, you must be able to guess. You have *no* idea if this is something she might do?"

He raised his eyebrows. "It's definitely something she would do."

"It is?" My heart fell a little. Then guilt squeezed it.

"Yes."

"Why?"

He shrugged. "Attention probably. Or something else. I don't know."

I took a small bite of my spaghetti. A moment later, I got up the nerve to ask him what I had been thinking. "Max, do you think she might have been pregnant?"

He froze. "I don't know."

"Really?"

"No. I have no idea." His tone had sharpened.

I stared at him for a moment. "I'm not very hungry. And I'm tired. The plane, you know." I waved my hand, as if to say, *Oh, planes, they put me right to sleep.* "I'll see you tomorrow."

He said nothing, and let me walk away. I said good-night to everyone else. Blake gave me a kind smile and waved.

I ran into Johnny on the steps.

"Hey," he said.

"Johnny." I breezed past him, not stopping until I got to the rotunda. I slumped down in one of the seats with itchy fabric.

"What's wrong?" Johnny had followed me.

I shook my head. "Do *you* think Becca might come back?"

"It's something she'd do."

"Well, that doesn't sound like the trait of a very lovable person, does it?" The question flew from my lips before I could stop it. "I mean...I mean..."

Johnny sat down across from me. "She wasn't all simple charm. She had more to her. Yeah, this is something she'd do, but...I don't know." He looked thoughtfully down at his own fingers. "If she did, there's more to it than just attention. I'm sure of that."

"I asked Max if he thought she was pregnant."

He looked stony. "Yeah, I've wondered that, too. Most everyone has."

We were silent for a moment. "Was he…really that in love with her?"

"I don't know what it was. It was something…different."

My heart sank. "Okay."

"He just couldn't tear himself away from her. I don't know why. But I mean, he wasn't the only one."

"What do you mean?"

"I just mean that…everyone was fascinated by her. She looked like a movie star, but partied like a rock star. I don't know. She was just endearing in that way."

I bit my lip and stared down at the floor. I'd never felt more drab in my life. I was like the gray, rainy skies outside, only less threatening and full of no mystery at all. Before coming to Manderley, I'd always thought I was worth knowing—certainly not worth admiring or obsessing over like Becca clearly was—but now I just felt like a mess. I bet Becca never had a hole in her socks, or a bad face day. I bet she never had puffy eyes in the morning or got hungover. She probably looked good in glasses—not that she'd have to wear them because she'd surely have perfect vision—and still look gorgeous without makeup. Probably had sexy, messy, bed hair instead of just ratty, messy hair.

She was the kind of beautiful we've all been comforted into thinking was just airbrushing in magazines. I was the "real" girl they always show before the airbrushing with a caption like, "But *here's* what the average real girl looks like! Can you even *believe* it? She was walking around like that!"

"I can't compete with that." My face was getting hot. "Everyone looks at me like they think that *I* think that I'm as good as her, and I'm not even *saying* that I am. And yet, why should it be just *so* obvious that I'm not?"

I couldn't figure out what exactly was driving my jealousy.

I didn't want to be fawned over and obsessed over. But I envied that she was.

"Look. Look at me." He waited for me to look at him. "Call Becca the most beautiful and charming girl in the world, and it has nothing to do with who you are. You hardly pale in comparison. Everyone here, they're just shallow. Becca wasn't a bad person on the inside, but no one here got to know her, either. They all liked her because she was unique. She was a new toy they never really got to play with. And now that she's gone, they just want her more than ever."

I looked up at him, not noticing my eyes were filled with tears until some fell from my eyelashes. It was nice of him trying to console me. But I knew what he was saying was just that. Consoling.

Johnny smiled a little, furrowing his eyebrows. "Don't. You have no reason to cry. You're bigger than this whole school and everything anyone might think about you inside of it."

"I never worry about this kind of thing. I've *never* been this person."

"You're still not, you're just being massacred by a popular girl's posse. It makes sense."

I took a deep breath and laughed. "Thank you."

Johnny looked over my shoulder and I turned to see Max.

"Are you fucking joking?" Max asked, looking at Johnny.

"Max, *stop* before your imagination goes crazy. I wasn't—" Johnny began.

Max clenched his jaw, and stared straight at Johnny. "I'm not going through this whole thing again, especially not with her." He threw a finger at me.

Johnny shook his head. "Max you gotta—"

"Fuck it, do what you want." He walked through the dorm door, and was gone.

Johnny and I both sat silently for a moment in the now very still air.

I didn't know what had just happened. I wanted to cry all over again.

He put a hand on my shoulder when he saw the expression on my face. "It's okay, you haven't done anything."

"I have to go to sleep. Thank you so much, Johnny."

I stood and went back to my room. I got under my covers and tried to sleep. Before I knew it, hours had passed and I was still not asleep. Finally my desire to talk to Max outweighed my desire to try sleeping.

I ran to the boys' dorm and then through it. I knew his room number. It had been a small, embarrassing fantasy of mine to sneak into his room for months.

He opened it after a few seconds. He was in shorts and no shirt. I collected myself and then said, "What's wrong with you? Why were you so mad earlier?"

"I'm sorry about that. I shouldn't have acted like that."

"But why *did* you? I was just talking to him."

He nodded. "Yeah. So was Becca."

"What do you—what?"

He opened the door he stood in front of. "Come with me.

"Becca and Johnny were hooking up for…I guess most of my relationship with her."

I practically did a double take. *"What? Johnny?"*

"Yeah. So that's why he and I aren't friends anymore."

"Weren't you two friends for a long time? I can't believe he would just do that to you."

"He wouldn't usually. It was just Becca. Just how she was."

I nodded. I was barely even aware of how cold it was outside.

"So when I saw you two," he went on, "it just felt like déjà vu."

"Well, I'm not... I don't have any interest in Johnny at all. I hardly even know him."

"You don't have to say that. We're not together."

He may as well have slapped me. "I know." My words were hard and restrained.

He took a deep breath. "I'm sorry about that. I really am."

"I never said—"

"No, I know you didn't. I'm sorry. I'm just..." He looked at me. "I like you. And I want to be with you. But I just can't."

"Max, I never said *I* wanted that. What makes you think you're the one deciding you and I aren't more than we are?"

He looked surprised, and that only made me madder.

"Seriously," I went on, my voice rising a little. "When do you imagine I said anything about feelings for you?"

His face fell a little but I had to ignore it. I opened the door and said, "I'm going."

A couple of guys were coming down the hallway. I felt my cheeks go red, and I closed the door behind me. They stayed silent, but I heard them start to laugh once I was past them. I flew out of the boys' dorm door, and heard a lot of noise coming from the hall below. I leaned over the balcony.

"Miss *Tobias!*"

Professor Crawley, in khakis and a Harvard sweatshirt, was standing and breathing hard at the bottom of the stairs. Susan turned around when he called her name. "Stop running, I've already seen you—*all* of you—so just stop running."

Susan Tobias was trembling and white as a sheet. "P-please, Mr. Crawley, I—I... My p-parents will kill me!"

"Come with me, and we might be able to work something out." He ushered her with his hand. "There are only, what, five hundred students at this school? I know who you all are."

He looked up and caught eyes with me. He crooked his finger to beckon me downstairs.

"We might have been out of bed after curfew, but she just snuck out of the boys' dorms!" Susan was saying as I descended the stairs.

My heart was pounding. I hated getting caught doing anything. It always mortified me.

"You come with me, too," he said, once I was next to them.

He led us through two heavy wooden doors and down a hallway. He switched on the lights and opened his office door with a key. "Sit."

He indicated the seats across from his own, where he sat.

"I'm sorry, I—"

Professor Crawley cut me off. "I'll talk to you in a second." He turned toward Susan. "Miss Tobias. You've had a lot of detentions lately, haven't you?" He turned on his computer and typed her name into a search box. "Yes, you have. Six in the past three months. I'm not going to ask you what's going on. I just need you to stop messing up. You're going to interfere with your own chances of getting into Northwestern. Also, I hate being dragged out of bed."

"Yes, Professor Crawley. I'm sorry."

"Don't apologize to me, apologize to your future if you screw it up."

"Yes, Professor Crawley."

He gave a nod. "Go on to bed now."

"Thank you, Professor Crawley," she said quietly, before walking out the door and leaving us alone.

"So what happened with you? The boys' dorms, really? *This* surprises me."

"I wasn't doing anything—I just had to talk to Max. Holloway. Max Holloway. I had to talk to him about something."

"Couldn't wait until the morning?"

I shook my head. My eyes suddenly started to burn, and I surprised myself by getting the urge to cry.

"What's goin' on?"

I shook my head and fought back the tears. "I don't even know. I'm just so frustrated. I feel like all he thinks about is *Her,* and everyone's always talking about it—Becca this, and Becca that—and I'm just *not* trying to be her—I don't want what she had. Well, I mean, I do, I want *him* but that's just a coincidence, it wasn't on purpose. And everyone thinks it is, I feel like. And I went home and even Michael knew. *Michael!* He doesn't know anything, and yet he knew about Her. And then we got in that big fight, and it's just like even if I wanted to, I can't even *go* home, and I don't want to go to school with Leah anymore, because she's just...*ugh* sometimes, you know? Plus then every time I go up to my room here, *there's* Dana, just waitin' to be weird as hell. Blake's nice and everything, so that's cool, and I mean, you know, sometimes it really *does* feel like Max likes me. But why does Dana care so much? It's like I *get* sticking up for your friend, but... And what if she really comes back? Not that I don't want her to be okay or anything." I took a deep breath. I'd been staring at a spot on the desk, my words getting faster and more high-pitched as I spoke. I looked up at Professor Crawley and shook my head again. "I'm sorry."

"Quite all right," he said.

"I'm okay. Really. Like...all that stuff is just pissing me off. It's not like I'm troubled or anything."

"No, I understand perfectly well what you're saying. I don't know that I understood half of what you *said,* but I get that you're frustrated. But you're okay, you say?"

"Yeah."

He nodded, and then opened his mouth to say something before closing it again. He leaned in on his desk and looked at me. "Listen. Kids your age love to obsess. Half of them didn't even know Becca. But once she was missing, they all appropriated the pain and suffering. It's just what people do. Also, they've idolized her. They took her from being a normal human being, and turned her into some kind of deity of popularity. I'm not saying anything negative about Miss Normandy. But you just have to remember that no one is perfect. Not even her."

"Right. I'll remember that."

"All right. Feel better."

"Thanks." I stood to leave.

"Oh, and don't sneak into the boys' dorms again. If you want gossip started about you, that's the fastest way to get it."

When I got to my hall, I saw that almost all the doors were open, and everyone was talking.

"What happened?" I asked Madison when I saw her standing against a wall, her hand over her mouth.

"We should have known this would happen eventually." She was shaking her head and looking upset.

"What happened?"

"Someone else was watching the tapes."

Julia took over. "There's this…slow guy who works with the security team, and he usually watches at night. Becca cut some deal with him last year. He usually points the cameras away for a little while or something. I guess he wasn't the one watching tonight, or something. Or maybe he just doesn't care anymore."

Madison wiped the black tears from her cheeks. "At least last year he listened to Becca."

"Listened to her how?"

Julia shrugged. "I don't know, she talked to him one time and he agreed to keep quiet about seeing us walk down to the boathouse and everything on the other cameras. He works the overnight shifts on weekends. It was really convenient."

I'd had no idea I'd been risking so much by going down to the boathouse those few times. I thought it…well, I guess I never thought about it.

"That sucks." I tried to look sympathetic. "Anyway. I'm going to bed. I'm sorry you guys got in trouble."

I pushed open my door and went in, threw off my clothes without bothering to find pajamas, and crawled into my stiff bed. A few minutes later, Dana came in. She said nothing, but started laughing. I lay there, without acknowledging her, until she sighed and went silent.

Welcome back to Manderley.

chapter 22 *me*

THE DINING HALL THE NEXT DAY WAS AWASH with "FIND BECCA" T-shirts.

I spotted my usual table easily in the sea of pink. I sat next to Blake, and ignored Max.

"Does it ever stop being cold here?" I asked, at a loss for anything else to say.

"Usually in April or May," said Blake. "So did you hear about the bust last night? Cam and I almost went!"

"Yeah, I heard a little bit."

"A bunch of people went down to the boathouse last night," Blake explained to Max. "But apparently a bunch of people got caught. Professor Crawley came down with security guards, and then Crawley chased a bunch of people up to the school."

"It's crazy, dude," Cam said, his mouth full of waffle. "Like fifteen people got a week study hall, and it's going on their record."

"I feel like it was more than fifteen." Blake looked at Cam. "In any case, it's a lot, and that *so* easily could have been us."

Cam's eyes were wide with the thought of it. "On any other day, it *would* have been us. I mean—"

Dana ran over before Cam could say whatever he'd been about to. She was wearing one of the pink shirts.

"I have to talk to you, Max." Her voice was higher than usual, and her words were running together. She looked pleased.

"What?" Max asked.

"Just come with me."

He followed her out of the dining hall, and the three of us sat watching the doorway until he came back in, looking green. None of us said anything.

Whatever she said, he looked to be taking it very seriously. When they'd finished, Max came back to us.

"What happened?" Blake asked him as soon as he found his way into the chair.

He ignored her and looked at me. "Dana saw her last night."

All of us froze, and I felt like I'd been punched hard in the chest.

"Becca." Blake gasped her name. "She *saw* her? Where?"

"At the boathouse, apparently. After everyone got caught, Dana stayed behind to hide. When she came out, she says she saw her. Becca told her she'd been about to come into the boathouse when she saw Professor Crawley, and hid."

Blake dropped her spoon and leaned back and away from her yogurt.

"If she's *back,* why won't she just come out?" she asked. "What's she doing, just creeping around the beach? Seriously?"

"Come on," said Max. "Can you not see how this would make perfect sense to Becca? She loves having people think about her. I can completely picture her just shrugging and saying it's funny to watch everyone wonder."

Blake nodded. "Okay, yeah, that is true."

I stood and ran after Dana. I caught up to her in the rotunda, where she was sitting in one of the itchy chairs and writing in a notebook.

"What's up?" She looked at me with all kinds of smugness in her smile.

"If this isn't true, you know that it's really wrong to lie, right? If she wasn't here, and she's somewhere else, then everyone will be looking in the wrong place."

She smiled toothily, and I noticed her canine teeth were sharp and looked threatening. "What's wrong, *new girl,* you afraid of what's going to happen to you and Max?"

"Stop calling me that! And I'm *not.* But if you're sure, don't you think you should tell someone?"

"I was just about to. Is that *all right with you?*"

"I'm just saying it's pitch-black out there, and I know you miss her. You were probably drunk, and maybe you just…saw what you wanted to see?"

I didn't know why I was saying it, or what I expected to gain. I felt my cheeks go hot with embarrassment. Dana's face, on the other hand, went paler than usual. Her eyes narrowed, and I could hear her heavy breathing.

"Why don't you just *back off?* What is *wrong with you?* It's like you're *obsessed* with her or something!" All of a sudden she was screaming. "You're just *psycho!* Aren't you? You just want to be her! You don't want her to come back because you want to be the new girl! You want to marry Max instead of her! You want to—"

Johnny walked out of the dorm and came over to her, and I felt Max come up behind me. I suddenly felt okay. I wasn't alone in this.

"Dana, hey," Johnny said as he grabbed her. "Chill out."

She shifted her gaze to him, looking crazed.

"Calm down. It's okay." He was speaking to her like an overemotional child.

But it was working. Her breathing slowed a little, and she collapsed into him. Johnny looked at Max and gave him a small shake of the head.

We all stood there for a minute with a quiet dining hall behind us. I could feel eyes on me. Then, very suddenly, Dana covered her face and turned to run up the stairs.

"What happened?" he asked Max.

"Becca. She saw Becca."

Johnny looked steadily at Max and I saw the vein throb in his forearm as he clenched his fist. "Really."

"Apparently."

Johnny looked like he didn't know what to do with the information. He was staring at the floor with wide eyes.

I wondered, as I looked at him, if he'd had real feelings for her. He certainly looked as though he had. I remembered the way he'd talked about her in the study room. He had said that there was more to her. That not everyone had gotten to know her. He and Becca had hooked up––but had it been more than that for them?

By the time I came back to reality, Max and I were alone.

"I have to go study." He didn't look at me. "I'll find you later."

I went back into the hall, and took my and Max's barely touched trays to the kitchen.

I wasn't hungry anymore.

The school was buzzing with gossip for the rest of the week. Everyone was whispering about how *she* had been seen again. *She* was back.

For whatever reason, the increased theorizing of Becca's imminent return made me a target of even more stares. Why this was the case was a mystery to me. It's not like if she came back, we'd have a Godzilla versus Mothra fight and she'd take back her old bed and send me out onto the curb to wait for a cab. If she came back, she wouldn't even be able to finish out the year, surely. I didn't know what her return would mean. Still, people looked at me as if that was exactly what would happen.

When Friday night came and there was no boathouse to sneak down to, every girl on the hallway had to scream and shout in their dorms. It was nearly impossible to sleep. Eventually I drifted into unconsciousness, my head killing me and my blankets wrapped tightly around me to ward off the chill coming through the shut window.

Time passed, and finally everything was quiet and dark. In the hall, in my room, in my head. But then something was stealing me from my nothing-dreams.

It was a small voice, practically a musical whisper in the blackness. My eyes snapped open like a baby doll's as I realized first that I was awake, and then that the sound I heard was real. I couldn't make it out at first. But finally I realized this was Dana's voice. Singing "You Are My Sunshine." To herself.

I felt paralyzed.

"…you make me happy when skies are gray…"

I felt a little panicky, and fully awake.

"…please don't take my sunshine away…"

And she finished singing, and went silent. As if it had never happened.

chapter 23 me

THE PINK BECCA SHIRTS WOULDN'T GO AWAY.
Particularly when Valentine's Day rolled around. I just wore
my uniform, making me stand out even more than usual. I
kind of wished the administration would ban those shirts, but
apparently they didn't mind.

Everyone's minds were on love, and so that's most of what
people were talking about. Every time I heard the words
love, *perfect* or *romantic* I wanted to punch something. Perhaps
because every time I heard those words I, and everyone else,
thought of Becca and Max.

I'd heard so much about how "perfect," "in love" and "romantic" they were. I knew they were "adorable together." So
when the words were flying around like cupid's arrows, I felt
like all I could do was duck for cover.

Max and I were not speaking. He asked to talk to me a few
times, but I couldn't bear to be told again that he just couldn't
be with me. I'd heard that enough. I also resisted the urge to
ask him what he and Becca had done last year. Probably flown

off to Paris and fed each other chocolate croissants while getting silly and light-headed off mimosas.

I headed to the Black Box Theater in the art department, where they were airing a movie *about* romance in Paris.

I passed by Susan Tobias, who said nothing to me. She tossed her long, straight blond hair over her shoulder. It *did* look a lot like Becca's hair.

No one was in the theater, but the lights were down, and the movie had just started to flicker on. I could hardly see around me. I sighed, feeling more lonely and pitiful than ever, and sat down in one of the seats.

The movie was slow, overacted and impossible to pay attention to. I hadn't even been tired, but I found myself falling asleep. At a certain point, I realized I didn't even know what the plot was. I was just watching this woman have emotions about something or other.

Then, quite suddenly, the lonely woman in her flat vanished and was quickly replaced by—what looked like—burning paper, and then a white screen. It stayed that way.

I looked around. I got up and looked in the projector box. The guy running the projector was gone.

My Valentine's Day date with myself even sucked. I trudged sadly up the stairs and into my hall.

It was filled with people, going in and out of rooms, laughing and dancing, looking woozy, making out, and/or fighting. Like any good party. Almost all of these things came to a halt as I rounded the corner.

Like any Manderley party.

Madison and Julia, never to be seen far from each other, came over to greet me.

"Hey, where have you been? All the guys snuck over while they changed the tapes in the security office." Madison smiled genuinely.

"I didn't know anything was going on. I was just down-stairs."

"Oh, well, yeah it was kind of a spur-of-the-moment... thing."

Right. "It doesn't matter."

"Anyway...Max seems a little down," Madison whispered to me.

"Does he?"

Julia nodded. "Yeah, he probably feels guilty, because he knows he shouldn't have...you know."

"Shouldn't have what?"

"You guys...everyone said you were in his room...he probably just feels guilty 'cuz he did that."

"What *am* I doing, Madison?" It was Max.

She cowered under his glare. It was obvious she regretted saying anything. She shook her head, looking sorry.

"No, go ahead," Max went on. "What am I doing? Furthermore, what horrible thing could I do that she *didn't?*"

It was quiet around us as people listened. We all knew who *she* was.

"Nothing. I'm sorry." Madison was struggling to keep her words and voice steady.

Dana crept, as always, from some unseen corner. "She can make up for it when she comes back. Especially after everything she's done in the past... Oh, how long has it been now?"

"Shut up, Dana."

I saw Johnny coming through the crowd. Good. He was always good at calming Dana down.

"I mean I'm just saying, things will change when she's back, won't they? It won't matter what she did last year or what you've...chosen to do in the interim." She looked at me.

"Maybe he actually likes me," I said. "Have you ever thought of that?"

I was hot in the cheeks, and I just wanted to yell at Dana. This desire heightened when she started to laugh. Everyone was listening now. Johnny put a hand on her shoulder, but she swatted him away.

"You are kidding me, right?" She looked gleeful.

"No, I mean he is choosing to spend time with me, isn't he? If he was just moping around he could do that alone. He doesn't need me for that."

"Is he *with you?*" she asked, looking skyward as if puzzling it out. "Because I thought you weren't actually his girlfriend. Couldn't give you that label, isn't that right? Why do you think that is?"

No, he hadn't. And she knew it. We never were actually together. I said nothing, but felt my cheeks go redder.

"Dana, cool it, okay?" Johnny's voice was low and personal. "You can't keep attacking her."

"You really can't." This came from someone I didn't expect. Julia.

Dana looked as surprised as I felt for a second, but collected herself.

"Oh, see, there it is. I always said you weren't her best friend. You and Madison always thought you were, but when it comes down to it, you really aren't, are you?"

Johnny took hold of Dana's shoulders. "Come on, that's enough."

He took her back to our room, a place I really didn't want to go back to.

Then, as if he'd read my mind, Max asked Julia, "Can she sleep in your room tonight?"

"No, no, it's—" I began.

"Of course she can," Julia said. "I still have the futon that Bec—"

She stopped herself, and Madison took over. "Yes, you can come sleep in our room whenever you want."

"If that's really okay."

"Of course."

Julia walked over and pulled out a rolled-up cushion from her closet and gave me a pile of blankets. She was just handing me a pillow when Madison emerged from the bathroom.

"I think I have f-food poisoning or something," Madison suddenly hiccupped and ran into the bathroom.

"Uh-huh." Julia rolled her eyes and got into her own bed. "I'm going to sleep. Don't step on our guest next time your 'food poisoning' says hello."

Max nudged me in the arm. "Can I talk to you for a second?"

"I guess."

I followed him back out of the room and down to the end of the hall, which was darker.

"I'm sorry."

I almost said that I didn't care how sorry he was, when I saw the look in his eyes.

"It's okay," I said. "I get it."

"I wish we'd hung out tonight."

I shrugged. "It's just another day. Whatever."

"Yeah. Well. I wanted to give you something." He reached in his pocket and laughed quietly. "It's really stupid. But I got my mom to help me with it over winter break. She used to own a jewelry store. I wanted to give it to you, but I didn't know if I should. Or when, or whatever."

He pulled out a small, delicate-looking bracelet from his pocket. It was black ribbon with a silver plaque in the middle, flanked by a pearl on either side. It had a small, silver clasp. He handed it to me and then ran a hand through his hair, looking embarrassed.

On the plaque, my name had been engraved.

"All the girls wear pearls here. I don't know, I just thought it was right that you should have some hint of Manderley on you, but…you're different, so I didn't want to just give you pearls."

"It's so pretty. It's gorgeous. Thank you, Max." I couldn't even believe that it was really happening. "I don't know what to say."

"You don't have to say anything. I just wanted you to have it. Here, I can help you."

I held out my wrist and he clasped the bracelet for me. "Thank you," I said.

He shrugged again. After a second he said, "I'm going to sleep. So, I guess I'll see you tomorrow or something?"

"Okay. Good night."

"Night."

We walked in our separate directions. A moment later, he caught up to me, turned me around and kissed me.

"Happy Valentine's Day." He smiled, and then walked out of the hall.

chapter 24 becca

"OH, MY GOD, IT'S *GORGEOUS!*"

"Isn't it?"

"I can't believe Max bought it for you! It's got to be expensive. I mean I know he's got money, but still—it's *so* nice!"

"Yeah, and look what he engraved on the back." Becca turned over the locket and showed it to Madison and Julia.

"To Eternal Love," read Madison. "Oh, my God! That's so sappy! It's crazy how he is with you. He's so not like that!"

"Yeah, well." Becca returned the necklace to her neck. "He wanted to spend the day with me today, but I couldn't lead him on like that. Especially on Valentine's Day."

She sipped her lobster bisque.

"Wow, he's so hung up on you, I can't believe it," Julia said.

"Oh, my God, you guys."

Julia and Becca looked at Madison, and then followed her gaze out the window. It was Max. He was sitting on a bench, leaning on his knees.

Had Becca's words come true?

"Oh, I'll go talk to him." She rolled her eyes, like she'd just been waiting for this. But she hadn't. In fact she was down-right shocked to see him.

"Max?" she said when she walked outside.

"Sit down."

She did as he said. "What's wrong? Are you okay?"

"Let me see your necklace."

"Max—"

"Let me see the necklace, Becca."

She removed it, hesitantly, and gave it to him. She watched as he read the inscription on the back.

"I just—" she began.

"Stop. Just…stop. I didn't give this to you, and now I'm wondering why the rumors going around all have to do with my undying love and how I'm obsessively buying you gifts."

She was all too aware of how they must look to Madison and Julia, who could surely see them on the bench.

"I'm sorry, Max. Please. Just let everyone think that I wasn't dumped." She looked at him with pleading eyes.

"Why should I do that?"

"Because I just don't know what I'll do. Please. I'll stop. This'll be the last time. But please don't tell anyone anything."

Max and she were done. He'd ended that. She was no longer part of the golden couple.

But she and Johnny were done, too. That, however, had been ended by her. She just couldn't be with him. Dana was her friend. And Becca had never been a real friend to anyone. She had to do this for her. She couldn't be with the one guy Dana had feelings for. It just didn't feel right.

"Please," said Becca again. "I just can't look like that big a loser."

"You're not a loser, everyone likes you."

She shook her head. "I just can't have everyone looking at me like I should be embarrassed. Please."

She looked him in the eye, and tried to show him how much she needed this.

"Fine," he said. "But this is the last thing."

chapter 25 me

ALL GOOD THINGS COME TO AN END. I HATE
when that stupid expression is right.

The first time I realized this was when I went to my room
the next afternoon and saw the word *WHORE* written across
the small mirror I had on my side of the room. I found that it
was written in my permanent markers, and had to throw the
whole thing away.

Over the next few days, the looks and whispers about me
got louder and more frequent. Even Madison and Julia seemed
a little chilly toward me, and just as they had started being so
kind to me, too.

Madison asked, "Why didn't you *tell* us you guys had sex?"

My insistence that we didn't fell on deaf ears each time
someone new brought it up. Blake swore she hadn't said anything, and I had to believe her. I *had* to feel like someone here
had my back.

Max did as I asked, and denied it to everyone. It hadn't
taken long for him to fall out of the hearts of everyone. Everyone seemed disappointed in him. He didn't care. He just kept

asking me if I was okay. He said he'd do anything he could to make them stop.

Over the coming month, the weather remained cold and biting. The snow was deep and thick, sometimes sharp and icy. There was one time of day when the sun shone enough through my window that when I lay in bed, I could almost pretend that it was warm outside.

One night, halfway through March, I'd been lying in bed reading *The Crucible,* when the witch in my own room shrieked very suddenly, *"Will you turn off that light, I can't sleep!"*

She'd been in a bad mood for weeks. It seemed that she thought Becca owed her more than just one quick visit.

I was unable to summon a civilized response, so I put on my flip-flops and a sweatshirt and went out of the room with my book. I left the light on just to be a jerk.

I headed to the dining hall for some hot chocolate. It was empty, except for one person.

"Johnny," I said, walking over to him.

The enormous hall felt even bigger and more echoing without all the usual voices and bodies filling it.

"What are you doing up?" He looked at me, and then at my pajamas and shoes.

"I've been kicked out of my room because I had the light on."

"Really?"

"She's been really upset lately."

He nodded, and looked concerned. "Like, how upset?"

"I dunno. Just moody as far as I can tell." I sat down next to him. "What are you doing down here?"

"Couldn't sleep. I've been having trouble lately. I don't know why."

I could see it all over his face. His eyes were dark and

sunken, and his hair was tousled in a very Axe commercial type way.

"I've been having trouble this semester, too. Though in part that could be due to Dana screaming at me for reading and singing to herself in the middle of the night like someone out of a Hitchcock movie."

"Singing?"

I shrugged. "Yeah. It was weird."

"What was she singing?"

"What's that song...oh, 'You Are My Sunshine.'"

He stared at me for a second, his smile fading. "That's weird. That's really weird."

"Yeah, I know."

"No, I mean...that was a joke she and Becca had. Dana used to say something about how..." He screwed up his face, trying to remember. "How Becca was like sunshine because of her hair. I don't really remember."

At that bit of creepiness, I couldn't think of anything to say, except, "I'm going to get some hot chocolate."

I was grateful that he changed the subject when I came back.

"So where are you going to college?"

"Oh," I said, "FSU. Florida State University."

He nodded. "That's cool, why there?"

"All of my friends are going there." I thought, with a pang, of Leah. "Sort of been a plan forever."

He nodded again. "Did you apply anywhere else?"

"Yeah, I got accepted to Boston University."

"Really?" he asked, raising his eyebrows.

"Yeah." I laughed. "It's stupid. I did it on a whim."

"That's not stupid, that's an awesome school."

"Yeah, I applied in junior year for an early bird kind of thing."

"I don't understand then, why are you going somewhere right by your house or with all of your friends? Don't you want to branch out?"

"I did branch out. I came here. Look how fantastically this went." I laughed.

"I think you've held up extraordinarily well. Don't you sorta feel like if you can handle all this, you can handle anything?"

I hesitated. "That's true but…I can't go to *Boston*…that's crazy, I don't even know why I applied. I could never go somewhere completely alone."

"Why's it crazy? Money?"

"No," I admitted, my voice small. "I got a scholarship."

He furrowed his eyebrows at me. "You should do it. I mean it. Go somewhere new. Don't stay so close to home. You'll go back, and find that they've changed—or maybe they haven't and they should have—or it'll feel like home isn't how you remember it. They'll be different, and you'll wish you'd met new people."

"Maybe," I said. "Maybe I'll think about it."

He just leaned back and rested his head on his clasped hands.

Well, since we were getting honest…

"Johnny, can I ask you a personal question?"

"Sure, go ahead."

I hesitated, and then went for it. "Were you…in love with her?"

"Who, Dana? I liked her a lot. Once upon a time. I don't know. I had a thing for her the whole time I knew her, but Becca got here and then told me Dana didn't like me at all. Not even like a friend. So, I guess I gave up."

I stared at him. "I—I meant Becca."

He raised his eyebrows and cleared his throat. "Oh. *Oh.* No. I wasn't in love with her."

I was still reeling at the idea of anyone having feelings for Dana. It was so impossible to imagine her as anything other than mostly crazy.

"Max told me you and Becca were hooking up. And it just didn't seem like you to do that to your best friend."

He looked at me, and seemed to make a decision before answering. "I don't know what we were. She was hard to read. I couldn't tell if she actually liked me or just loved the illicitness of what we were doing. I hated myself the whole time, but I just couldn't pull myself away from her."

"What was it about her?"

"I honestly don't know. I know why she was fun and why she was exciting. But I can't figure out why I felt so strongly about her. I think I just believed there was more to her than that. And I think she felt something for me. I really do. She must have. And if there was more to her…I don't know, she went missing before I really got to find out."

I looked at him, and saw in his eyes that he had really cared about her.

"Well, I should go up to bed," Johnny said suddenly, rising.

"Oh, okay, yeah. It was nice running into you."

"You, too."

He gave me a weary smile, and left. He'd had feelings for Dana.

Huh.

I got up to my room, which was blessedly empty. I opened the window and breathed in the air. It was a little chilly, but I wanted to feel the breeze and hear the sounds of outside.

I sat on my bed for a few minutes, thinking of what Johnny had said and listening to the wind. I kicked off my shoes and looked at the floor. There was a thumbtack there, left over from one of Dana's and my fights. I reached down to get it and spotted the Louis Vuitton suitcase under the bed that I'd grown to ignore.

An idea struck me.

Dana wasn't here. I could look inside it. For what, I wasn't sure. But I was curious.

I locked the door. Dana had a key, but at least I'd hear her coming and could push it back under the bed. I did *not* want her knowing that I had touched precious Becca's precious stuff.

I crouched down on the floor and slid the case out. It was strange to touch something of *hers*. I unzipped it and pulled up the top.

Right on top was a jewelry box. It was silver and heavy. I sifted through the tangle of delicate chains and charms that lay in it. I spotted a silver necklace with half of a heart. It looked like the best friend necklaces that Leah and I had worn as kids, but it was heavier and shinier and had a diamond. Clearly, it had not been bought for twenty-five cents from the toy machine at the grocery store. Leah and I had spent all of our money, a whole dollar each, when we were six as we tried to get the set of necklaces. We ended up with a bunch of plastic spider rings and Mickey Mouse tattoos before finally getting them. When we had, they felt hard-won.

I remembered now that I'd thought of this last September. I had seen what must be this necklace's other half hanging from Dana's neck. I shut the jewelry box. As I did, the door behind me rattled—Dana and her key. I threw the suitcase shut, and shoved it back under the bed. I was sitting back on my bed, my heart pounding, when Dana stepped into the room.

She looked at me, with my approximation of relaxation, and her already narrow eyes turned to mere slits.

Feeling panicky, I said hello. Like I never do.

Dana shut the door and stepped in. She looked at me for another few seconds before her gaze dropped down to the suitcase, and my stomach plummeted with guilt. And then Dana did something I did not expect. She smiled.

"You're curious about her."

I shook my head. "What?"

"It's okay. We can look together."

I couldn't move. It was like my dream about Becca all over again. I was paralyzed as a strange scene unfolded before me. I watched as Dana pulled the suitcase back out, much more slowly and ceremoniously than I had done.

"Come here," she said in a whisper. When I didn't move, she looked at me and spoke a little louder. "Come *here*."

I was shaking. I suddenly did not want to know the secrets that lay within Becca's things. I didn't want to see things that she'd seen, any more than I already had. I didn't want to touch this person's stuff or look at any more pictures.

"I don't know why you never asked me before," said Dana. She sounded kinder than she ever had. It was like she could not remember all the things she'd said to me in the past. "But today, of all days, is a good one to introduce you to her."

She pulled out the jewelry box and smiled down at it. "I suppose you know what can be found in here. These are mostly gifts from all the boys she dated. Also the other half of this." She laid a hand over the half of her broken heart. "What you won't find in here was my other gift to her. I got her a charm bracelet. She was wearing it on the night…but of course she was wearing the locket from Max, too…she always wore *that* after he gave it to her. 'To Eternal Love…' She often wore both necklaces, but that night…just the one you found in the closet at the boathouse…"

Her voice trailed off as her fingers ran gently over all the silver and gold within the box. After a moment, she shut it and set it aside. She sifted through more of her clothes, trinkets and pictures, seemingly gaining her own comfort from looking at them but not saying anything out loud. I wanted to get up and run away. I didn't want to watch her do this.

She lifted from the suitcase a soft silky slip trimmed with lace. She handled it carefully, as though it might shatter. Before I could stop her, she had raised it to my face, and had run the fabric across my cheek. "Isn't that the softest thing you've ever felt? She bought it to wear for Max. She showed it to me. She wanted to sneak into his room that night, since his roommate had already gone home. But...she never got the chance... She had it laying out on the bed when she..."

Dana pulled it away from my cheek and folded it neatly. She picked up a Polaroid picture I had not seen, and looked lovingly at it. "Look how beautiful."

Only my eyes moved down to the photograph. It was the same one I'd seen in his room. Max was behind her hugging her with both arms, and looking happier than I had ever seen him in life. He was holding her tighter than he had held me, and they looked closer than I felt I had even imagined being with him. She was laughing and looking away. It was the prettiest I had ever seen her look. She was not posing or trying. She looked like a real person. And that might have been the worst part.

It was one thing when I thought of her as a marble statue, always posed and so very *intentionally* everything she was. It was another to think of her as most people must, and to imagine that she was probably out there somewhere living and breathing like a real person, Or worse, that she wasn't. Everyone loved her. Everyone talked about her. Everyone showed it by wearing T-shirts in her name. She must have had something special. It was only me who hated her. Resented her. Envied her.

Dana set down the picture, and took out an envelope. It was filled with folded notes. She opened a few of them.

Meet me at the beach at midnight.

I can't wait until later.

Same thing this time—you know I'm looking forward to it.

"No more." I said it without even meaning to. Dana smiled and closed the envelope.

I looked down at my own bracelet. Suddenly it didn't seem as sweet. He'd done almost the exact same thing for Becca.

"Maybe you can see now what I've been trying to tell you?" Dana looked from my wrist up to me and folded the notes in my hand. Only then did I become aware that my face was hot and that there were cool streaks from tears on my cheeks.

The second she looked back to the suitcase, I stood and ran from the room. I ran all the way down to the boys' dorms, without even glancing to see if I was going to be caught.

This was it: my breaking point.

I knocked on his door, and Max opened it looking concerned. "What's wrong?"

"Everything!"

My voice was not low.

He glanced around. "Why don't we go outside or something?"

"No. I want to talk now."

"People are going to listen if we're in here." He said it very matter-of-factly, and as if he knew what I was going to say.

"I don't *care,* they're all just going to make up stuff about me anyway, it may as well be true."

He didn't listen. He pulled me from the hall and all the way outside.

"What isn't *good* enough about me?" I asked, my chest hot with the fire of everything.

I felt like it was all crashing down on me. Guilt and embarrassment for being so childish, but frustration and anger at Max for still never telling me what all the secrets were that had to do with Becca.

"Where is this coming from?" he asked.

I took a second to breathe and not spew childlike complaints. He waited quietly for me to compose myself.

"It's because…" I started. "Dana just showed me a bunch of Becca's things from her suitcase. A picture…her jewelry… her present to you…*your* present to her…"

I cringed as I thought of the silken nightie that Dana had touched my face with. Max looked down at his watch.

Impatience rose in me. "What, do you have plans to get somewhere? Why are you looking at your—"

"No."

Then it occurred to me. "Was that from her?" It was a wild guess.

He said nothing, but unlatched it and started to put it in his pocket.

I held out a hand and asked quietly, "May I see it?"

He hesitated but then handed it to me. It was as if I knew what I was looking for. There it was, engraved on the back of the face.

Max and Becca, for the rest of time.

I nodded and handed it back.

"When you say my present to her…do you mean the locket Dana found in the supply closet?"

I suppressed the memory of that night, and how it had been to be so close to Max in the dark. "Yes, that one."

"I didn't buy that for her. She just said I did."

"Really."

"Yes. It was a ploy to make everyone think we were the happiest couple or whatever."

"Well, *I guess it worked*." I knew it was immature. I knew that I wasn't helping my case if I wanted to be appealing. But I just couldn't help it.

"I'm sorry. Please just don't think about her. It doesn't have anything to do with…"

He trailed off, because there was no "us." There was no "this."

I stood. "I'm sorry, too. I should have known better."

I turned and went back inside. He didn't follow me. The farther I got without being chased, the bigger the lump in my throat got and the hotter my cheeks turned.

chapter 26 becca

HE USUALLY SLIPPED HER THE NOTES, AND SHE always saved them. She didn't know why, but she always had trouble throwing them out. But this time, she slipped one to him.

Boathouse. One last time.

It was twelve-fifteen now, and Becca was walking down the wooden steps that led onto the sand. It was almost pitch-black, but she could see that he was there when he dragged on his cigarette. She walked toward the orange burn. It was because of her that he smoked. It was fucked-up, but she liked that she'd affected someone like that.

"Hey," Johnny said.

"Hey." She reached up for a kiss. He always tasted the same, every night they met. Like cigarettes and peppermint gum. She so preferred that to Max, who always smelled of soap.

He held out the cigarette for her.

"Thanks." She breathed it in.

They said nothing for another moment while he finished it and then, as usual, they went into the boathouse. He pulled the string that hung from the exposed lightbulb by the door, and they walked across the dusty, dirty, creaky floor and over to the couch. It smelled like mildew, and the fabric was frayed and matted. It was the kind of couch you'd never want to hold a black light over, and you couldn't be paid to stick a hand between the cushions.

He popped in a piece of his gum and sat down. As he did, a cloud of dust filled the air.

She felt guilty being here with him whenever she thought of Dana. But she'd missed him so much. His touch, his kiss, his words...

He scoffed. "I just can't do it."

"Why?"

She hated it. She hated feeling like this. She should have known better than to try to see him again.

"Because," he said. "I've been trying to get over you. It was never right that we were together. And now we've been apart. We're fine. We should have just stayed that way."

She wanted to tell him she'd tell Max everything if he didn't stay with her. But that's not what she wanted from Johnny. She wanted him to really want her.

"B–but don't you like me? Don't you *want* me?" Her heart skipped a little. She was the girl he wanted. "If you want me then why not just say *screw everyone* and do it?"

"It doesn't work like that in real life, Becca."

"Screw real life."

"I'm sorry, Becca." He stood and went to her. He leaned over to kiss her head. He lingered a moment, and all she wanted to do was grab him and kiss him back. But she couldn't do that now. She just stared at her shoes and listened to his footsteps until they were gone.

"Can I tell you a secret?" Becca asked Dana, staring up at the ceiling from her bed. She'd been counting the embossed fleurs-de-lis there, but Max had been in her head the whole time. It was April. There was only a month left of school. And she'd been flying solo for months now. No Max, no Johnny. No Johnny at all.

It's not that she'd been floundering. Being single had provided her with the chance to flirt with and be chased after by everyone else. But that wasn't what she wanted. And now, with this, she wanted that boy more than ever.

"Of course," said Dana, putting down her book. "You can tell me anything."

"I…" Becca was losing her nerve.

"I won't tell anyone."

"Well…I haven't even told Max." Or Johnny. She took a deep breath. "I'm…I'm pregnant."

The room fell silent as the news sank into both of them.

"You—what? How do you know?"

"I went into town last weekend. I stopped at the drugstore. I…I just found out."

She hung her head. She felt blood rushing to her cheeks and head.

"Are you serious? Are you…are you sure?"

"Yes, *Dana,* God! Am I serious? No I'm not fucking kidding. It's not *funny.*"

"You haven't told Max? Don't you think he has a right to know?"

Becca shook her head. "I don't know. It doesn't matter now anyway. It would only make things harder."

"I don't know, Becca…."

"Look, just forget it."

Dana nodded, and studied the end of her bed intently.

chapter 27 me

I SPENT THE NEXT FEW WEEKS MOSTLY ALONE.
I went to classes. I painted. I called my parents and told them
the bare minimum of what was going on. I pulled away from
Max and everyone else I knew. Blake still sat down with
me every time she saw that I was alone in the dining hall or
wherever, but at this point all I was doing was counting down
the days until graduation. The one final social thing I had
left to do was go to Blake's birthday party. I'd promised her I
would, and had decided that just *maybe* it would cheer me up.

Blake's mom had paid for a school bus to take us from
Manderley to Eastgate. Blake was wearing a dress and a flash-
ing crown that blinked the number eighteen. She was standing by the door to the bus with Cam, getting hugs, birthday
wishes and sometimes presents from everyone passing by her.

"Happy birthday, Blake—I'm sorry I didn't have time to
get you a present or anything."

"Are you kidding? I don't expect anything from anyone!
I'm just glad you came. Is… Do you know if Max is coming?"

I was growing a bit practiced at answering questions like this. "I haven't talked to him."

She looked pityingly at me.

"It's fine," I said. "I want to have fun tonight."

I might as well. What did I have to lose? Next year I'd have another fresh start. I'd be back with my friends at FSU. Or I'd have a fresh start at BU.

I took a seat on the bus, and a few minutes later I heard Blake squeal outside, and looked out to see Johnny picking her up and wishing her happy birthday. "You're finally a grown-up like the rest of us." He laughed. Their voices were muffled, but they were right beneath my window.

"Oh, I've been more grown-up than you guys for years."

"That's probably true. We'll have fun tonight." He kissed her on the cheek, and then pounded fists with Cam. The three guys with him said happy birthday and got on the bus.

I brushed the hair from my eyes and looked fixedly out the window. I couldn't help but glance back just in time for Johnny to notice me. He cocked his head with concern, and I felt grateful he was there.

"You doin' okay?" he asked when he got to my seat. He let his friends go ahead of him and take their seats.

"Yeah, I'm fine."

"You sure?"

"Yeah."

"Johnny, dude, come see what that chick from back home just texted me." Ricky was snickering in the back and calling him.

"Do you want me to sit up here?"

"No, no, of course not. Go. I'll see you in, like, a block."

"Okay. I'll be your chaperone tonight, 'kay?" He winked and went back.

Blake finally got on the bus and said we were ready to go.

"Now I know it's not much of a surprise probably, but my brother, Wes, bought me all the alcohol we could possibly need for tonight."

There was a collective cheer on the bus. I looked out the window. Max definitely was nowhere in sight.

Cam stood up. "But hey, everyone remember to be respectful to the hotel rooms. This is Blake's present to all of *us* for *her* birthday, so let's not make her regret it. Okay?"

I envied their relationship. They were both so good to each other, and always seemed happy. Cam was even willing to play bad cop, doling out the warning.

Someone started singing "Happy Birthday," and then everyone joined in. I couldn't help but smile.

I would have fun tonight. I had to. Plus, what did I have to lose?

Three hours in, all thoughts of Becca and the mystery surrounding her were gone from my mind and everyone else's. Maybe it was the change in scenery and routine that did it. Perhaps I felt it less immediately because Max wasn't there. Instead of being at dark, cold Manderley with its cobwebs and secrets in every corner, we were in a fresh and clean hotel room. There were soft, comfy beds, clean, white walls and a phone to connect us to someone who could bring us towels or pillows if we wanted them. I didn't know who'd been in this room before, and whoever it was, they hadn't left behind their suitcase or a lot of questions for me to wonder about.

It was one of those nights that had few activities but was fully occupying for every moment. I chatted with people, played card games and finally felt like myself. I was confident and happy. I also watched what I drank, because I knew I never, *ever* wanted to feel like I had earlier in the year.

We were playing Kings, a simple game in which everyone

sits around in a circle, each person taking their turn pulling a card from a facedown circle and obeying the rule connected to each card. After drawing the card, we placed it in the space under the tab of a beer. Whoever makes the tab pop loses and has to chug the beer.

Blake pulled a seven and, as the rule goes, put a hand in the air toward the rhyming "heaven." Cam was the last one to do it, so he took a sip of his drink.

"Oh, *Cam,* you should have known! I'm your *girlfriend,* aren't you supposed to know what I'm thinking?" She smiled at him, and he smiled back.

"I did, sweetie, I just wanted to take one for the team."

"Ha!" Blake scrunched up her nose and kissed him.

Johnny was next. He pulled one. "Poorly shuffled. I got an eight."

"Pick a date!" one of the guys Johnny had arrived with, said. Tony? I didn't remember his name. And right now I didn't care.

Johnny looked at me and grinned. "You."

"Me?" I asked, laying a hand over my heart in mock honor. I knew he was just doing it to make me feel better and more included.

He nodded.

"Well, I'm touched. After all, being your drinking date means I have to drink every time you do. Considering how bad you are at this game, we'll both be wasted."

Everyone laughed, and the girl next to him took her turn.

Johnny, probably intentionally, lost almost every round for the rest of the game. I glared at him, unable to wipe the smile from my face. In the end, Blake lost when she popped the tab. Cam drank the beer for her.

When he finished, he pulled his phone from his pocket and then looked at me.

"Max is on the way. He's taking a cab."

My heart lurched.

"Wha— Really?" That was uncharacteristically spontaneous of him.

"He said he needs to talk to you."

Everyone looked at me, and there was a flip in my stomach.
What could he need to say now?

Fifteen minutes later, he walked in and directly to me. He
laid a hand on my cheek and kissed me. In front of everyone.
He'd never done that before.

I could feel the eyes on us. At first no one noticed, but then
the conversations died down one by one. I almost laughed as
I realized they all wondered what was happening. Had this
been going on, had they been *right* about Max and the new
girl?

I reveled in the beauty of showing them all that I was
worthy of more than just gossip and drawn conclusions. I was
worthy of my own storyline. I wasn't just an unreal character
in their lives; I was someone who had secrets. I was someone
Max wanted to kiss. And that was something none of them
could say.

My stomach did a few more flips, and when he pulled away,
I didn't know what to say.

"Let's go outside."

We walked out of the loud room and into the far quieter
hallway. We moved away from the muffled sounds coming
from our room, down the stairs and then outside. The cool
air felt good on my flushed cheeks.

"I think this is the first time I've been glad it wasn't hot
outside."

"Yeah, it feels good." He took a swig from a Pepsi he'd
swiped on the way out. "You look…good. You look good
tonight."

"Thank you. You, too," I said, trying to find the wall behind me. I turned to see that there wasn't one. "How cold do you think that pool is?"

"Freezing."

I walked toward it, my gait one of slight figure eights. "Dare me to jump in?"

"Absolutely not." He looked past me. "I dare you to jump in there though."

I followed his gaze. There was a hot tub behind a clump of trees. I turned back to him, smiling, and bit my lip. I kicked off my shoes and ran to it. It would feel good to be submerged in water again.

I heard him following me. I kicked off my jeans and pulled off my shirt, feeling confident and glad I'd worn a black bra and underwear.

He laughed. "You're really getting in?"

"Pfft. Of course. I never reject a dare." I took a tentative step in. "Ooh!"

"Hot?"

"Ohmygod," I said, breathing methodically. "Well, wait, you're going to have to get in, too."

Max looked back at the hotel and then raised an eyebrow. "Okay, you got it." He set down his can and took off his shirt.

I looked at his stomach and chest, and felt the surge of desire I always did with him. He was strong. He was...not like most of the guys I'd known in high school—he looked like a movie star *playing* a high school student. I tore my eyes away as he lowered his jeans, exposing muscular legs. I glanced at them, and he caught me.

"Hey," he said, "no guy looks cool in only his boxers."

"Sure." I tried to play it off like that had been what I was thinking.

"This is hot as hell." He sucked air in through his teeth as he got in.

"You'll get used to it." I dipped my hair in the water and slicked it back and out of my face.

He smiled at me. "You're gorgeous, you know that?"

Before even feeling flattered, I thought immediately of Becca. I didn't want to, but I couldn't help it. I knew he didn't think I was all that she was. What words had he used to describe her, I wondered?

But I just smiled back. "Don't I have mascara all under my eyes?"

"A little."

I wiped with my fingertips. "Did I get it all?"

"Not even." He came over to me, still smiling. "Here."

He took his thumb to my skin. This might have been the closest we'd been in months. And I felt the same wave I'd felt the first time he'd kissed me and told me he liked me. I wanted him.

He moved his hand down, and then his thumb was on my cheek and his fingers were in my hair.

I stared back at him. Daring him.

A small line appeared between his eyebrows. His grip tightened slightly on me. Our breath in the air mingled with the steam, and I was surprised to find I was practically whispering. "It's been a while since we…"

"I know. Believe me, I know."

My heart started pounding hard as soon as he kissed me. He pulled me on top of him as he sat down on the bench under the water. The steam gathered around us, and the jets shot out ferocious bubbles that covered the sounds of our breathing with their loud simmering hum.

I was afraid every second that he was going to stop. I didn't want him to. For once, I wanted him to *please* just kiss me. I didn't want him to pull away and shake his head or to apologize or to make up an excuse and disappear. But he didn't. His arms wrapped strongly around my back, and then he unsnapped my bra with an effortless twist. He ran his hands around my ribs, constantly pulling me closer. He didn't care if anyone saw. Neither did I.

But even so, I was very glad we were alone.

"Do you want to go back into the party?" Max asked.

It was half an hour later. I looked at him and immediately saw what he was feeling. No, he hadn't pulled away from me this time, but he was about to now.

"Whatever you want to do."

"She gave you a key for a room, right?"

I fumbled in the wad that was my jeans to find the pocket that had the card. "Yep. Room 402."

"You want to go hang out there?"

"Sure."

He followed me up the stairs, past the noisy party, and into 402. Once inside, I sat down on the end of one of the two full-size beds and stared at the pattern on the floor.

He reached into his pocket and pulled out some change. "You want chips?"

There was a tension between us that I couldn't quite lay my finger on.

"If you're going."

I sat in silence while he walked down the hall to the vending machines. Max returned a few minutes later with two bags of chips. One of them was sour cream and onion, my favorite. He knew that much about me.

He handed it to me, but I didn't open it.

"What's wrong, Max?"

He sat down next to me. "Nothing."

"I feel like this…whatever we've been has been really hard for you. But why did you continue on with me, if you only ever thought of…Becca?"

Maybe it was the alcohol. Maybe it was the fact that finals were a stone's throw away and I'd never see Manderley again. Maybe it was the fact that I had finally hit my limit.

"I'm with you because I like you."

"No," I said, and shook my head, "you don't. Every time we touch I know you're comparing me to her and thinking about her. I know you think about her constantly. I know you can hardly *stand* being around me because I pale so much in comparison. Which is *bullshit* because there is nothing wrong with me. I don't care how perfect she was or whatever, I'm pretty damn good, too."

He said nothing for a moment, and stared down at the design on the carpet, his expression very serious. Without looking at me, he responded.

"You're the best thing that ever happened to me. And I feel like I squandered my chance with you."

"Don't just say that because you feel bad, seriously I've had enough of—"

"I'm *not*. I— You're just amazing." He shook his head. "There's no way for me to tell you exactly how much you've meant to me. This just makes me hate her so much more."

"Hate who?"

He paused. "Becca."

"Hate her? What do you mean *hate* her? I get that you weren't as in love as everyone thought, but—"

"No, I really grew to hate her."

I didn't know what to say. "I had no idea."

"She was just a girl. Just someone to hook up with and have fun with. But somehow my life became all about her trying to find happiness. Through that whole year, she just got more and more unhappy. I felt bad then for not loving her. Even though she didn't love me. I just wanted to be able to give her the admiration she wanted. But I didn't. And that night…I screamed at her. I was at the end of my rope. I was frustrated. I was angry. If she's dead…I don't know. I accept some kind of responsibility for it. I've felt guilty forever. I was one of the last people to talk to her."

"But she's been spotted, right? So I mean, there's hope."

He waved away the suggestion. "I don't know. There are a lot of blonde girls that could look like her."

"But Dana…"

"Dana's practically a nut job. She doesn't want people to stop looking."

"The Facebook update, there was that."

"Someone could have hacked it. Some kind of prank or something." He shrugged. "I don't know. I just feel bad. She was really unhappy in the end."

We were there for a few minutes, both of us thinking and saying nothing, just being together and alone in the quiet room listening to the quiet hotel sounds around us.

"I left my purse in the other room," I said.

"Let's go get it. I kind of want a beer anyway."

We walked out of the room and across the hall. The party had died down for the most part. Some people were passed out, and others were still drinking. I looked outside and saw that Johnny was making out with some girl. For a moment I wondered if it was Dana, but then I saw blond hair.

"There you guys are!" Cam exclaimed, taking a gulp from his beer.

There was a movement on the couch, and I saw that Dana was lying down. She looked around and her eyes caught on Johnny. She stood and crept to the balcony door. It was like watching a zombie rise from a grave.

She slid it open, with much struggle. She was obviously very drunk.

"Johnny..." she said.

He turned, and let go of the girl. It was Susan. The Becca look-alike.

"Dana's already puked," Blake said, as she walked up next to us.

"Really?"

She nodded and looked concerned as she walked to the other side of the room. "I don't think I've ever seen her this bad. She's like...weird drunk. She looks like she's on something else. But Ricky swears he didn't give her any pills or anything."

"That's good," I said.

"Johnny, why'd you..." Dana leaned on the door frame and then slid down onto the ground. Her skirt came up past her underwear. She was too wasted to care.

Johnny came over to her and fixed her skirt. "Come on now, Dana, get up." The way he spoke to her was gentle and kind. I remembered his feelings for her, and wondered if they were still there.

"Johnny, I've love you, 'n you doe c-care."

She couldn't form words. Her eyes were out of focus. I wondered if she even knew she was conscious.

"I didn't mean to, you know," she said. "I didn't... It wasn't... I didn't mean to. I just didn't mean to, you know."

"Stand up, sweetie, come on. Please."

"Don't call me *that*." Her face contorted, and she started to cry. The room was silent as we all watched her. She was weeping now, like a person does when they are alone. "I just wanted you and you didn't—and then *she* took you, and then, then her, too, and now Susan, too. Why did you do it?"

She smacked his hands as he tried to get her to stand up. My face went red as she shifted her unfocused gaze to me.

"And why did you?" She pointed to me. "You could have had anyone…but you had to do it with him. Why did you have to do it with *Johnny?*"

"M–me?"

"Why did you have to hook up with him? Johnny is the only one I wanted. And you…you *had* to…"

She tried to breathe, but couldn't stop crying enough to do it quietly.

"I didn't, Dana. If you mean me…I never did anything with Johnny." Everyone's gazes shifted to me.

"You didn't? You did. You said you did, you were talking about it with Blake, you said so. In the bathroom."

I shook my head. "No, no, no, no, no. I never did anything with Johnny. I never said I did. And I won't."

"She did. Becca did." She nodded, her head moving in huge motions. "She did that. She knew I liked him. She knew everything. But she did it anyway."

Everyone seemed to be waiting for me to respond. "Um," I said. "I'm not actually Becca, you know…and I'm sure she didn't know. Or she wasn't trying to hurt you. Maybe she just…couldn't help it or something."

"But he loved her. You loved her." She pointed to him. "And then she got pregnant. It was your baby. She was pregnant. When I found out…when I found out she'd been hooking up with you, it made so much more sense."

Now we all looked to Johnny. The color was gone from his face. "Why do you think that?"

"She told me. She knew. And that night…the last night. That's when you said you'd have been with me—" she pointed lazily at herself "—if she hadn't messed it up. And then she said she wanted to be with you *still*. *Still* is the operative," she said, stumbling over it, "word there. You guys were hooking up all along. And the baby was yours."

No one said anything. I looked at Max. He was as pale as Johnny. He reached for my hand, and held it hard.

"I didn't mean to do it," said Dana, who was now lying flat on her back. "I didn't mean to."

chapter 28 becca

IT WAS THE LAST NIGHT OF THE SCHOOL YEAR. Some people had already gone home, but Becca was at the boathouse with Max and most everyone else. Including Johnny.

A few weeks had passed, and Johnny had not tried to re-kindle anything with her. It was killing her. She had to talk to him tonight. Had to tell him about the baby. Had to ask him what he wanted her to do.

Becca also had to figure that out for herself. Every time she thought about it, she felt sick. Her parents would kill her. Seriously. They might literally disown her. She shivered whenever she thought of having to tell them. She wanted someone to lean on, someone to share the burden with. She had Dana, but she couldn't tell Dana the whole truth.

She had to talk to him tonight.

It was still cold out, even though it was May, and rain had been pouring down in buckets for hours. Becca couldn't drink. She didn't know why she cared…there was no way she could keep the baby.

She tried not to let the thought into her mind that maybe having it was what she wanted.

"Hey, Ricky," she said as she walked up to him. "Give me something."

He raised an eyebrow. "Like *something* something?"

She nodded. "I need confidence. I need energy. I need to be—"

"I have just the right thing." He went over to his backpack and removed a pillbox she'd only really ever seen used by old people so they could keep all of their "keep me alive" medicine straight. He pulled two yellow pills from a compartment.

She took them without hesitation. "Thanks."

"Come talk to me for a second!" she shouted over the music at Johnny.

The world around her was getting stranger and stranger. She was fighting to stay aware, but too messed up to realize that the pills she'd been given were screwing with her.

"I can't," he said, not making eye contact with her.

"Come on!" She smiled, resisting the uncharacteristic and sudden urge to cry. "Just for a tiny second?"

He looked around, too, and then let her lead him. They went outside and shut the door behind them. Beyond the awning, it poured down rain.

She pulled him into the rain and kissed him. He kissed her back for a second and then pushed her away gently. "Please, Becca, don't make this harder."

"It doesn't have to be hard, Johnny." She blinked away the rain and smiled. Her face felt numb. "I want to be with you. I love you."

It was out of her mouth before she could stop it. He stared at her. "You...what?"

"Come *on!*"

She ran out farther into the rain, her bare feet sinking into the muddy, so-cold-it-stings sand. Every sensation was heightened. The air was warm, but she was sharply aware of the cold air and the pricks of rain. She felt like she could feel every grain of sand.

He followed her, looking reluctant. "Please come back, Becca, I don't want to play this game with you."

"Oh, stop." She went up to him and planted a kiss on his neck, the only part on him she could get to.

"We can't, what if—"

"What the *fuck?*"

They both turned to see Max standing in the doorway. "Are you serious, dude?"

"No, Max, I—"

He threw open the door and ran at Johnny. He tackled him to the ground and then punched him hard in the face. Johnny tried to speak, but Max wouldn't let him. He just cracked him hard again in the jaw. Johnny didn't fight back. He only tried to stand and to speak.

Becca screamed at them to stop.

"Shut *up*," said Max, standing with ease. "Just stop, for *once* in your life just shut up!"

She nodded and tried to keep her mouth shut. She was crying. She was losing her mind. Everything was heavy on her shoulders.

She ran to Max. "I'm sorry—"

She put a hand on his arm, and he whipped it off him. *"Do not,"* he shouted, *"touch me."*

He had never raised his voice to her like that. He had never sounded so furious. He went back into the boathouse. Johnny stood.

"Why didn't you fight back?" she asked, her chest convulsing with every breath she tried to take.

"Fight *back?* I can't fight back, I *fucked his girlfriend*." He stared at Becca with all the rage she'd ever seen come from Johnny before, ever. "God, I'm *mad* at you. You know, before you got here, I had a best friend. And I probably would have gotten with Dana, and things would have been a lot easier. I liked her, you know. I know you say she didn't like me, but she seems to, and you just *messed it all up*."

Becca glanced at a movement in the door, but then saw nothing. She collapsed onto the ground. She was suddenly crying harder than she ever had in her life. She looked up at him, blinking the tears and rain out of her eyes. She tried to speak, but couldn't.

Johnny's face softened, and he closed the door. "I'm sorry. Just…just come inside."

She shook her head violently. "I can't. I can never see those p-people again. I—I—I can't. Johnny, I've never felt anything like what I have with you. Please, just, just…" She was hyperventilating. "I'm begging you. I'm *begging you*…tell me we have something real… I know we do, I love you…I *love* you…."

"Becca, please, calm down."

She was shaking so bad she couldn't move. She let out a pathetic moan over the thunderous waves and the pounding rain. Blood was pulsing through her body. She couldn't feel okay.

"Something is—is really wrong, I can't…breathe…."

"You're probably just having a panic attack. Just try to breathe. You'll be okay." He ran his hand over her hair. "It's okay."

"I can't—please, Johnny, I can't— I'm going to lose it— please…"

JOHNNY

He'd never seen her like this. She was weak and miserable. She'd always been so strong and sure of herself. It had been nearly impossible to stay away from her these past few months, but he'd thought it was for the best. He'd never have imagined that she'd be anything but okay.

She was laboring to breathe. Johnny had his arm wrapped around her tightly but then slowly unwound it. "I'll be right back." He stood and ran into the boathouse.

"Ricky, come here."

Ricky followed Johnny. "What's up, dude?"

"Do you have Xanax or something? Something to calm a person down?"

"Sure." He went to his box and grabbed a pill. "Wait, who is this for?"

He didn't want to say who it was really for. That'd make her feel even worse when she found out. "Uh, me. I'm just feeling all panicky for some reason tonight."

"All right, all right."

"Thanks." Johnny patted him on the shoulder and was set to go back outside.

"Whoa, dude, only girls don't pay. Thirty bucks."

"Dammit," Johnny said under his breath. He pulled out his wallet and threw it at him. He ran outside, to find Becca lying in the wet sand, being rained on. She was still crying. Her blond hair was clinging to her face, and she looked like she had no idea where she was.

"Becca, take this, it'll make you feel better."

She shook her head. "Nothing, it's not… No, I can't."

Her breathing was still labored, and she looked like she might pass out at any second.

He put the pill on the tip of his tongue and leaned over her body. He kissed her. She kissed him back.

Damn, he'd really missed that.

He pushed the pill into her mouth with his tongue. She seemed too out of it to notice. He picked her up, and carried her up the stairs and all the way to her room.

DANA

It was hours later, and Dana was drunk. She'd heard that Max and Johnny had fought over Becca.

Fucking great.

Dana had done everything in her power to stop herself from freaking out. And she hadn't. She hadn't been anything but good about it all so far. She lay in her bed, silently seething at the girl in the bed only a few feet from her.

Becca had everything. Dana didn't need *everything*. All she'd wanted was Johnny. And Becca had *of course* gone and taken that, too.

Suddenly there was a movement in the dark. Becca was standing up and walking…to the door? She opened it. And then shut it behind her. She was in her white slip—the one Dana had always admired.

I can't let this go, Dana thought. *I have to talk to her, even if it's in the bathroom while she gets sick.*

She put on a jacket and ran out into the hall. But Becca was gone. She looked in the bathrooms and in the dining hall before stepping out of the door and looking out in the rain. She saw Becca's white slip catch the light of one of the lights along the field. She was walking down to the boathouse.

Dana wondered with a pang if this person who she'd never been anything but nice to was going to meet Johnny. She wouldn't say anything, then. She'd just wait until they were both together and then she could confront them both. That was better anyway.

Dana followed her silently. She stepped down the stairs, as quietly as she could. Once on the sand, she looked around for Becca, but only caught a silver glint, in the sand, by her feet. Bending down to pick it up, she saw it was the locket from Max. Why...?

She hadn't heard the door to the boathouse open. She squinted, and saw that Becca was at the end of the dock. She opened her mouth to yell her name, but something stopped her.

What was Becca doing?

BECCA

The necklace had felt heavy on her skin. The locket was heavy with holding all the lies she'd told just to be happy. Ignoring the pain that ensued when she ripped it from her neck, she let it fall to the sand.

She now stood on the waterlogged wood. This was her end. It had to be. She couldn't even think about anything else. The baby in her stomach (how was that even *real?*), whatever drug Ricky had given her was now making her thoughts turn to mush. She felt rippling with electrical currents, but she also felt she might fall asleep at any moment. She couldn't stop clenching and unclenching her hands. Her eyes were foggy and her mouth felt dry.

But most of all, she felt hollow.

The dark, ferocious waves were fighting each other to swallow up the sand. Everything was wet. Everything was black. Everything was threatening to engulf her. The water hit her like small bullets.

She looked up at the dark sky, and breathed. From this angle all the air above looked like it was coming at her fast.

Nothingness was all she wanted now.

The dock swayed. She glanced back at the boathouse. People might look for her in the morning. But now she was alone. She untied the boat and climbed onto it.

Something was guiding her. Something besides herself. She wasn't thinking or deciding. It was like she'd made a choice, and now her body was holding her to it.

She climbed into the boat and immediately drifted too far away from the dock she'd released it from. She turned on the light, partly to battle the sky, and it cast a dim and dirty glow on her surroundings.

Very quickly, the ocean ripped control away from her, and fear ran through Becca. The waves were ripping the boat from its sturdy position and rocking it back and forth like a bath toy. She held on to the side. Water smacked her in the face. It was all she was breathing, hearing, seeing, tasting or coughing up. She'd had enough trouble standing on the beach. She was slipping on the slick floor of the boat, and barely holding on to the side.

More thunder and lightning, simultaneous. She was right in the eye of the storm. She was more nauseous than ever, and puked, not even seeing or feeling where it landed. She let go of the side to try and get to the pole of the sail. In that moment, her side of the boat was whipped into the air, and her light body was thrown into the waves. The powerful waves curled her within them, and she was helpless against them. She couldn't find the bottom, and she couldn't find the top. She opened her eyes, and everything was black. Her foot smacked painfully into the hull of the boat once, but she was unable to do anything but flounder helplessly.

Her head came above water once and she started to take

a breath, but was then swallowed back into the water. She would be gasping for breath but instead she was just filling her body with the salty, black water. There was no up, there was no down. There was a steady, nauseated life five minutes ago, but nothing five minutes from now.

And then, very suddenly, there was no "now."

chapter 29 me

THE NEWS HIT MANDERLEY LIKE A THRASHING
storm. Becca Normandy was dead. Her body had been found.

And Manderley became colder than ever.

Even though it was May, the sky was flat and gray with
clouds that raced across the sky, threatening icy rain. The air
was foggy and thick, and my mind was much the same.

I was guilty and sick for my jealousy. I had been selfish. The
world was bigger than just me. I should have realized that and
stayed to myself.

But nothing was worse than the assembly where we all
found out. All we'd known were the rumors: that it had something to do with Becca's whereabouts.

"We should have *known* she'd wait until the end of the
school year. It makes so much sense!" I overheard one girl
saying to her friend as they passed by. We all thought she was
alive.

We all assumed it was good news.

The noisy talking and laughing ebbed as Professor Crawley

took the stage. He cleared his throat and adjusted the microphone. Max squeezed my hand.

"Hello, everyone. I'm sorry to have to call you all here on one of your last nights at Manderley. But..."

Professor Crawley spoke calmly and gently to us. He told us in the only way he must have known how. He gave us the facts.

An initial din quieted to only a few hushed sobs. Everyone listened as Professor Crawley explained, quickly and without gruesome detail, that her body had been found in the water.

I thought back to the recurring dream I'd been having all year long about being whipped around beneath the waves, unable to find air. I knew the feeling well, having grown up next to the beach. You go in the ocean enough and you'll eventually get caught in a riptide that sends your brain the thought that this time, the water is going to...

Swallow me whole.

I remembered the ghostly Becca I had seen in my dream on the night of the Halloween Ball and how she had asked if I could hear the ocean, and how she told me that no one knew if it had swallowed her whole.

Why had she gone near the water? *Had* she taken out the boat, like Blake had wondered? If so...did she know she was going to die?

I barely listened as Dr. Morgan took the stage, to urge us all once again to come talk to her. Her small face contorted with worry as she looked out at the auditorium filled with sobbing teenagers. I spotted Johnny along our same row. He looked etched out of marble he was so still. His eyes were fixed on the seat in front of him, but I could tell that he was not really seeing it.

I didn't find Blake and Cam until the end, and when we

did they were as somber as we were. Neither shed a tear, but
the shock had clearly affected them.

"Are you okay?" Blake asked, looking to Max after nodding
a hello to me.

He hesitated. "Yes, I'm okay."

Blake nodded and then looked concernedly at him. "If you
need anything…"

"I know." He glanced up at them. "Thanks. I'm going to
bed for right now. I'll see you guys tomorrow."

"Dana's mom is here."

"What?" I asked.

"Her mom. They told her before us. I guess she wanted to
tell Dana herself, but got here too late…"

Max and I both muttered something about that being too
bad, and then our conversation wound down to good-nights.
Max walked me up to the girls' dorms, where we, too, said a
quick, polite good-night and then parted ways.

I floated up the stairs in a haze, and then into my room.
The door was cracked, so I pushed it open quietly. I was
walking to my side of the room when I heard Dana in the
bathroom. It was muffled through the door, but I could tell
she was weeping. Her sobs were unbridled and deep. It stung
my eyes and throat to hear.

"It's okay, it's all right. You're okay."

The person who must be her mother was speaking in a
slow, calm voice.

"I watched her…I watched her on the dock and I didn't
stop her. It's my fault…"

"No, honey, it's not. It's not because of you. It's not because
of anyone. You're okay." Her voice was still measured and
soothing. I imagined that she was soothing Dana in the way
my mother always had me, by running her hands through her
hair and wiping tears from her cheeks.

"She was my f-friend! I could have done something. Should have gone after her or…or…" Her voice trembled, and I could hear her trying to catch her breath. "No one was there for her and *I* should have been! She had enough time out there alone to…to…"

"You didn't do anything wrong. You did all you could. You are okay."

Dana broke into tears again. A few seconds later she had caught her breath. "What was the last *thought* she had? When she…when she woke up that day, she didn't know it was the last time she ever would. Did she know she was going to die? When did she stop being aware of what was happening? She must have been cold… I can't…I can't stop imagining it…."

This time her mother said nothing. I didn't blame her for being stumped. After all, I had thought the same thoughts, too.

"I want to *die!*"

There was a twinge in my chest. *No, Dana, you don't want to kill yourself,* I thought.

"I know that you feel that way now, but you *will* change your mind. It's going to be okay."

I snuck back out of the room, not wanting them to know that I had been there. It was the last time I'd see Dana until the funeral.

For the next few days, the students that filled the halls of Manderley were in constant funeral march. No one spoke, it seemed, and when they did it was almost always in hushed voices.

The last few lacrosse games we had, we were crushed in. No one could fight hard, playing or cheering. Everyone was lethargic with the loss.

Becca was dead. We were all about to graduate. A feeling of finality was pushing in everywhere.

For a lot of us, I think it was the first time we'd thought about life or death that way. My grandfather had died when I was too young to understand, but that was it. I might not have known Becca, but it didn't matter. She was our age and she was no different than us. I might not have stumbled into the ocean if I had been her that night, but maybe I would have. The possibility that it could be any of us at any moment for whatever reason was shaking us all to the core. The mystery around her disappearance had kept these thoughts at bay, that we were seventeen, maybe a little older or a little younger, and we could, all of us, just die like that. We could be as dead as anyone who'd lived to be a hundred or as someone who was given a lethal injection. Our lives could be over at any moment.

We were not invincible.

I think that thought was a new one. We all knew it of course, but we had never really felt it. And as we were all getting ready to end our high school lives and begin our new ones, I realized that these were thoughts worth remembering.

For me, it made me decide that I needed to live. Really *live*. I could not be afraid or timid; I had to make my life worth living. I couldn't push anything off. As I realized that, I thought of my friends back home and the college life we'd planned out. We'd be friends forever, we had decided, and college would be no different than high school except we'd be older and freer. Whenever I had thought of a life beyond those friends and the streets I already knew, I had always thought: *Later. I'll tackle the real world later.*

Maybe it didn't have to be later. I remembered my acceptance letters to Florida State and Boston. They had both come on the same day. When I opened the letter from FSU,

I had expected to get in. I hoped for an acceptance because it would be embarrassing not to get into the school my friends did. I wanted to be accepted because that was the plan. And when I was, I was happy…but there was something else I had squelched and ignored. I thought of it now, and wondered if that was the part of me who wanted to be pushed from the nest. Maybe what I wanted was a reason to leave the comfort of my plan.

I'd opened the envelope with the big blue letters *BU* in the left-hand corner, and there was a quiver in my chest as I'd read the words telling me I was accepted. I ignored that feeling, too, it turned out. Here a door had opened right next to the one I planned to walk through, and another, more daring and spontaneous version of myself had strode through it.

Maybe that's who I wanted to be now. I'd already taken the first step and left home. Would I regret it if I sank back into an old routine with the same people when I'd already gotten the worst of it over with?

I'd been homesick a lot, but I'd also been okay. It had been a difficult year, but I had lived. I didn't even have to take a leap into the cold water of newness; all I had to do was keep swimming.

I thought about it all night until I fell asleep. Then suddenly I *was* swimming.

The water was cold and biting. It was the same old dream, I figured, where I was caught under the waves and couldn't find the surface. But this time it was different. Two hands grasped me and pulled me up out of the water. I breathed desperately, coughing water from my lungs. When I opened my eyes, it wasn't a rainy scene on turbulent waters as I had expected. It was that moment right before the sun sets, when all the sky is golden, and the water sparkles invitingly as if it had never done any harm to anyone.

And there was Becca again, as perfect as she had looked the last time we'd met in my dreams.

She smiled at me. "Hello."

My throat was tight, but this time I could speak. "Becca."

She considered me for a moment. "I wish I had met you."

"M-me?"

"Yes, you. You would have been a worthy adversary for me. I think I would have liked you." She laughed the coquettish laugh I'd always imagined she would have. "You would not have liked me, however."

She paused and her smile faded. "You are everything I ever wanted or pretended to be."

My voice was gone from me again, and all I could do was listen.

"I went about it all wrong. I lied and cheated and craved attention, while never seeing why I should deserve it. But you didn't scratch your way to the top. You lived a year in my shadow, but somehow you still never lost your light. You wondered what was so wrong about you that people wouldn't want to be around you, but then you realized that you were someone worth knowing, and did not understand why no one else could see that. I was popular and adored for pretending to be a person like you. But I hated myself, and felt ugly and shameful."

She shook her golden head and looked down at her lap. "Max never wanted me, but I made him stay by making him feel guilty. Johnny never wanted me either, but I appealed to his weaknesses to obtain him. The main weakness being that he'd never felt that he was as good as Max, and I made him feel like he was better. My family wanted me to be more, but all I could do was push them away. You never would have done the things I did. And I'm sorry that you ever had to feel like there was something wrong with you. Believe me, *I was the messed-up one.*"

"Th-this is all just a dream."

She raised an eyebrow. "Right." Her face went very serious, and she kneeled in front of me. "I was never going to change. And I let my own internal misery end my own life and ruin everyone's around me if they got close enough. Please find Dana. Tell her to step down. Ask her what I ever did to earn her friendship. Tell her she will be okay."

I shook my head, not understanding. Becca grabbed my shoulders and spun me back around. Suddenly I was walking in the darkness, but I couldn't see where to. Finally my surroundings materialized around me, and I saw that I was on the top floor of the old mansion, where some storage rooms were and I didn't know what else. I'd never been up here. There was a dim light at the end of the hallway. I blinked, becoming more and more aware as I grew closer. It was a balcony that looked out at the ocean. There was someone there. I blinked again. It was a tall, thin figure standing on a chair, about to step onto the wide ledge of the balcony.

"Dana!" I yelled her name, and it echoed in the hallway. She started, and then righted herself. She wanted to see who I was. Her eyes grew wide.

"Becca?"

She was looking straight into my eyes. Something besides my own volition led me to nod.

"This is a dream, isn't it?" Dana said it quietly, sounding resigned.

"Yes. Dana, you have to get down from there. You don't want to do this."

"I don't. I know. But it's going to happen anyway, isn't it? Why should I live, if it's just going to be awful like this forever?"

"It won't be." The words came from my mouth without my ever thinking them. "You will be okay. I never earned your friendship. You gave it all to me, and I never gave you anything back. You did nothing wrong other than being my friend to begin with. You didn't have to try and save me. You knew I was screwed up, but you couldn't stop me from ruining my life. You tried to be nice to me and listen, but it's not your fault that you couldn't change me."

She looked as though she was taking in what my lips were saying.

"It'll be okay. It'll be okay." I said the words, and then slipped into dreamless unconsciousness.

I could not remember my dream. But when I awoke, I felt as though a weight had been lifted.

chapter 30 me

I DON'T THINK I BELIEVED SHE WAS REALLY DEAD until I was at her funeral.

I had spent ten months building up a case against Becca in my mind. I had turned her into my rival. All the while, she'd just been an unseen body being whipped around by currents and undertow.

She was supposed to be the reason for everything that had happened this year. She was supposed to come back. Not that I'd wanted her to. How many times had I wondered what would happen to everyone if she did? I never had a happy answer for that. And that's a terrible thing to think.

But here she was. Here was everyone else. Here I was. In a church.

I wasn't being selfish; I knew this wasn't about me. That was the problem. I had spent a year thinking about this girl, resenting her at times, and that entire time, she'd been just a ghost. She wasn't even real anymore. She couldn't fight back. She was innocent. The dead always are. I think it would be hard to stand over a dead body and ever feel like they completely deserved it. Once someone dies…I don't know, I don't want to spout off something about how we come into this world the same way we leave it—alone—because I don't think that's so.

We come into the world the furthest *thing* from alone. We come into the world with everyone fawning over us, and helping us. That's just not how it is when we die. I don't know what's different. Maybe it's the fact that when you look at someone's dead body you see their entire lives flattened, with an end point. When I was eight, and went to my grandfather's funeral, I had that realization. I didn't even know him. But you look at that person…and you see everything they ever felt, thought, cried over, worried over, was thrilled by, and you realize that someday someone will look down at you when your brain is quiet and you're lying in your last bed. You realize that everything you think and feel now will be encompassed in the hyphen between two years. It's not even that depressing, it's just true.

But of course we couldn't see Becca's body, thanks to the ravages of the deep waters. She was just the mystery she'd always been and would be to me. She was on the inside of that chestnut box, only inches of wood separating her from us. Her body anyway.

It was colder than it should be in May. Not just for me, but for everyone. Rain was pounding against the tall, stained-glass windows and no doubt reminding everyone grimly of the night she died, almost a year ago. For me it was just a haunting sound track to the dour scene in front of me, and the gruesome one from the past that my subconscious couldn't help but imagine.

I was out of place. I knew that. Everyone else knew that. I didn't know Becca Normandy. But I had to come.

I went to the service kind of early, in an effort to not arrive late and have a rerun of my first assembly at Manderley. So from my seat, somewhere in the back left middle, as inconspicuous as possible, I just watched. Her parents were sitting up front, quietly sitting a respectful and quiet distance from each other. Her mother wore a hat with that net down in front of her face like the girls in old movies. I could see that she had the same blond hair as her daughter. The neat waves met the shoulders of her black dress. She was still, like her husband. There were a few other people on the same bench that I supposed were the rest of Becca's family.

More people trickled in that I didn't know. All of the men were wearing dark suits, which made it seem like we were all being transported to another time. All the women and girls wore black panty hose and sensible heels. Everyone looked neat, no one stunning. This wasn't the time for that.

There were more people on my row now, and no one seemed to notice me. I was exceedingly grateful for that. If I could have come to the funeral and been invisible, I would have chosen to. Eventually, I saw people I knew. Dana, Madison, Julia, other people I'd seen around, many of the teachers. Professor Crawley. Johnny walked in toward the end, but didn't see me. He sat at the edge of one of the rows nearby. Max saw me and acknowledged me with a nod. But we couldn't sit together, I knew that. It would feel wrong somehow.

Cam and Blake walked in, hand in hand, behind him. Blake and I locked eyes, and she gave me a sweet smile. I think all I did was give a watery look back at her, but she continued walking silently and took a seat. She was the one who'd convinced me to come. I'd insisted that it might be weird; I never even *knew* Becca.

"Funerals are about saying goodbye, and about the ending of a person's life. It's not like showing up to someone's birthday when you don't know her," she'd said sagely to me. "It's about showing that you care."

I was in a haze as the priest spoke. Everyone was absolutely wordless and motionless. It was a horrific reason we were all here and there was nothing good in it. He went on for a while, saying all of the comforting things he had probably said a hundred times to groups like ours.

When it came time for the eulogies, I braced myself. Dana was first. She stood in front of the black sea of people, and breathed visibly.

"This is my first funeral," she began, "and I don't know what to do. I know to be sad, and I know to honor Becca. That's all I know. Maybe that's all there is." She furrowed her brow. "I worried about Becca when I knew her, and I only worried more about her from that night on. The night it happened, I guess. And ever since then…up until a few days ago, I mean, I was sure she'd come back. But she's really gone. I don't know what I can say. I wish I could have done something to help her. So with the help of Mrs. Normandy, I collected these pictures and made this slide show. I thought it would be a good way to remember my friend."

A minute later, the lights were dimmed, and there was a projection on a screen.

And there it was. Right beneath her name, Rebecca Elisabeth Normandy. The two dates with the hyphen in between. Then the music started.

The first picture was of a pretty blonde child holding a pumpkin and smiling under a golden sun, one of her front teeth missing. The projector light faded out and then back in to show another image, from a Christmas morning, gaping excitedly and animatedly at a book I couldn't see the title of. Another, her blowing out ten candles on a pink birthday cake, surrounded by friends at a dining room table. More childhood pictures passed by. Then what looked to me like her first year of public high school. She was smiling gamely, wearing corduroys and a white, long-sleeved T-shirt, and her hair was in a tight ponytail.

The quiet hush of the room was filled now with the echoes of sniffs, a sob here and there, and some uncomfortable shifting.

Some of the pictures after that were ones I'd seen on the wall at Manderley. It was obvious that she'd changed a lot in her last few years—not only in age but in posture and attitude. I gave an almost involuntary shake of the head as I thought of it.

She was laughing in one picture, and holding a red Solo cup, and I saw that she had her tongue pierced.

There were suddenly no pictures from home. All of them were taken at Manderley or with other friends I'd seen and interacted with but never gotten to know.

The slide show faded for the last time, after the picture of Max and her where she was laughing. Then the church lights came back up.

I hadn't noticed, but Dana had stepped down already.

Max took her place. He didn't rush into talking. He stood there for a moment, and everyone sat comfortably, letting him take his time. A line came between his brows as he leaned on the sides of the podium.

He straightened up and cleared his throat. "This is very difficult for me, of course. And I have very few words for how I feel. I'm not a big talker." I noticed people, especially women, looking sympathetically up at him. "She was beautiful. And really vibrant." He shrugged. "There was just something about her. She would have loved having you all here. Everyone coming here today is a really great way to honor her." He looked down at the podium, seeing something beyond it. "I will never forget Becca. I know that much. I will never, *ever* forget her."

He stepped down, and stopped in front of her parents. He shook Mr. Normandy's hand and leaned down to kiss Mrs. Normandy on the cheek. She took and held on to his hand for a moment and then she rose, and he patiently remained standing there until she let him go with a pat.

She was next. I hadn't seen her face yet, and was surprised to see that it was not puffy or red. It was stone-cold as she walked to the podium.

"I want to thank all of you for coming today. It means a great deal to our family."

And then she stepped down, and back into her seat. *What?* Blake, who was sitting a few rows in front of me, looked back at me. I shook my head, baffled. That was her *mother*. That was all she had to say?

I thought for a moment maybe her husband would step up and speak for both of them, but no. It came to a close. Becca and her coffin would be flown back to her home in Chicago for the burial at the family plot.

Everyone poured out of the chapel, and I veered off up some stairs. I felt strange, and a little overcome. I needed to break away. I didn't want to stand outside with everyone or mingle, or feel how I was feeling in front of anyone else. They would think I was assuming their grief as my own, and I didn't want that. There was a bathroom at the top of the stairs, and I ran in.

I leaned against the wall, not entering one of the three stalls, and felt the cold tiles through my dress. I shut my eyes and breathed. So much had changed for me. So much had happened. And I couldn't even think about any of it without feeling blasphemous and selfish.

A moment later, I jumped as the door opened. It was

Becca's mother. Her face had changed. She still wasn't crying, but I could see something like desperation in her eyes. It reminded me of when Max had taken me down to the beach and had looked so hollowed.

"Oh," she said, surprised to see me, too.

I couldn't think of anything to say, and leaving immediately would seem rude. She stood in front of one of the mirrors and tried to stand up straight. A few seconds later, she had collapsed onto the floor into tears.

I didn't know what to do. I didn't know her. I didn't know Becca. I didn't know how to soothe someone even, not for something like this. So I just did what I felt compelled to do. I knelt down next to her, and put a hand on her shoulder. She leaned almost imperceptibly toward me and laid a hand over mine.

Neither of us said a word for a few minutes. I didn't ask if she was okay, because what a useless question that was. She wasn't okay. I could see that. I didn't ask if there was anything I should do. I knew I couldn't do anything. I didn't ask if she wanted to talk. If she wanted to, she would.

When her sobbing subsided, she patted my hand as she had Max's, and took a deep breath. She whispered an apology, and I shook my head.

"Don't apologize."

"Were you one of her Manderley girls?"

"I— No. I just transferred this past year. I never knew her." She nodded slowly. "Heard of her, no doubt."

"Yes, I've heard a lot. Everyone talks about her all the time. She really made an impact."

She raised her eyebrows knowingly. "Oh, I'm sure she did."

"I had to come to the funeral. I know I didn't know her personally, but…I don't know, it sort of felt like I did." My honesty flowed out of me before I could stop it. "I hope that's okay."

"Of course." Mrs. Normandy stared at her slightly aging hands. "I don't know what to do with Becca gone."

I didn't know what to say.

She shook her head and went on. "I don't know why I feel that way. She hated me. She wouldn't let anyone *near* her. I'm so...I'm so *mad* at her for that. Why couldn't she just let me know her?" Her tears began anew. "I want my *baby back*. I want her to come home and I want to do it right this time! I just let her do whatever she wanted. I shouldn't have done that."

She needed to say this, I could tell. She still didn't look at me. I listened, and said nothing.

"She was always loved, but she was always cold. She was never happy with what she had. Nothing moved her. *Nothing.* I don't know that she ever loved anyone, or hated anyone." She waited a few seconds before narrowing her eyes as if trying to figure something out. "But she hurt people. She would say hurtful things, and do things just to *do* them. I just...I just want her back. I want to understand her. I want to try *harder* to understand..." She breathed deeply again. "It's my fault. It must be. I don't know what I did wrong...."

I felt motivated to speak up. "Sometimes things happen, and they aren't because of anyone. Sometimes they just *are*."

She looked up, as if she was startled to find me next to her. "Maybe."

I nodded, not knowing what else to say as she didn't take her gaze from me.

"I'm pregnant." She whispered the words. "I haven't even told my husband yet. It feels wrong to be bringing someone else into the world after losing Rebecca. But what if this baby is the same?" She laid a hand on her stomach. "What if I can't raise a happy child? What if I'm just...unfit?"

She was pleading with me for an answer I knew I couldn't give. So I just shook my head and said, "You will be fine, and so will your baby. I'm sure you didn't do anything wrong with Becca. She just was who she was. It's not your fault."

The woman searched my eyes, and a small, sad smile appeared on her face. After another few seconds, she started to stand. I helped her up, and noticed she smelled a little bit like alcohol.

She recovered herself, as if morphing back to a former self, to what she had been when I'd first seen her. As if this had never happened.

She looked at me for a long moment, mouthed the words *thank you* and left. I would never see her again.

I was in the bathroom for fifteen minutes after that. Recovering, or something.

When I went back downstairs, most people were gone. Cabs, cars, town cars and one limo were sloshing out of the parking lot. I stepped out of the tall open doors and under the awning.

Now it was time to graduate.

Somehow the kick of graduating had ebbed. But seeing my family felt like surfacing for air for the first time in months.

My parents and Lily flew up the morning of graduation, and we'd be flying back together that night because that was the cheapest way. I only had time to hug them all, and then direct them to the auditorium to wait. The ceremony was starting in an hour.

I put on my cap and gown with everyone else. No one was saying much. I wanted to leave throughout the entire ceremony, which seemed to drag on for days. Some people

were back to chatting and laughing, whispering and thinking already of their futures and not of their pasts. But I just
couldn't.

I wouldn't have even gone if it hadn't have meant so much
to my parents. When it came time for my name to be called,
a sense of finality washed over me. I was finished, I thought,
walking across the stage to shake hands with the administration. I was finished with high school. Finished with Manderley.

My parents stood and cheered at my name, and I smiled
for what felt like the first time in too long. They were proud
of me. They'd never have to know about the whole past year,
and how awful it had been in some ways.

Could I look at it now with a wise eye and say that it had all
been for the best, and that I was better from the experience?

As we all stepped out into the hall to take pictures with
our families, I think all of us felt the oldest we've ever felt.
So much was coming for us. There was a small twinge in my
stomach when I thought of Becca, who had never gotten this
far. She was gone, and had nothing in her future. I wondered
how long that thought would plague me.

"Congratulations, honey!" My dad picked me up and spun
me around.

"I am bursting with pride," my mother said with tears in
her eyes. "You have done so much. You should be so proud
of yourself."

I hugged her, too, and then Lily. She was jumping up and
down next to me. As I hugged her, I caught eyes with Johnny.
He gave a half smile, and a nod. I smiled back.

"So introduce us to your friends!" my mother cooed. "I
want to know who you've been spending all this time with!"

"Oh, I don't know. Everyone's with their families...."

Just then, Max walked up. I suppressed whatever was rising in my chest. I didn't want to say goodbye to Max. I just wanted to start over. Not that the thought of reliving the past year was any kind of appealing.

"Congratulations," he said.

"You, too," I said. "These are my parents, and this is my little sister, Lily."

He shook hands with both of them and introduced himself. He even held out his hand for a high five from Lily. She blushed and then hid behind my father's legs, peeking out at Max.

"Your daughter is amazing. I just wanted to tell you that I feel better for having known her."

I smiled and looked at my shoes.

"She sure is amazing, isn't she?" my father said, rustling my hair.

"Together for a picture, please!" my mom gleefully said and stepped back.

Max and I stood together, his arm around me. He kissed me, as he so often had, on top of the head as the flash went off. I would always love the picture, even though my smile was small and his brow was furrowed. It held so much in it.

"Adorable," she said. "But both of you try to look *happy* this time!"

We took one more picture, both of us smiling like you're supposed to in pictures.

"Thanks," I said to him.

"No problem. Do you want to meet my parents?"

"Sure."

He walked me over to them, and I did as he had done. I held out my hand and met each of them.

"I saw you up there, congratulations on your graduation," said Mr. Holloway. "Couple of cords, I see. Smart girl, huh?"

"I try to be." I smiled as genuinely as I could. I was too

aware of Max next to me, and the fact that he would soon not be.

His mother said nothing, just looked at me.

"Max is…" I looked up at him. I wanted to return the favor and say something nice to his parents about him. But emotion was filling me. "Max is…" I smiled and breathed very intentionally to stop from getting watery. I felt like they might be able to see that.

"I have to show my parents around and then leave. It was so nice meeting you."

They said their goodbyes to me. Max hugged me and told me he'd talk to me soon. Then I turned, feeling like I'd said goodbye all wrong. That couldn't be it. I hadn't held on to him long enough.

"That's the kind of girl you ought to spend your time around," I heard his father saying as I walked away. I smiled to myself, still biting my lip to keep from crying.

My mom put her arm around me, and ran her hand up and down my arm.

I led them around, showing them the dining hall where I'd spent the mornings with Max and his coffee and newspaper. Where I'd gotten my hot chocolate for the nights I spent alone. I showed them the senior study room, my haven from the rest of the place. I remembered when he'd kissed me there.

I showed them my room, which was empty and character-less. I remembered all the nights I'd thought about him as I fell asleep. I also looked under the bed, which was now empty and void of the mysterious Louis Vuitton suitcase.

My mother was enchanted with every last corner of the place, taking pictures every time we'd let her. "Ooh," she said, "this place is just *wonderful*. Would you like to come here some day, Lily?"

"Yes!" she shrilled.

I privately wondered what ghosts would haunt these halls by the time Lily got here.

We ran into Cam and Blake, who were on their way out. They were polite, as always. Blake squeezed me hard and told me that we just *had* to stay in touch. Cam smiled and told me he was happy I'd come to Manderley.

When they left, I already missed them.

Dana was already gone. The funeral was the last time I'd ever see her. She hadn't come to graduation. I told my parents that when they asked about my roommate.

"Why didn't she go?" my mom asked, looking concerned.

"That girl who was missing, Becca Normandy? Do you remember when Michael told you about her over break?" They nodded. "They just found out she died. Dana and she were really close."

"That's a shame," my dad said, shaking his head. "I feel that everybody loses someone during their teen years."

"Did you know her best friend?" Lily asked.

I hesitated. "No."

"That's good."

At last, we went out to the front circle with our suitcases to wait for the cab. I saw Madison and Julia, who dashed over to me and told me they'd miss me. They both still looked very depressed. I wondered how long it would take for them to be okay again. They were just telling me they'd find me on Facebook when Johnny walked over. Madison and Julia went off to talk to Susan, who said nothing to me.

"Hey, new girl." Johnny smiled as he came over to me.

"Hey."

"I'm gonna miss you."

"I'll miss you, too. I don't know what I would have done this year without you."

"You better shoot me a text every once in a while."

"I will. You, too. Here, give me your number."

He took my phone, put it in and handed it back. He gave me a quick hug and said, "Seriously. Texts."

"Come on!" Lily shouted.

"I'm coming!"

"I really do hope we see each other again," he said earnestly.

I nodded. "Goodbye, Johnny. Thank you for everything." I went off to join my family.

"That's us," my dad said when a van pulled up. "Number seventy-two."

I got in the car, and had a sinking feeling as I realized I wasn't going to see Max again. But just as I thought it, Lily exclaimed.

"Look, it's that guy!" She was pointing at someone running through the crowd of waiting people.

It was him. I beamed when I saw him. "Go ahead, I'll get in in a sec."

I ran to him, and met him about thirty feet from the car.

"I thought I wasn't going to see you again before I left," I said into his shoulder.

"I know. I know. I'm sorry. My parents wanted to talk to the headmaster about my performance and wouldn't let me leave. I wanted to. I had to say a real goodbye to you."

"Me, too."

He gave me one last, long look, and then cleared his throat. "You'd better go."

"I know."

Max leaned down to kiss me on the cheek, and I held him there. I turned to look at him. He moved a fraction of an inch toward my lips.

"Lily!" my mother shouted.

I turned to see Lily running up to us. "She has to go!" she

said sternly to him. She then turned and marched resolutely back to the van.

I was just starting to apologize for her when Max kissed me. I felt everything fall away, and kissed him back. When we broke apart, I realized how much I was really, really going to miss him.

"We wasted time," he said with a laugh that didn't quite meet his eyes.

"Yes, we did."

"Go," he said with a sly smirk, "or that sister of yours is gonna punch me right in the knees."

I gave him one long look, and then ran back to the van.

"Hey, Callie," he said, when I was a few feet away.

I turned at the sound of my name. "Yeah?"

"I'll see you next year."

I smiled and looked at him. "What do you mean?"

"I got into Harvard."

I walked back to him. "*What?* I didn't even know you were trying!"

He smiled. "I didn't want to say anything. It was a crazy dream. I didn't think it'd actually happen."

"That's amazing, Max."

He nodded. "So if you make the right choice…and pick BU, we'll be right next to each other."

The urge to cry happened all over again. "I already accepted." I smiled. "I'll see you next year."

We both knew there was nothing more to say. I ran to him, just to feel him one last time. He kissed me and then pushed me off toward the van.

I looked at him as we drove away. He didn't move, but just stood with his hands in his pockets.

"You certainly had your choice of them here, didn't you?" my mom said happily. "Where to for dinner, do you think?

I saw this cute little place next to the...what was it, Eastgate Hotel? We have about four hours until the flight, and we simply must have a celebratory dinner."

I was barely listening as the school receded out the back window. I remembered Manderley as it had been on my first day. The inside had been a mystery; the outside was a breathtaking facade of ivy and promise. Any story could have unfolded within its walls. When we drove back down the narrow road, and Manderley finally disappeared from view, I felt oddly nostalgic for the place I'd been so eager to leave. I knew now that I would never be back again. It may have burned to the ground as I drove away, and I would never know.

And as I left for the last time, I could have sworn I saw a tall, thin, blonde girl standing at the entrance of Manderley.

★ ★ ★ ★ ★

They say that before you die your life flashes before your eyes

You think it's going to be the good stuff.
Don't count on it.

I was Bridget Duke—the uncontested ruler of the school. And if that meant being a mean girl, then so be it! I never thought there'd be a price to pay.

Until the accident.

Now, trapped between life and death, I'm seeing my world in a new light. And I've got one chance to make things right. If I don't, I may never wake up again…

www.miraink.co.uk

EVERY GIRL WHO HAS TAKEN THE TEST HAS DIED.

NOW IT'S KATE'S TURN

Kate's mother is dying. There seems to be no hope. Then she meets Henry; dark, tortured and mesmerising, but Kate thinks he's crazy. Yet when he brings a dead girl back to life right in front of Kate's eyes, she's not so sure any more…

Claiming to be Hades, god of the Underworld, Henry offers Kate a deal.

He'll keep her mother alive while Kate tries to pass seven tests. If she succeeds, she'll become a goddess—*and Henry's bride*.

If she fails she'll never see her mother again.

www.miraink.co.uk

Coming soon... Book one in the new
Blood of Eden series

In a future world, vampires reign.
Humans are blood cattle.
And one girl will search for the key
to save humanity.

Allison Sekemoto survives in the Fringe, the
outermost circle of a vampire city. Until one night
she is attacked—and given the ultimate choice.
Die...or become one of the monsters.

www.miraink.co.uk

Join us at facebook.com/miraink

Bound by darkness, forbidden to love...

Savannah Colbert's family have warned her to have
nothing to do with the Clann, but when she
recovers from a strange illness, her attraction
to Clann golden boy Tristan Coleman
becomes nearly irresistible.

For years, Tristan has been forbidden to even speak
to Savannah Colbert. Then Savannah disappears for
a week and comes back...different, and suddenly he
can't stay away. Tristan has to fight his own
urge to protect her, to be near her no matter
the consequences....

Read Me. Love Me. Share Me.

Did you love this book? Want to read other amazing teen books for free online and have your voice heard as a reviewer, trend-spotter and all-round expert?

Then join us at **facebook.com/MIRAink** and chat with authors, watch trailers, WIN books, share reviews and help us to create the kind of books that you'll want to carry on reading forever!

Romance. Horror. Paranormal. Dystopia. Fantasy.

Whatever you're in the mood for, we've got it covered.

Don't miss a single word

 twitter.com/MIRAink

let's be friends

 facebook.com/MIRAink

Scan me with your smart phone

 to go straight to our facebook page

MIRAINK_SM